PRAISE FOR JILL SHALVIS

"Bestseller Shalvis (*Love for Beginners*) launches the Sunrise Cove series with a charming, emotional romance featuring a cast readers will quickly come to see as old friends."

—*Publishers Weekly* on *The Family You Make*

"*Love for Beginners* is quintessential Shalvis, with humor and heat (whew, Emma and Simon give us heat), and a cast of characters you'll hate to leave behind when you turn the last page. But even so, we promise you'll finish this book feeling warm from the inside—and maybe the outside too. This is the summer's perfect beach read."

—Christina Lauren, *New York Times* bestselling author

"Jill Shalvis has a unique talent for making you want to spend time with her characters right off the bat."

—Kristen Ashley, *New York Times* bestselling author

"Sisterhood takes center stage in this utterly absorbing novel. Jill Shalvis balances her trademark sunny optimism and humor with unforgettable real-life drama. A book to savor—and share."

—Susan Wiggs, *New York Times* bestselling author, on *The Lemon Sisters*

"Jill Shalvis's books are funny, warm, charming, and unforgettable."

—RaeAnne Thayne, *New York Times* bestselling author

ALSO BY JILL SHALVIS

The
Sweetheart List

A NOVEL

JILL
SHALVIS

AVON

An Imprint of HarperCollins*Publishers*

THE SWEETHEART LIST. Copyright © 2023 by Jill Shalvis. All rights reserved. Printed in the United States of America. No part of this book may be used or reproduced in any manner whatsoever without written permission except in the case of brief quotations embodied in critical articles and reviews. For information, address HarperCollins Publishers, 195 Broadway, New York, NY 10007.

HarperCollins books may be purchased for educational, business, or sales promotional use. For information, please email the Special Markets Department at SPsales@harpercollins.com.

FIRST EDITION

Designed by Diahann Sturge

Title page and chapter illustration © Danussa / Shutterstock

Library of Congress Cataloging-in-Publication Data has been applied for.

ISBN 978-0-06-323569-4
ISBN 978-0-06-323570-0 (hardcover library edition)

23 24 25 26 27 LBC 5 4 3 2 1

CHAPTER 1

Harper Shaw was a single snack-getting-stuck-in-a-vending-machine away from an anxiety attack. But hey, that was what happened when you decided nothing in your life sparked joy. You wiped your slate clean like an Etch A Sketch and started over.

A heavy sigh came from the shotgun position of her car.

"I know, I know." Harper leaned forward a little, squinting into the dark night, broken up only by the white slashes of snow coming down. "We've been on the road for twelve hours and you're hungry and bored. I get it, believe me. Who knew it could snow in Tahoe in July? But hey, it's pretty, right?"

No response from the peanut gallery, so she reached into the passenger seat for her skinny popcorn, pulling the huge, one-pound bag into her lap to munch on. "The point is, we agreed to stop being Eeyore. It never gets us anywhere or anything but heartbroken and shoved aside. We're done with that. We're only looking at the silver linings now. Positive thinking. Gotta dream it to live it and all that crap." Sure, she was exhausted and frazzled on the inside, but she meant it. She'd just turned thirty *and* a corner on her life path. If it didn't bring her joy, then *forgetaboutit.* And speaking of joy, she found some driving over the majestic summit, taking in the staggeringly high peaks that were nothing but inky outlines against the stormy night sky.

She was pretty sure her beat-up sneaks weren't going to stand up to this storm, and she didn't have any sort of warm boots. She reached for her phone to access her notes and start a new list before she remembered—she no longer made lists.

They hadn't brought her joy. They, along with her ex-almost-fiancé, Daniel, had brought only pressure, unrealistic expectations, and heartbreak.

But she still had Ham. Aka Hambone, her 125-pound, five-year-old perpetual puppy Bernese Mountain rescue. The perfect male, he was loyal, sweet, and always kind. His only fault was that he got carsick—like, really carsick—unless he had his huge head out the window. This meant Harper was currently freezing, even with her heater blasting.

Most of her belongings were in a moving pod that would arrive next week. But the things that mattered most to her were in this car. Ham, of course. Her mom's recipes—one of only two things she had of the woman she'd loved more than anything. She also had her own beloved and essential baking tools, including her mixer and food processor, not to mention her jar of homegrown, irreplaceable sourdough starter and a tin of her chocolate and mint chip cookies, both out of this world, if she said so herself. She planned to use them to bribe people into wanting to be friends with her, because she could really use some. Or even one.

And then there was the small building she'd rented to open her own bakery. Scary, but as she had zero regrets, also incredibly thrilling. She'd happily walked away from her stressful job at the busiest bakery in all of San Diego, then also walked from things she'd considered her responsibilities, like helping her ex-almost-fiancé through law school or making sure her dad was happy, as she'd promised her mom she'd do. But since Daniel had graduated and dumped her, and her dad had remarried and moved on, she was free.

And looking forward to living life as she wanted—without obligations or anything that preyed on or drained her emotions.

Not that anything could drain them at the moment. Nope, her emotional gas tank was currently on *E* for Empty.

She looked out at the dark night. She knew the route to the lake, but she needed help from here, so she unmuted her GPS.

"Crikey!" an Australian male voice immediately yelled, startling her so badly the bag of popcorn went flying in the air like the snow on the other side of the windshield.

"Turn left at Sunrise Cove in one hundred feet, mate."

Past Harper had been amused by the accent, but Current Harper's nerves were shot and now her popcorn was all over the car.

Ham was tap-dancing on the seat, craning his neck to catch each piece.

"Do not hork up popcorn in my car or you'll walk the rest of the way." A hollow, empty threat, because Ham was family. Plus, they were almost there, and excitement had her heart pounding.

What she remembered most about Tahoe was camping with her mom on the lake, and also Sunrise Cove, a small mountain town perched on the north shore near the head of the Truckee River. The memories of the beautiful, woodsy lake and a walkable downtown community with all sorts of shops and places to eat lived in her heart.

"Turn left, mate! And then left again into your final destination, hidey-ho!"

She made the first turn, and her car slid a little, eliciting a startled squeak from her and a surprised "gak" from Ham when the seat belt he wore tightened around him, halting his forward progress. He resettled with what she was pretty sure was an eye roll.

Ham was no stranger to sitting shotgun with her.

She slowed way down for the second left, but it still wasn't enough. Her tires didn't grip on the ice, and she slid into the parking lot and right up against one of the huge bushes lining the lot.

Her car came to a sharp stop, but not her pounding heart. She put a hand to her chest and gulped for air as she turned to Ham. "You okay?"

Ham was doing his happy tap-dancing again. He had a piece of popcorn stuck to his forehead and was wagging his tail, because in his mind, stopping meant food.

Food was Ham's entire reason for existing.

"Okay, okay," she said, removing the popcorn from his face and then gently pushing him back so she could take stock. She was fine, Ham was fine. Everything was fine.

Well, maybe not *everything*. Her driver's-side door was jammed up against some seriously Amazonian-size bushes that didn't give when she tried to open her door. Damn.

When she'd stopped for gas on the summit half an hour ago, the attendant had taken one look at her two-wheel drive and told her she would need to buy chains or risk getting turned back away by California Highway Patrol. She'd asked him to put the chains on, but he'd wanted an arm and a leg for the service, so she'd decided against them since they weren't required right at that moment. The attendant swore that they'd be "easy-peasy" to put on herself if she had to.

She was really hoping that was true, because she figured her car wasn't going anywhere without the traction the chains would provide.

"Scootch," she said to Ham as she crawled over the console and wedged herself into the seat with him. He took the opportunity to lick her face. "Thanks, buddy." Reaching past him, she shoved open the passenger door and basically poured herself out to take stock. "Stay," she said, and gently shut the door. He pushed his big face out the open window and whined at her.

"It's okay, this'll be quick." She hoped, because damn, it was cold.

"Hey, you okay?"

Harper nearly leapt out of her skin at the voice behind her. Heart still pounding from the slide, it threatened to burst out of her chest as she whirled and came face-to-face with a man. A big one. He wore a jacket against the cold, hood up shadowing his face but not hiding the fact that he was tall, broad shouldered, and built for strength. In a swift move that only a girl who was used to walking alone at night between her work and car could be, she had her handy-dandy pepper spray out of her pocket and showed it to him.

"Whoa," he said. "I come in peace."

Swallowing hard against the slam of adrenaline, she pushed her hair back from her face and gulped some air.

Several pieces of popcorn fell from her and hit the asphalt.

A corner of the man's mouth twitched as he sniffed the air. "Ranch flavored?"

"Yes, what do you want?" Because where she was from, women didn't talk to strange men who could turn out to be serial killers.

He pushed his hood from his face, allowing her to see his wavy brown hair on the wrong side of his last cut, along with at least a few days' stubble. He wore dark jeans and a sweatshirt under a leather jacket that looked like it might've survived combat in World War II. "Just making sure you're okay."

"Why wouldn't I be?" she asked, trying to be a cool cucumber.

This got her another mouth twitch. "I don't know, Speed Racer, maybe because you came in hot and just lost a fight with a manzanita bush. Do you need help?"

"No, thank you."

He gave her car a look of doubt.

"I'm fine. You should probably go before I let my dog out. He's not men-friendly." And neither was she.

Ham's head was still out the window, and he let out a long, dramatic I-wanna-lick-the-new-person-to-death whine, accompanied by his sweet come-pet-me smile.

The man smiled back and flashed a dangerously sexy dimple on the left side of his mouth that in no way lessened his rough-and-tumble appearance. And anyway, why was he smiling and standing there all calm and relaxed when she still had her pepper spray in hand?

"You're right," he said. "Your dog looks terrifying."

Having been a city girl all her life, suspicion and caution were part of her DNA. "I'd like you to go now."

He raised a brow. "Before or after I help you disentangle your car from the bush?"

"Definitely before," she said, proud that her inner trembling wasn't audible in her voice. "I'm going to put on chains to make it easier."

"All you need is some kitty litter."

"For what?"

"Sprinkled behind your tires. It gives you traction on ice and snow."

Okay, and now she knew why the gas station had a stack of kitty litter bags for sale next to the chains. Damn. "I've got this, but thanks." Opening the trunk of her car, she eyed the chains.

"You probably don't see much ice and snow in San Diego," he said.

Try zero . . . "So is that your party trick? Guessing where people are from?"

"Nah. You've got a Toast Your Buns in San Diego sticker on your back window."

Oh. Right. She pulled out a piece of paper folded up in the chains that listed what to do in what order.

She read it twice. She considered herself fairly intelligent, but in this instance, she'd have appreciated pictures. Crumbling the paper, she tossed it into her open window. "Don't eat that," she told Ham.

The dog sighed.

"You might need to keep that—"

"Look," she said, spinning to face him. "I gave up lists, okay? They don't spark joy. So thank you, but as I've mentioned, I'm fine."

"You gave up . . . lists."

"I gave up everything that didn't spark joy. Obsessive list-making. Kale. My high-stress job. My ex . . ." She was sure there was more, and if she hadn't given up list-making, she'd probably have it written down.

"Everyone should give up kale," he said.

She snorted, and maybe it was the long drive, maybe it was her life, but suddenly she felt a little too close to a breakdown, and she *really* liked to be alone for those. "Please, just go."

He lifted his hands in the universal I-give-up sign, turned, and walked away. She caught herself watching him because he had a way of moving that was inherently sexy male, and also possibly the best ass she'd ever seen. But it was something else that made her call out to him. "Are you hurt? You're limping a little."

He either didn't hear her or didn't want to answer, because he vanished into the night.

Fine by her. She eyed the chains again. "I'm a strong, independent woman and don't need no stinkin' man. But easy-peasy, my ass."

"You don't need chains. Some common sense, maybe, but not chains."

Again Harper whipped around and found a woman this time, somewhere around her own age. She had bright red hair cut in a bob, complete with bangs, thick black-rimmed glasses, and freckles dusting a pretty face. Her orange turtleneck sweater, red miniskirt, orange knee socks, and red patent leather Mary Jane pumps all brought to mind a cartoon character, but Harper couldn't quite place which one.

Ham whined and tried to jump through the window. For a brief second, he got stuck in his seat belt, and though he might have been short on brains, he had determination in spades. He managed to wriggle out the window. He hit the wet asphalt on all four paws and also his chin, recovered quickly, and started for the woman—who calmly held up a hand, palm out. "Sit. *Stay*."

Harper stared in shock as Ham skidded to a stop and indeed sat and stayed.

"Good dog," the woman said, and Ham wagged his tail so hard he nearly took off airborne like a helicopter. "You two okay?"

"Um," Harper said, taking in her attire. "Are *you*?"

The woman looked down at herself. "Oh, right. I'm Velma. You know, from the *Scooby-Doo* gang." She waved a hand again, this one dismissive. "Book club night at the bookstore. The theme was famous female detectives. I stayed late to clean up. You took out my manzanita bush."

"Actually, your bush took out my car." Harper watched Ham, who never "stayed" for more than five seconds. And sure enough, he hoisted a leg and further insulted the bush by peeing on it. "And I'm putting on chains so I can free your manzanita."

"Ah, man," Velma muttered. "He was right. You *are* a tourist."

"The guy on the summit said I should have chains on me. What 'he' are you talking about?"

"Bodie. The guy who tried to help you. He had to get to work and didn't want to leave you out here alone. He asked me to watch out for you. And bring you this." She hoisted a ziplock bag, which appeared to be filled with . . . kitty litter.

"I told him I was fine." Harper opened the passenger door and gestured for Ham to get back in the car.

"Tell me the asshat who sold you those chains didn't charge you like a hundred bucks."

Nope. He'd charged her $150. Not that she'd admit it.

Velma shook her head. "Let me guess. You're a city girl who heard we were getting snow in July, and you wanted to relive that time in college when you fell for a ski bum."

"Wow, judgy much?"

Velma actually laughed. "Yes."

"Well, save it, because I'm a local." As of five minutes ago, but still . . .

Velma eyed her car. "You sure?"

Harper sighed. "Look, thanks for the kitty litter. I'll pay for any damage to the manzanita."

"It's okay. I hate manzanita." Velma began searching through her purse for God knew what. Not one, but two bottles of pain reliever fell out. "Welcome to your thirties," she muttered, shoving them back into her bag, "where you keep two bottles of ibuprofen on you at all times."

True that . . .

Finally, Velma pulled a pair of serious gloves from her purse, tossed them to Harper, then crouched low and carefully scattered some of the kitty litter around the rear tires. "Pull out slowly, you'll be fine now. And for the record, Bodie could've gotten you out of this with or without the kitty litter." With that, Velma stood up, dusted a nonexistent speck of dirt from her skirt, and walked away.

Harper got into the car but first had to nudge Ham out of the driver seat. "Fingers crossed," she said, but the kitty litter indeed gave her traction, and she pulled away from the bush and parked several spots over.

"Let's try this again," she said to Ham, and they got out. Now that her panic and adrenaline rush had receded, she took a moment and looked around. She'd checked out a lot of places when she'd been online shopping for a place to lease. The four buildings in front of her had stuck out. In the pics, they'd been lit up like a postcard for holidays at the North Pole. The second building had been available, and she'd immediately signed the lease without a single ounce of doubt.

That had come later. In buckets.

The pictures hadn't done it justice. The cottage-style buildings were connected by a cobblestone walkway that wrapped around pine trees, each of them lit with twinkle lights, looking like she'd just stepped into some long-ago Swiss Alps village, complete with pitched roofs with front gables and wide eaves and exposed rafter tails. There were faux balconies and balustrades as well, the walls stone with wood accents, all of it welcoming and warm and . . . perfect.

The first building had a wooden sign that read OLDE TAHOE TAP and it was busy, even this late. The next one, hers, was dark, no sign. The next two were also dark, but their signs read MOUNTAIN TRAILS ART GALLERY and THE BOOK SPOT, clearly the bookstore Velma had mentioned.

"Guess what, Ham? We're home." It hadn't come cheap, but she'd been the beneficiary of her mom's life insurance, and she'd not spent a single penny of it until now. She was a woman with a savings and a business plan—which was to open within a few weeks and be in the black by the end of the year.

The first floor was eleven hundred square feet—the perfect size for a small bakery—and even better, there was a small apartment on the second floor.

Compared to some of the places she'd called home, it felt like a huge luxury.

She and Ham walked up to the front door to peer in the windows, but she couldn't see anything. Her lease didn't formally start for a week, but she'd asked to get in early. The plans had been for her landlord to meet her here with the keys, but when she knew she was going to be held up by traffic and weather, she'd called and he'd promised to leave a note on how to get in.

She knew there were three access points to the building: the front door, the back door—which led directly to the bakery kitchen—and there was also a set of exterior back stairs that led up to her apartment. Maybe the note would be on one of the back doors? Turning on the flashlight on her phone, she walked Ham down the narrow alley, grateful to not find a boogeyman or spider, her two biggest fears.

Okay, not true. Her biggest fear was being used, played, then shoved aside, unwanted and unneeded.

Halfway down the alley, Ham stopped. Then hunched, tail up.

"Oh, for the love of—" Harper broke off when two bikes came barreling down the path. It was two boys, the smaller one yelling to the bigger one, "Don't crash into the old lady! Watch out for the old lady!"

"Hey, I'm twenty-nine!" she yelled back, stepping off the path in the nick of time. Okay, so she lied by one year, sue her.

The boys on the bikes were long gone by the time she realized . . . they'd run over the steaming mountain of poop Ham had left.

He smiled up at her with pride, and she had to laugh as she pulled out a doggy bag. After she made use of the dumpster at the end of the alley, she used her phone flashlight to look around.

She had a stoop! And there was indeed a sticky note on the back door of her bakery. It made her giddy. *She had a bakery!* She felt accomplished, and also, for the first time in a long time, like she had her shit together. Possibly an illusion, but she was going to go with it.

The note was short and to the point: *keys at the bar.*

Hmm. Not exactly chatty. But what had she expected, a welcoming committee? She led Ham back through the alley and then to the front of the bar. Going inside was the absolute last thing she wanted to do. She was tired, and thanks to the weather, her naturally curly light brown hair had turned into a Chia Pet. Plus, at some point during the day, she'd smeared chocolate on her right boob. Yep, she most definitely had her shit together.

She put a leash on Ham, and he shot her a soulful, insulted gaze from his warm chocolate brown eyes.

"I know," she murmured, squatting to give him a hug. "You're an angel. But you're an angel who likes to shove your nose into strangers' crotches and also sometimes jumps on those same people to demand love. So the leash stays. We want friends, not irritated neighbors, okay?"

Guilty, he sighed and set his big head on her shoulder, nearly knocking her to her ass on the icy cobblestones. With a sigh, she hugged him again, then rose. "I hear Tahoe's super dog friendly. Hopefully you can come into the bar with me."

The extrovert of the two of them, he panted his happiness about that plan. He didn't care that it was 10:00 p.m. and she was freezing cold and exhausted, or that her old friends Panic and Anxiety were brewing behind her eyes in the form of a tension headache. But she'd started this, and she would finish it. She liked to think she was doggedly determined, but it'd been suggested to her that she didn't know when to walk away and cut her losses.

The bar was busy. There were a bunch of cars and trucks in

front of it, and delicious scents slid through the night. Just outside the double wooden doors sat a huge bowl of water on a mat. Next to the bowl was another bowl with doggy cookies. Relief made her knees weak. "I think you're welcome here," she said to Ham.

He smiled up at her like, *Duh, who wouldn't want me?*

With a snort, she led him inside and was immediately enveloped in warmth from the huge stone fireplace against the far wall, the waft of burgers and fries, and the sounds of music, laughter, and talking.

The place was packed, and for a beat she felt self-conscious about walking in alone. But this wasn't about being single in a bar. This was about the first day of the rest of her life, and all she needed was one little key. She looked around. There were two bartenders, one at each end, both multitasking: making drinks, taking orders. Both doing so effortless with ease, one smiling and engaged, the other not smiling, giving nothing of himself away.

The latter was the guy from the parking lot, all six feet of hard muscles, thick, unruly sun-kissed brown hair, and questionable attitude . . . and his sharp, see-all gaze had her in its grip.

She told herself to head to the other bartender. The friendly one. But her feet had other ideas, taking her on a collision course with the other one.

Nice Ass, aka Bodie.

CHAPTER 2

Bodie Campbell watched as Ms. I've Got This stepped inside his bar. She was wet, her hair had rioted about her face and shoulders, and she looked uneasy as she hesitated just inside. It didn't surprise him when their gazes met across the tavern. After all, he stood behind the bar. He expected her to move toward him and order a drink.

Instead, she spun on a heel and walked toward the other end of the bar, as far from him as she could get, her big goofball of a dog at her side, taller than some of the smaller tables.

"You're scaring away the customers again," his brother Mace said. "Thought you were past that. Didn't your government alphabet-agency-issued therapist tell you to try to stop alienating people?"

"You take out the trash yet?"

"You've got other employees for that. You know, the ones you actually pay."

Bodie gave him a level look, and Mace sighed. "You're still

mad I told Mom that you were back to running, even though your doc hasn't said it's okay."

Bodie used the same low-pitched voice he had once used on bad guys in his previous profession. "Just remember, I don't get mad; I get even."

Mace grinned.

"Just take out the damn trash." Bodie watched him go, tamping down on the niggle of worry at the back of his mind, because his baby brother hadn't been acting like himself.

Okay, so none of them had been, including himself. The Campbells hadn't been okay since Bodie's dad died six months ago now.

Bodie glanced down at the other end of the bar and once again caught Ms. I've Got This's eyes. She purposefully turned away. Okay then. He took a few orders and wiped down the bar, all while keeping track of everyone and everything. He was good at that, courtesy of his training with good old Uncle Sam.

He had eyes on the back left corner of the tables section, where four twentysomethings were getting loaded, but they were self-contained for now. A young woman, too young, sat alone in the back right corner, either waiting for someone or hiding out. It wouldn't be the first time an underage kid had tried to order alcohol here. Or the last.

At the bar, the guy to Bodie's right had hit his limit. If he asked for another round, he was going to be disappointed. The table against the left wall was a rowdy group of bachelorettes. In Bodie's experience, a group of inebriated women made the worst customers, as they tended to harass the male staff. And sure enough one of them reached out to pat their server's ass. Jason quickly turned, picked up their empties, and pocketed his tip, all while smoothly avoiding any and all hands. He looked up at Bodie and nodded. He was handling himself.

Normally on a July night, they'd have all the doors open and the front patio filled with tables for outdoor dining. The unexpected snow had taken care of that. Either way, it was a relief everything was running smoothly. He'd been out of the ATF, the Bureau of Alcohol, Tobacco, and Firearms, for six months, but three of those months had been spent in a rehab facility back east recovering from four gunshot holes in various parts of his body. He wouldn't say he was as good as new, but he was getting there. Fact was, he knew how to do a few things exceptionally well. Track down bad guys. Keep himself alive under any circumstances. Oh, and fight. All great skills for felons . . . and the people who pursued them.

He'd done the latter for a long time, until his luck had run out. Now all he wanted to do was just be for a while, with a good view. Running a bar on Lake Tahoe was close enough. Except he wasn't just running it—he owned it. There were four buildings on this lot, five if you counted the ramshackle warehouse behind the bar, and his dad had left one to each of his sons.

Even the dead one.

Bodie had gotten the bar and the warehouse, which had been his dad's fondest possession. It was impossible for Bodie to stand inside Olde Tahoe Tap and *not* think of the man who'd indelibly shaped his life and molded him into the man he was. A hard thing to think about while surrounded by a packed house. But, man, his dad would've loved this. The bar was making decent money, which meant Bodie *could* go home and do nothing if he wanted.

But he'd never really gotten the hang of doing nothing. So here he was, licking his wounds, both physical and mental, while trying to figure out how to put his life back together.

His phone buzzed, which he ignored. It buzzed again a few times in quick succession, and thinking it must have been an emergency, he pulled it from his pocket. No emergency, just the Campbell family text thread.

> **MOM:** Bodie, your brothers tell me you're working too many hours and looking too thin. Have Mace close up tonight and stop by, I've got a lasagna for you to take home. Love you. P.S. If you don't, I'll come by the bar with Hazel and her daughter Janie to set you two up. She's very nice.

> **MACE:** Go Mom!

> **ZEKE:** Mom, wait until I get there. I need to get a pic of Bodie's face.

Jesus. Zeke, their older brother, had a smart, hot attorney wife, three kids, and a white picket fence and was annoyingly perfect—according to their mom. And the US government should hire Mom Campbell, since her intimidation techniques were better than anyone he knew. Hazel was her BFF, and she'd been attempting to set her daughters up with the Campbell boys for years. Janie was perfectly nice, but *he* wasn't. Plus, he needed another complication like he needed . . . well, this stupid text thread. He hit reply:

> **BODIE:** Mom, I love you and your lasagna, but if you try to set me up on a date, I'll work 24/7 AND stop eating.

MACE CAME BACK from taking out the trash, tucking his phone into his pocket with a grin. Which faded when he looked across the bar and saw his ex, Shay, sitting calmly at a table, steadfastly ignoring him. "She just get here?"

"Yep," Bodie said, pleased to see someone else miserable. "I'm about to text Mom to let her know that you're ignoring the love of your life so she can get down here and facilitate your reconciliation."

Mace didn't bite. Nor did he take his gaze off Shay. "Why does she look like a cartoon?"

Bodie looked at Shay and felt a stir of amusement and affection for the woman they'd all grown up with, the one who still held Mace's heart in the palm of her hand. "She's dressed up as Velma."

"Who?"

"Velma, the cutie-pie detective from *Scooby-Doo*."

Still nothing from Mace.

"It's book club night," Bodie said. "The theme was fictional female detectives. Man, you should know this about your woman. Or read the family newsletter Mom emails us weekly."

Mace's expression was pure broodiness. "Shay's not mine anymore."

"Look, whatever you did, go grovel and get her back. She's been your better half for years."

Mace made a sound like a snarl, shook his head, and continued to take in Shay's short skirt, the wig, the high heels. "She was always after me to join the book club. I never did."

"Because you're an idiot." Bodie shook his head at Mace's hound-dog expression. "Just go over there."

"Can't."

Mace and Shay had been high school sweethearts, then college sweethearts, perfectly paired and wildly in love until about a month ago, when it was suddenly just over. Bodie hadn't been able to pry the story out of either of them, but hell, if those two couldn't make it work, the rest of the world was doomed. "Are you ever going to tell me why she dumped you?"

Mace's mouth tightened grimly, but he said nothing.

"Fine," Bodie said. "Don't talk to me. But talk to *someone*."

"Oh, like *you* talk about what happened to *you*? You think I don't know you stopped seeing that therapist the ATF was paying for?"

They stared at each other.

Chris, one of their chefs and also their cousin, put two plates up on the warmer station and hit the bell for Jason. "You're both messed up. But Bodie's worse."

Mace held out his hand, like, *See?*

"Though not by much," Chris said.

Bodie did the exaggerated hand-out gesture right back at Mace.

Chris shook his head. "Look," he said to Bodie. "Are you all broody and shit? Yeah. And we get it. You lost your longtime work partner through no fault of your own, and now you run a bar where the toughest decision you have to make anymore is when to cut off a drunk. You're also deflecting."

That this was true was little help at all. Well, except for the part where it hadn't been Bodie's fault that Tyler was killed. Because it had been.

"And," Mace added helpfully, "he also doesn't have to make any real connections because everything in a bar is superficial. Like what happens here, stays here."

Chris nodded. "He's also struggling with getting involved with anyone, not wanting to expose the fact that beneath that sharp edge of his, he's lost."

Bodie narrowed his eyes at both of them. "*Seriously?*"

"It's the college classes I'm taking," Chris said. "You're *classic* Psych 101."

Mace snorted.

Bodie gave both of them a classic middle-finger gesture and turned away.

Mace caught his arm. "Look," he said, softer now. "You were ratted out and betrayed by your CI, had to watch Tyler die, and then were left for dead yourself, all of which sucks and makes the rest of us feel murderous on your behalf. So I'll 'talk to someone'"—he used air quotes—"when *you* talk to someone."

Bodie shook his head. "You're the one 'deflecting.' You just don't want to deal with this Shay thing. But fair warning, Mom put Zeke on the hunt for the story of what happened between you two."

"Zeke can kiss my ass."

"Agreed. Now get your head in the game and start taking some orders so I don't have to fire you. Start with Shay."

Mace took another look at her and shook his head.

"Man, whatever. Cover me." Bodie slipped out from behind the bar and headed over to Shay's table. His leg and shoulder ached like hell thanks to the cold weather—and bullet holes— but he ignored them both. Habit had his gaze scanning the room again. The young woman was still there, though she ducked when she caught his gaze. And shit. She was even younger than he'd thought. He'd have to deal with that, but Shay first.

Shay stopped perusing the menu that she surely had memorized after all these years and lifted her face to Bodie's, not speaking, her eyes a deadpan stare.

"Hey, Velma," he said, and tried out his best I'm-just-a-normal-guy smile.

She snorted. "Still needs work. Too much teeth. You want to look friendly and open like a bartender, not crazed like a serial killer looking to add to his collection."

Bodie blew out a breath and gave up on the pretense.

Shay smiled. "You do the silent, mysterious shit better than anyone I know. It's all that dark, sexy intensity you have going. It works for you. Just stick with that."

He gave her a long look.

She laughed. "Yeah. That one. It's good. You could probably get laid every night if you wanted."

"Those years are long behind me. And stop trying to derail the reason I came over here."

"Can't blame a girl for trying."

"Come on," he said. "You and Mace have been together since ninth grade. Whatever happened can be fixed, right?"

Shay drew a deep breath and looked away. "Not up to me." She ran The Book Spot for her grandmother, but everyone thought of Shay as their resident fixer. She could fix anything. Unless . . . She hadn't been the one to break them.

It'd been Mace. Bodie felt the shock of that reverberate through him, because his brother was a dumbass sometimes, but not usually stupid. "Shay—"

She stood. "Never mind on a drink. I'm going to call it a night." Her gaze slid across the tavern to Mace, still standing behind the bar.

Mace stared right back.

"I'm sorry." Bodie gave her a quick hug. "If it helps, he's miserable. Maybe you could—"

"No." She gently squeezed Bodie's hand. "Mace and I said all we had to say." And with that, she turned and walked out into the night.

He moved back to Mace. "You want to tell me what happened?"

"Nope," Mace said, popping the *P*. "Oh, and the pretty woman at my end of the bar with the curls is looking for the keys to the building next door. Apparently she leased it for a bakery. Did Zeke tell you?"

At the time of their dad's death, his will hadn't been changed since he'd created it. Which meant that his fourth child, Austin—Mace's twin—was still in it, despite having been dead for fourteen years. Their mom had gotten the family home and the retirement funds. The remaining assets—the four buildings on Lake Drive—had been divided among the boys. Bodie had been gifted the first building, which held Olde Tahoe Tap and the small warehouse behind it. The second building, soon to be a bakery, apparently, was Austin's posthumously, and each of them pitched in with it, the profits going by unanimous decision to their mom. Mace, who worked in construction, had been left the third building, which held Shay's abuela's bookstore. Zeke, who ran his own property management firm, had been left the last building, currently leased out to an art gallery.

Zeke managed all the financials. Handy, since neither Mace nor Bodie wanted anything to do with that side of things.

Which had made it convenient for Bodie to come home broken, because all he'd had to do was show up and run the day-to-day at the bar.

The three of them pitched in and helped one another as needed, which didn't go nearly as peacefully as it might sound. Still, with Bodie short-staffed, Mace often stepped in as bartender. And Bodie helped on his construction sites as needed. Neither of them helped Zeke much. Their eldest brother knew everything and they knew nothing, ever—just ask him.

Bodie looked down the bar and once again met Ms. I've Got This's gaze. "Zeke told me he had someone starting August 1, and if he wasn't around, I should give them the keys to get in." Although he'd said nothing about her being a sassy, feisty, sexy, adorable hot mess. "She's a week early."

"Early *and* annoyed. I told her you'd be with her soon. She didn't seem thrilled."

Bodie set aside his towel and reached for his phone to text Zeke.

BODIE: Name of lessor?

ZEKE: Harper Shaw. Be nice.

Asshole. Bodie headed Harper Shaw's way. She watched him move toward her and didn't waste any time when he got within hearing distance.

"You," she said.

"In the flesh. How can I help you?"

"My name's Harper Shaw, and I've leased the building next door. A man named Zeke from the management company said I could get the keys here." She held out a yellow sticky note with Zeke's unmistakable messy scrawl.

Nice of him to call and let him know. "Sure," he said. "Do you have some ID?"

She pulled out her driver's license. "I signed the lease digitally and have a copy if you need to see it. So . . . do you have the keys?"

"I do. Welcome to Sunrise Cove."

"Thanks." She shrugged, making a visible effort to relax. "I haven't been here since I was twelve, but it's the last place I remember being truly happy, so . . ." She gave a small smile. "Here I am."

Understanding this more than she could know, he nodded. "Without your lists."

Her laugh was rueful. "Looking for spontaneity. Fun. Pleasing myself for a change."

He found his first smile of the night, and a flush immediately hit her cheeks. "I didn't mean it like that," she said quickly.

He laughed. So Ms. I've Got This would be right next door. He wasn't sure if that was a good thing or a bad thing. "You're early. The building isn't ready." They were slowly bringing all the buildings up to par, but this past month alone they'd been swamped with repairs from a small fire in the art gallery. Bodie thought they'd have at least another week to get next door all cleaned up and freshly painted.

"Zeke said it'd be okay for me to show up early."

Another thing Zeke had neglected to tell him. Probably he'd forgotten with his brain turned to mush by three kids under the age of eight. "He was mistaken. The building hasn't been cleaned or painted."

She looked disappointed but shook her head. "No worries. I can clean, and I'd rather pick out the paint colors anyway, if that's okay." She put her hand out for the keys and wriggled her fingers in a "gimme" gesture.

Good thing he wasn't looking for a sexy woman with a bad

attitude. Or any woman at all. He went to his office and came back with the keys but didn't hand them over. It was dumb, but just the keys reminded him of Austin, and hell, he missed that kid so fucking much. "The building's been empty for a while. We had to turn off the utilities a few months back when a pipe burst. We were scheduled to get them turned on this week anyway, and I can try to make that happen tomorrow. But obviously, you can't stay there tonight without them. You've got someplace to go for a few nights?"

"No worries," she repeated, wriggling her fingers again. "Look, not to be rude, but I've already signed all the paperwork. It's late, and I've just driven a million hours, most of it in the pouring rain, so if you don't mind . . ."

This was Zeke's mistake, but Bodie felt responsible for the lack of communication just the same, as well as the mess of a building she didn't deserve. "Can I offer you a complimentary hot meal first?"

"No, but thanks."

He leaned over the bar and took in the big, dorky, but beautiful dog sitting at her side, tall enough that his head was even with the barstools. "How about you, big guy? Want a burger to go?"

The dog straightened, ears going up in interest, and Bodie laughed. "Two seconds," he said, and went into the kitchen. His leg was bothering him today, which he ignored as he commandeered not one, but two burgers—with Chris swearing as he added fries and all the fixings—before heading back to Ms. I've Got This. "Here you go, Harper Shaw."

The frown line between her eyes vanished as she took the two loaded boxes and inhaled deeply with what looked like great pleasure. Then she met his gaze straight on for the first time. "Thank you," she said genuinely. "For everything. Feel free to stop by Sugar Pine Bakery as soon as I'm up and running for your choice of something sweet to eat."

That had him grinning again, and she clearly ran back through what she'd just said. "Not that," she said on a rough laugh, like she was rusty at it. "It's never going to be that!"

Something else they had in common.

"You tell her the place isn't ready yet?" Mace asked, materializing at his side to watch Harper and her dog head back out into the night.

"Yeah. She didn't seem to care."

"She will when she sees it."

"She's not going to stay there tonight, and we'll get on it first thing tomorrow. Cover me." He started out to the tables.

"Shit," Mace said. "Are you limping again?"

Bodie ignored him and headed toward the teen, still at the table in the back. He heard her give a small squeak when she saw him coming. Why was she out this late by herself? Actually, he could think of several reasons, none of them any good. She wore a knit cap with long dark hair coming out of it, was slender to the point of being painfully thin, and was licking the last of a Kit Kat bar from its wrapper.

"The kitchen's closing soon," he said. "But we still have appetizers available. Can I get you something?"

She was a deer in the headlights but recovered with admirable spunk. "Whatever you have on tap."

He raised a brow. "Size?"

"Um . . . medium."

He had to squelch his laugh so as to not insult her. "How old are you?"

She lifted her chin. "Old enough."

"Uh-huh."

"So is that a no on a beer, bartender?"

"Hard no, Kit Kat. How about a ginger ale and a burger?"

She snorted. "Only a grandpa would offer ginger ale."

"And only someone lying about their age would come into a bar and try to order a *medium* beer. How old are you?"

"Seventeen."

He gave her a long look.

She blew out a breath. "Okay, sixteen, but before you get any ideas about making me call home or whatever, I'm emancipated."

He could buy that she was sixteen. She was shivering and hugging herself. He realized she was wet straight through her thin sweatshirt. Her jeans had holes in them. The kind that were from genuine wear, not artfully precut. "We've got a lost and found box in the back," he said. "Let me get you a coat."

"No, I've got one in the car."

He eyed her doubtfully. "You have a car?"

"My mom's at Vons getting us some food."

There were no Vons in Sunrise Cove. They had only one grocery store. "You mean Safeway?"

"Right. Safeway."

He appreciated the bravado. Admired it, even. "A burger is my last offer. Take it or leave it."

She eyed the stand-up menu on the table, clearly trying to figure out how much a burger would cost. She had nothing with her except a ratty backpack at her feet. He figured the chances of her being homeless, broke, and hungry were high, and he felt a pang in his chest. "It's on the house."

"Okay." Her eyes slid to his, hooded and wary. "But what's it really going to cost me?"

The pang turned to an actual ache. "On the house means on the house."

She chewed on her lip, clearly debating whether to believe him. "Everything costs something."

Wasn't that the truth.

When he didn't speak, she stood. "Forget it. I'm outta here."

"Whoa. The food's completely free, no strings."

She eyed him for a long moment. "Do you have curly fries?"

Bodie gestured for her to sit back down, and he quickly moved to the kitchen, once again grabbing a burger and fries from the ready shelf, eliciting another long oath from Chris.

"Man, you suck."

"You can remind me of that when we're having your next employee review," Bodie said on his way out.

He brought the plate to the teen, and before he could even release it, she had the burger in hand.

"Maybe," he said as she began to shove food in her mouth, "after you eat, we can talk about calling your parents."

She was noncommittal on that, probably because she was inhaling the hamburger. Hopefully because she was inhaling the hamburger.

When she was down to her last curly fry, she looked up at him shyly and gave him a small, conciliatory smile. "Can I have some water?"

He smiled back. "Sure." He was gone for sixty seconds, but it took only half that time to realize his mistake.

When he got back to the table, she was smoke.

CHAPTER 3

Campbell brothers ongoing text thread

BODIE: Thanks for the head's up that the new renter was coming early.

ZEKE: Oh, excuse me, do you have a wife who's locked herself in the bathroom, a 7 year old who's smarter than you, and a 3 year old who's teaching the 2 year old how to stalk me? Do you?

Harper led Ham back to her building and took a moment to stand at her front door and take it all in. Yes, she'd just moved far from everyone and everything she'd ever known.

Without a list.

She felt good about it. Hell, she felt *great* about it. Sure, no one had so much as blinked when she'd left. And maybe that had hurt, but this . . . *This* was her new start, and the first thing she'd ever really done just for herself and no one else. She smiled down at Ham. "Welcome home, baby. It's just you and me."

His tail gave a loud thump-thump as he smiled up at her like she was all he needed.

She accessed her flashlight on her phone and pressed her face to the big picture window. Okay, so the landlord hadn't been kidding, there was indeed a lot to do. She could see dust on every surface. But all it needed was some elbow grease, new paint, and the scent of her homemade goods. *That* would make it feel like home. "We start in the morning," she told Ham, who panted happily up at her.

Pulling out her new keys, she reached for the door, then nearly swallowed her tongue. Staring at her, with a whole bunch of eyeballs, sat the biggest and fattest spider she'd ever seen—perched right on the door handle like he owned it.

Fear was a funny thing. It was also irrational. One second she nearly and very accidentally touched the spider to open the door, and in the next she'd jerked back, tripped over Ham, and was flat on her ass on the wet cobblestone walkway, swearing and sweating in spite of the cold night.

The bookstore next to her opened, and out came Velma, muttering something about too-long days at work and how life sucked. She stopped short at the sight of Harper on the ground, Ham in her lap. Or at least trying to get in her lap. Hard to do when he weighed more than she did, but he was giving it the old college try.

Velma went brows up. Apparently, she didn't believe in wasting words.

"M-m-mutant spider!" Harper managed, pointing at her door.

Velma came close, her knee-high boots click-clicking. She bent to eye the monster, then casually flicked it off. It went sailing into the air and . . . right at Harper. In the middle of heart failure, she ducked. "What the—" She raised her head. "You just flicked the biggest spider I've ever seen right at me!"

"He missed you by a mile." She patted Ham on the head, and he looked up at her adoringly.

Harper nudged Ham off her and got to her feet. "I thought you were gone for the night."

"Forgot my laptop. I'm surprised you haven't run back to San Diego by now."

"Hey, I'm not that big of a wuss." She eyed the now spider-free door. "Though I'm really regretting the whole no-lists thing because then I'd have remembered to bring *mutant* spider spray."

Velma laughed. "Wait until you see a bear. Or mountain cat."

Harper put a hand to her chest, because nope, it hadn't been heart failure before, but it was now. "Don't they live in the woods?"

Velma threw her arm out at the forest behind the buildings. "You live in the woods now, City Girl. Wolf spiders, bears, mountain cats, and coyotes are your new norm. Take it or leave it."

"Harper," she corrected distractedly. But it was true. She was a city girl. Who'd moved to the woods. "My name is Harper. And I'm going to take it."

"Uh-huh." Velma looked doubtful. "Shay. Have a nice move back to the city, Harper."

"I'm not moving back!" she yelled into the night after her.

Then she realized that by standing there, she was fair game to the wolf spiders, bears, and . . . good God . . . mountain cats. She turned back to her door and gulped.

Be brave.

With a nod to herself, she unlocked and opened the front door. Ham, no dummy, stayed behind her. She automatically reached out to hit the light switch. When nothing happened, she remembered: no electricity until tomorrow. So she once again used her flashlight app, beaming it around, taking in the remnants of the abandoned pizzeria that had been here before. This building was fewer square feet than the bar, but it was perfect for her. It had an open floor plan: the kitchen in the back, counter and displays in the center, and an area for customers to gather while they waited in the front. No furniture, though there were two booths against a wall. She moved to the kitchen and took her first deep breath. The kitchen was everything. Industrial, modernized, and, in spite of the dust, *perfect*.

In the narrow space between the front counter and kitchen was a locked door, which she knew led to the upstairs apartment. "Here goes nothing," she told Ham.

They went up the stairs, Ham so close at her back that he tripped her twice. She had no idea if he was protecting her or if he was just as nervous as she was that they'd find more creepy-crawlies, but the company was nice.

There was a bathroom and two small rooms, one of which she'd use as an office. Her furniture wouldn't come for a week. Until then, she'd use her trusty sleeping bag. "It'll be like camping," she told Ham.

Ham didn't look impressed.

She looked into the dark bathroom and caught several sets of red eyes aimed at her. "Ohmigod!" Quickly backing out, she slammed the door.

Ham let out a "ruh-roh" sound, and she took a deep breath. "We've got good news and bad. Good news first, since I'm a cup-half-full sort of gal . . ." She totally wasn't, but sometimes a girl had to fake it to make it. "We've got a bathtub. The bad news is that there's a raccoon and at least two babies with her."

Ham looked deeply concerned.

"I know, but hey, we've lived in far worse conditions, right?" Besides, she had no backup plan. Failure was not an option.

Going chin up, she gingerly opened the bathroom door again. Mama raccoon stood in front of her babies in a defensive pose, doing a pretty great imitation of a mama bear.

"You know what?" Harper held up a hand. "You take the bathroom, no problem." She slowly backed out and shut the door. "It's not like we've got water anyways," she told Ham. "They can be tomorrow's problem."

Twenty minutes later she'd settled in the sleeping bag she'd gotten out of her car. She lay on one of the bench seats of the booths, feet hanging off and all three of her extra blankets on top of her for added warmth. Her steadfast steed was on the other bench. He sighed.

"I know. Nice Ass warned us not to stay here, but we need every penny to make this work. We're fine." And she hadn't lied to Nice Ass—okay, so she now knew his name was Bodie, whatever—about having a place to stay. She did have a place.

Here.

A "puuuuffff" sounded in the dark, accompanied by an instant stench. "Seriously, Ham?" She scooped the neckline of her sweatshirt up over her mouth and nose. "Wow."

Her only answer was a soft snore. He could sleep anywhere, at any time. This was not in her skill set. She was more of a lie-awake-and-angst-about-every-problem-she'd-ever-had kind of person.

Her tummy growled, reminding her that she'd not eaten the food Bodie had given them. Excited, she sat up, then froze at the sound of something at the back door. Dear God, if that was the spider coming back with his entire family, she was going to expire on the spot.

But unless the spider had opposable thumbs, it was someone else—and that someone else was testing the handle to see if it was locked. She had a moment's panic during which she couldn't remember if she'd locked it after going out for her sleeping bag. "*Ham*," she whispered.

He climbed up on her side of the booth and tried to hide behind her. She patted him in reassurance. "Okay, baby, I've got this."

This was a lie, of course. She had bravado in spades, but *real* bravery? Not an ounce. Still, she slid out of her sleeping bag and did a quick circle, looking for something to defend herself. She had nothing. Latching on to Ham's collar, she urged him off the bench. No easy feat since he did not want to go. "Look, all I need is for you to stand with me and look fierce," she whispered. She had her cell phone in hand, having punched in 9-1-1, but hadn't activated the call yet. After all, it could just be Daddy Raccoon coming home from a long day at the office.

But she knew it wasn't when the back door slowly creeped open. Yep, she'd indeed forgotten to lock it. Rookie mistake, especially seeing as she'd survived the drive up here, faced a wolf spider and a badass raccoon mama . . . only to possibly die from a bakery invasion.

A shadow crept in and stopped in the open doorway as if taking in the lay of the land.

Harper, heart in her throat, rose up and aimed her flashlight at the shadow, her thumb hovering over the green "connect the call" circle on her phone at the same time. *"Who's there?"* she demanded.

The shadow turned toward her, and Harper stepped closer and beamed the light right into the shadow's face, hoping to momentarily stun them while she ran past.

But what she caught in the light made her freeze.

A teenaged girl.

CHAPTER 4

vy Roberts forced her chin up, even though her heart was in her throat as a flashlight was shoved in her face, blinding her. "Okay, so you got me," she said with as much sarcasm as she could muster. She'd dealt with enough hostile adults to know she had to stay cool and tough, not that it eased her fear. And she hated how her body had curled in on itself, expecting the worst.

The flashlight shifted away slightly, letting her see. "I'm sorry," her attacker said. "I didn't know you were a kid."

"I'm not a kid." She hadn't been a kid in a long time. "I'm eighteen." She no longer stumbled over the lie. She puffed herself up, trying to look bigger, because no way was she sharing her crash spot. Or the forty dollars left of the two hundred she'd, um, borrowed from her stepsister. "And you should get out of here before I call the cops."

The woman shifted her weight, and something fell from her sweater.

"Popcorn?" Ivy asked.

"Dammit," the woman muttered. "This is embarrassing."

If the situation hadn't been so tense, Ivy might've laughed, but the urge faded fast at the woman's next words.

"And I'll call the police for you. Since this is my place."

No. Ivy didn't buy that for a single second. She knew that she looked like a street kid, and that was exactly what she was now anyway. But this woman, whom she'd seen at the bar earlier, seemed only a step up from a street kid herself, with her long curly hair that looked like it was a bitch to tame so she hadn't even bothered, oversize sweatshirt falling to her thighs, and fake Ugg boots. "If this is your place," Ivy said, "why are all the lights off?"

"Temporary problem. Electricity's coming back on tomorrow. I've leased this building, which makes you the intruder."

Was she for real? "You leased this dump? You know there's, like, mountains of dust in here, right?"

"Yeah. Nothing a little work can't fix."

Oh great. A positive-attitude sort. Ivy hated positive-attitude people. They were always so . . . positive. And now she had to find another place to crash, which was making her anxious. "Okay, then. I'm outta here."

"Wait." Harper blocked the door. "Where will you go? Can I call someone for you?"

"None of your business, and no thank you."

"Look, you clearly have nowhere else to go. I can't just let a kid go off and fend for herself."

"Told you. I'm eighteen."

"Uh-huh."

Keep your cool or she'll call Child Services. "Fine," Ivy said. "I lied. I'm sixteen, but I'm emancipated and on my own."

The woman backed up a step so they could more easily see each other. "But where are you going to sleep tonight?"

Ivy looked her right in the eyes and lied again. It really was her one and only true skill, and it was well-honed. "Home."

She shook her head. "If you were going home, you wouldn't be breaking into my shop with what looks like everything you own in your backpack."

"It's laundry day."

"Great," the woman said. "Because I've got a washer and dryer. I mean, once the utilities come on tomorrow."

And that was where Ivy screwed up. "I'd settle for a blanket."

"Great, because I happen to have a little blanket problem. I keep buying them. I've got enough for both of us."

This was not the reaction Ivy had expected from a grown-up.

Nor was what the woman said next. "Look, can we be real for a minute? It's my first night here, and I'm kinda freaked out. You could stay if you want. You'd actually be doing me a favor."

Tempting, especially when compared to sleeping outside or at the bus station, which was a few miles' walk that she didn't want to make alone this late at night.

Plus, this shopping center, which held four buildings, linked together by a cobblestone sidewalk, looked like something right out of a European Alps village. Huh. Look at that, she had retained some high school history after all. "Maybe you're an ax murderer."

She laughed. "My name's Harper Shaw. And I'm not fond

of axes. Or murder. I can't even watch those true crime shows without having nightmares."

A smile escaped Ivy before she could bite it back. An adult admitting a weakness . . . "It's almost colder in here than outside."

"Like I said, I've got extra blankets. Ham and I don't mind sharing."

Ivy eyed the huge dog leaning against Harper's legs. Like, massive. She'd never had a dog growing up, but this one, monster size or not, had sweet brown eyes that said he wasn't a killer, unless licking to death counted. "A real attack dog, huh?"

Harper bent down and hugged him. "Hambone here is more of a lover than a fighter." She lifted her head and met Ivy's gaze. "Please stay rather than finding another spot to sleep. You'll be safe here at least."

Ivy didn't want to admit just how tempted she was. "What do I have to do for it?"

Harper looked shocked, then offended. "Nothing." She looked around. "Tomorrow I'm turning this place into the best bakery on the lake. Once I do that, there'll be all sorts of amazing things to eat here. You haven't lived until you've tasted my buttery croissants."

Ivy's mouth was watering, but she snorted. "You think you're going to do all that tomorrow?"

Harper ran a finger over the older wainscotting on the wall and came away with a lot of dust. "It'll be a work in progress, for sure. With some elbow grease and new paint, a week. Two tops."

Ivy snorted. "Good luck." She started toward the door, tensing for the cold night ahead of her.

"You're turning down a lovely stay on a hard bench seat in a dusty, cold, empty building? How can you pass up a deal like that?"

Ivy turned. She didn't care about sleeping in the booth or on the floor. She cared about what it would cost her. "Still waiting for the catch."

"No catch. Unless you want work cleaning. And if you stay long enough, I'll need a bakery employee. I'll pay you, of course."

"Without even asking why I broke in here or calling the cops on me?"

Harper held Ivy's gaze. "You didn't break anything or steal, so I don't see any reason. Unless you've done something you want to tell me about."

"No," Ivy said, because no way in hell did she want this lady digging into her past. She'd done so many things wrong, she wouldn't even know where to begin. And she sure as hell wasn't going to open up to Oprah here, who'd offered her a free place to stay. "Okay, fine. I'll stay. Tonight only."

"Great." Harper smiled. "Should we call your parents and tell them where you are?"

Ivy was surprised she could still feel disappointment. She was at the door when Harper spoke again.

"Hey, just because someone asks you a question doesn't mean you're obligated to answer."

Ivy slowly turned back. "So if I don't answer, you're cool with that?"

"Yes."

Ivy thought about that, and also why she wanted to trust this lady she didn't know a single thing about. "When you open, would I have to wear one of those stupid hats, like the employees at drive-thru places wear?"

Harper smiled. "How about we just wear whatever we've got that's clean? Clean is the only requirement."

Ivy thought about what she had in her backpack. Clean might be a problem.

"Don't worry about it now," Harper said. "I'm not opening for at least a few weeks."

And Ivy planned to be long gone by then. She'd be off starting her new life, far from everyone who'd never loved her. Maybe Santa Barbara. It seemed like it might be warm there, and she'd always wanted to live at the beach. "I'll think about it."

"Want to think about it while we sleep?"

Ivy knew she was going to cave, because after days of sleeping with one eye open, she knew this was a good choice. "Okay."

Not five minutes later, Harper and Ham were on one of the benches of the booth, with Ivy settling in on the other, wrapped in blankets that smelled fresh and clean. Harper had set up her phone like a little lantern, and they'd locked themselves in. They shared burgers and a bunch of fries between the three of them—Ham loved fries—and other than it being the same meal she'd eaten earlier, from the same place, nothing had ever tasted so good.

"So why are you sleeping in a booth instead of a bed?" Ivy asked, curious in spite of herself.

Harper smiled. "You tell me your story and I'll tell you mine."

"Forget it."

Harper sighed. "Fine. My stuff doesn't arrive until next week. I've got the apartment upstairs too and would sleep on the floor in my new bedroom, but there's a very protective mama raccoon and her babies in my bathroom."

Ivy snorted. "How tough are you if you're letting the raccoons run all over you?"

"Hey, it's a mama and her babies. I can't just kick her out."

Ivy was stymied by this. That Harper would worry about anything other than her own survival didn't compute. Then she sneezed, and Harper got up. "What are you doing?" Ivy asked.

Harper was on her knees in front of her duffel bag with her flashlight, pulling out two pairs of fuzzy socks. She tossed one to Ivy.

They were neon yellow with pink polka dots. Ivy found a smile. "What, are you three?"

"They were on sale. Put them on."

Ivy had on one and was wrestling with the other when a thick sweatshirt hit her in the face. "Hey," she said, pulling the sweatshirt away, only to be hit with a soft knit cap. "What the—"

"We're cold. Put it all on."

Ivy held out the sweatshirt, which read BAKERS DO IT BATTER, and snorted. "Nice."

"Crap. Nope. Give that one back." Harper yanked it out of Ivy's hands and then tossed her another.

This one read: A CUPCAKE IS JUST A MUFFIN WHO BELIEVED IN ITSELF. "You want me to wear the sappy one?" Ivy asked, amused in spite of herself.

"I want you warm," Harper said, and then waited until Ivy got it on before dressing herself.

Wearing socks, a tank, a T-shirt, and a sweatshirt—hers—and now also Harper's sweatshirt, hat, and fuzzy socks on top of it all, she had to laugh. "I feel like the abominable snowman."

"But a warm one, right?"

"I guess." Ivy watched as Harper slid back into her sleeping bag. The woman had taken care of Ivy before taking care of herself. In fact, Ivy was pretty certain Harper had given her the thickest of the extra clothes.

Why would she do that for a perfect stranger?

"You okay?" Harper asked.

No. No, she wasn't. But she had no idea how to ask about her greatest fears. Like, where did she belong? Her mom was currently on a monthlong honeymoon, which included a cruise from New York to London and back with her fourth husband, completely unreachable. When her mom had remarried again and Ivy had found out she had an older stepsister named Kylie, she'd really thought she'd have an ally, even a *real* older sister. And in fact, that was where Ivy had been told to stay during her mom's trip. But she'd quickly realized Kylie had her own family and didn't want to take care of anyone else.

Ivy's mom probably still thought Ivy was at Kylie's house. But between Kylie's own three kids, there hadn't really been room for her. Hell, when she'd said she was going to stay with a friend, Kylie had been all "Cool, just be sure to tell your mom when she calls to check in."

That had been a week and a train and two buses ago. Her mom hadn't checked in once.

"Ivy?"

She drew a deep breath, her courage bolstered by the dark. "Do you ever feel like you were put in a world that wasn't meant for you?"

When Harper didn't immediately say anything, Ivy rushed out a quick "Never mind." She rolled over, because she knew Harper was going to spout something stupidly adult. Like, *Give it time*, or *Things will get better*. Or her least favorite, *You just need to stop being so dramatic*.

To her surprise, Harper sighed and said quietly, "More times than I can count. But tonight . . . tonight I feel like we're both right where we're supposed to be."

Ivy didn't say anything. She couldn't. Her throat felt too tight. She closed her eyes in order to not let the tears fall, but they fell anyway there in the dark. Refusing to make a sound, she sucked it all in, giving herself a headache to match her heartache.

Ham jumped down from his side of the booth with a grunt, then padded over to Ivy, shocking her when he climbed up to lie with her, squishing her under a gazillion pounds of soft, furry dog she wouldn't have pushed away for anything.

"He thinks everyone's his best friend," Harper said. "You can just give him a nudge, he'll get down."

Ivy looked into Ham's warm eyes. He delicately licked her on the chin, low on saliva, heavy on love, and her heart squeezed.

"Is he too heavy?" Harper asked.

"No." Ivy wrapped her arms around him, and he dropped his

big head on her chest, letting out a heavy dog sigh of relaxation. "He's perfect," she whispered.

HARPER WOKE FROM a dead sleep to a noise she couldn't place. Heart pounding in her throat, she took stock. Dawn's early light was filtering in from the two big picture windows in the storefront. She sat up, head cocked. Whatever it was, it wasn't coming from inside, unless she counted Ham's snoring. She glanced over and found Ham and Ivy wrapped around each other, still fast asleep on the opposite bench.

Ivy was right—a watchdog Ham was not.

Slipping out of her sleeping bag was a real loss.

Ham lifted his head.

"Stay," she whispered. "I swear I'm not doing anything important and I'll be right back. One of us should get to be cozy." With her exhales turning into little clouds in front of her face, she moved to the window. The morning sky was a stunning rainbow of colors as dawn gave way to a new day, the storm long gone.

Then her gaze locked on her car. "What the—" Her driver's-side door was open, with a big brown hairy bear butt sticking out. It wasn't Winnie the Pooh. In fact, he was nearly as big as her car, and she stood there frozen in place, stunned, because if she wasn't mistaken, he was eating the last of her popcorn, the bastard.

And possibly her steering wheel.

A man appeared in her peripheral. Bodie. He was yelling something she couldn't catch, waving his arms over his head, and . . .

The bear lumbered backward out of her car and slowly turned to face Bodie.

Was the man nuts? They were face-to-face, separated by maybe ten feet, and he was about to get eaten right before her eyes!

But Bodie stood his ground, each move he made calm and deliberate, looking every bit as big and bad and menacing as the bear.

Then suddenly the bear turned and ambled off into the woods.

Harper shoved her feet into her sneakers and yanked on her jacket before taking another peek out the window. Now it was Bodie in her car . . . cleaning up? She had no idea why he'd be doing that. In her experience, no one just did nice things—not her dad, her ex, or the friends who had vanished along with her ex . . .

She yanked open the door but wasn't stupid enough to step out. "What are you doing?"

Bodie straightened and looked at her. "Saving your car. Did you sleep here last night?"

She ignored the question. "You yelled at that bear like he was a wayward teenager," she said, marveling.

"Let me rephrase," he said. "*Did you sleep here last night?*"

She cupped a hand around her ear. "What?"

"Wow." He shook his head, maybe at her bravery, probably at her stupidity. "This is the Sierras," he said. "We've got bears. *Smart* bears who help themselves to tourists' vehicles when they're dumb enough to leave food in them. You practically issued an evite."

She opened her mouth to get defensive but knew he was right.

"Thanks for saving my car, but you should go before he comes back to eat you."

He flashed an unexpected smile. "Worried about me?"

"Worried you'll get killed and Zeke the landlord will blame me."

His smile remained. "Yeah. You're worried about me. Oh, and Zeke's one of my brothers. We own these four buildings."

"Oh my God," she said. "You're my landlord?"

"Well, one of them anyway." He turned to go. "Also, the bears here are American black bears. For the most part, they avoid dealing with people. They're mild and meek."

As opposed to the rugged, incredibly sexy man who'd chased the bear off without concern for life or limb. Her ex wouldn't even fight the field mouse that once tried to share their apartment. "That bear didn't look afraid of anything, not even you."

"Oh, he wasn't. But neither did he want to start a fight." His smile faded. "You need to lock up every night and never, ever leave any food in it. Not even gum. And . . ." He reached into her passenger door and pulled out what looked like the passenger-seat headrest. "You're going to need a new one of these." He eyed her sneakers as she came toward him. "And some snow boots."

"It's July."

"And?"

She sighed. "I didn't expect snow. Nor for that snow to be so . . . cold."

He reached back into her car and pulled out a round tin and a large jar. "The bear was just about to get into these."

She gasped at the sight of the jar. "My sourdough bread starter! You saved her!"

He looked down at it. "Her? This . . . *gunk* is a her?"

"Yes." She snatched it from him. "She's the best sourdough bread starter on the planet. It was my mom's secret recipe." She hugged the jar to her chest, feeling ridiculously emotional. What if the bear had broken the jar? She could re-create the sourdough starter, but she couldn't replace her mom's jar. "Thank you," she said when she could talk again. She nodded to the tin still in his hands. "That's filled with my specialty chocolate and mint chip cookies. Take some."

He shook his head. "You don't have to—"

"Eat one and then tell me you wouldn't kill for the rest."

He opened the tin, picked up one of her huge, fluffy cookies, and took a bite. "Oh my God," he murmured, and closed his eyes.

"Right?"

He held up a hand, like he needed a moment. Not opening his eyes, he finished the cookie before looking at her. "They're all right."

She arched a brow and took the tin back. "Since you didn't want them—"

"Whoa, no need to be hasty." He grabbed a few more cookies.

She smiled, quite pleased with herself and her cookies.

He looked back at her car. "Anything else valuable in there?"

"Nothing like this. Seriously, thank you."

"So, I'm guessing this is your first experience with snow."

"Of course not. I used to go to Disneyland every single Christmas." She smiled. "They blow snow onto Main Street."

"I stand corrected," he said, and looked her over, clearly taking in her pj's. "Please tell me you didn't really sleep in there last night."

"Okay, I won't tell you."

"Harper, it dropped down to twenty-one degrees."

Yeah, she'd noticed, and damn, certain parts of her noticed something else—the way her name sounded on his lips. "It was fine," she said. "The raccoon mama hardly objected."

"Ah, damn. Roxy's back?"

"Roxy?"

"A pesky raccoon fond of finer living."

"She has two babies with her."

Bodie ran a hand down his face. "I'm sorry. I've caught her twice and let her go out in the woods. Before my brother and I get going on cleaning and painting your place, we'll relocate her again—"

"No! She's got babies! She'll leave when she's ready."

He looked at her as if she was bonkers, and hell, maybe she was.

"Look, Harper, if I'd known you didn't have a place to stay, I'd have given you my buddy's number. He runs a B-and-B down the road."

She shook her head. "It was fine," she repeated.

"It's not fine, it's a mess. You've got no utilities and a bunch of other problems, like the kitchen sink's slow leak. It mostly just needs a wrench every once in a while, which is why there's a toolbox beneath your sink, but we intended to get everything fixed before you moved in."

"Hardly matters when I don't have water anyway."

He grimaced, like she wasn't making him feel better. "The utilities are coming on by noon."

"Great, thank you." She wasn't sorry she'd stayed. Yes, she was saving every single penny she had as capital for getting her bakery up and running. But more importantly, if she'd gone somewhere else last night, Ivy might've frozen to death. "Thanks for facing down the bear for me, I really appreciate it. But I'll clean the place myself. I like to clean, it's my thinking time. So don't worry, I've got everything under control." This was pure bluster on her part, because honestly, between her and . . . well, her, she wasn't at all sure she had anything at the moment, much less anything under control. But she intended to get there, raccoons, bears, and spiders be damned.

CHAPTER 5

Campbell brothers ongoing text thread

ZEKE: Which of you told my kids that the Tooth Fairy leaves *ten* bucks a tooth?

BODIE: Ten bucks? Mom used to leave a quarter. I feel cheated.

ZEKE: Mace, you owe me ten bucks.

MACE: Hey, I told them five bucks a tooth. You're being played, bro . . .

ZEKE: Wait until you jackasses have kids . . .

After the bear scare, Harper walked back inside. She was greeted by chocolate brown eyes and a wagging tail. She smiled as Ham's tail slapped the floor when he sat.

She hunkered down and scratched behind his ears. He licked her face and twirled, waiting for her to follow him to the big container of dog food she'd brought with her. "Oh, so you're not happy to see me, you're just hungry."

He sat patiently.

Harper laughed, fed him, then grabbed a broom she'd found left behind in the kitchen closet and started on the dust bunnies. She was trying to reach up into one of the ceiling corners to nail a cobweb when Ivy said, "Do you know you whisper 'okay' and 'all right' over and over?"

Harper turned to face her. "Talking to yourself is the definition of being an adult."

"Yet another reason to never be an adult," Ivy said.

"How did you sleep? Since you were wearing Ham . . ."

Ivy smiled. "Great. It was nice. You know, not to sleep with one eye open."

Harper did know, and her heart ached that Ivy knew too. "You really can stay as long as you want." She paused, wanting to tread lightly here. "But if you were my daughter, I'd be so worried—"

"My mom's out of the country for a few weeks. No Wi-Fi. I'm supposed to be staying with my stepsister Kylie, but she's too busy with her own kids."

"Can we just call Kylie to let her know you're safe?"

Ivy looked away. "You letting me stay here could get you into trouble, right? Like if Child Services found out you were harboring a minor—"

"I don't care about that." And it was the absolute truth. "I care about you."

"Kylie knows my number, and I don't have any missed calls."

Harper already hated this Kylie person. "Okay, then just text her that you're safe and she can reach you if she needs to." She watched Ivy think and eventually nod her head.

"Okay, I'll text her. But that's it." Ivy turned away. "This place really needs some work, doesn't it?"

Harper recognized a subject change when she heard one. "It's a diamond in the rough."

"Why don't you just make your landlord fix this up?"

"Because I'm a strong, independent woman and don't need no stinkin' help."

Ivy laughed but then began pulling off the borrowed clothes.

"Wait, you don't have to do that."

Ivy hesitated. Like maybe she thought she should leave. "You don't have to go," Harper said. "I meant what I said last night. I could really use your help."

Ivy looked away. "I've got some things I have to do."

"Okay, but you'll come back tonight to sleep? Unless you're leaving the area?"

"No. I . . . I've got some things still to do here."

"Then I'll see you later," Harper said, knowing she was pushing, but she was willing to risk that in order to make sure Ivy knew she wanted her here.

The teen drew a deep breath, like she wanted to say something, but then seemed to think better of it. "I'll be back in an hour to help you clean. Do you want me to bring anything?"

Harper looked into her eyes, which admittedly didn't give much away. The girl was good at hiding in plain sight, and Harper suspected the skill was hard-learned.

Her own survivor skills sure had been. And there was just something about Ivy that reached through the walls Harper had built around her heart. Maybe because she suspected they'd been through a lot of the same shit. Ivy clearly didn't have much, but that she'd offered to bring back something told Harper everything she needed to know about her. "Just bring *you* so I know you're sleeping somewhere safe and sound."

Ivy looked bemused, either at the thought of someone caring about her or that Harper thought she couldn't take care of herself. "Thanks," she said.

She hadn't been gone three minutes when a knock came at the kitchen door.

Ham went skidding from where he'd been snoozing in the front room, straight through to the back, pressing his nose to the door in hopes that whoever stood there was his new best friend.

It was Bodie, who accepted Ham's nose to the crotch with good grace. He was carrying a big cage in one hand and a mop in the other, an open bin of cleaning supplies at his feet.

Surprised at the thoughtfulness, she smiled. "Thanks."

He set down the mop and ruffled the top of Ham's head. "Is it okay if I go upstairs and get Roxy and the babies out of your hair?"

"Don't take her too far. She might have more family nearby."

"Understood." When he headed up the stairs, she followed, doing her best not to notice that his jeans were faded to a buttery softness that seemed to perfectly hug his body. Same with the long-sleeved shirt that stretched taut over his broad shoulders and fell loose to his hips. But what she really noticed was that slight limp she'd seen last night. He was most definitely favoring his left leg.

"You'll have electricity, gas, and water by noon," he reminded her.

"Thanks. Are you hurt?"

At the top of the stairs, he glanced into her empty bedroom.

"Everything's in a packing pod, which doesn't arrive until next week."

He nodded and paused to open one end of the cage, pulling treats from his pocket to set inside. "So why Sunrise Cove?"

"Excuse me?"

"Just wondering why someone would leave San Diego for Lake Tahoe."

Two could play at the not-answering-personal-questions thing, so she looked pointedly at his leg.

A corner of his mouth twitched. "Touché," he said.

His eyes were fascinating, she realized, a combo of gold and brown the color of warm brandy. Not that she'd ever had warm brandy. Or any brandy, for that matter.

He walked the cage into her bathroom.

She automatically followed but stopped short just inside the door. One, because she was a city girl, born and bred. Raccoons were cute—in pictures. She had no idea how cute they might be close enough to scratch her eyes out. And two, it was extremely tight in the tiny bathroom. And someone smelled good. Like man good. Like *really* man good. In fact, she took one more deep inhale. When he turned to look at her, she nearly choked by accident.

"Did you just try to inhale me?" he asked, looking amused.

"Ha." She crossed her arms. "You wish."

He raised a single brow. She tried to do it back, but she guessed she had failed miserably when he snorted. And right then and there, she promised herself she'd never try to smell him again, *ever*, not even if hell froze over. Besides, she didn't care if he smelled good, because though she didn't believe in diets in general, she *was* on a man-free diet. A strict one.

Bodie crouched low in front of the tub. "Hey, darlin'," he crooned softly, presumably to Roxie, not that Harper could see anything past those broad shoulders. "You know the drill. And look, I've brought liver jerky. Your favorite. Aw, that's a good girl," he murmured. "One baby at a time. No rush, sweet pea, I've got all day for you."

Harper still couldn't see, but if she'd been Roxy and that low, sexy voice was talking to her, she'd probably do whatever he wanted.

And more.

When Bodie rose and turned with the cage in his hands, Roxie and her babies glared at Harper. "I'm so sorry," she told them.

Bodie laughed low in his throat. "Don't let her make you feel guilty or she'll bring the rest of her family next time. And trust me, it's a large one. Do you really want to do the cleaning by yourself?"

"Yes," she said. "But I appreciate the supplies."

He nodded, and their shoulders brushed as he shifted past her, giving her a spark of . . . *damn*.

Sexual awareness.

Not what she expected to spark joy.

"I'm also going to have your sign fixed. The wooden one out front. What's the name of your bakery?"

"Sugar Pine Bakery." She smiled. "I used to camp at Sugar Pine Point with my mom."

"One of my favorite places," he said. "If you want to pick out paint colors for the interior, that's great. But we can handle the actual painting for you."

"We?"

"My brothers and I. But fair warning—Zeke's wife's a lawyer and she's super busy this week, so he'll have the puppies, which means they'll be more work than help. But they provide good comic relief."

"He's got puppies? Plural?"

"Worse. Kidlets. And I'm pretty sure they're feral."

Harper was fascinated by this. Her own family was small. Just her and her dad, and they rarely saw each other. There was no extended family, so all she knew about big clans were what she'd seen on TV and in the movies. "How many brothers do you have?"

"Three." He paused, and something passed over his face

quickly. "Well, two now. We can hit the local hardware store whenever it works for you." And then he was gone, leaving her with more questions than she had answers.

Like what had happened to the fourth brother?

Why did he seem so charismatic and open, but at the same time closed off?

What was wrong with his leg?

And . . . why did he smell so damn good?

AN HOUR LATER the power, water, and gas came on as promised, and Harper scrubbed the bathroom to within an inch of its life. Roxie had been cute but also stinky. When she finished, she was thrilled to get a long, hot shower. She'd just finished dressing herself in fresh clothes when Ivy showed up with a breakfast burrito that she split with Harper and Ham.

After, Ivy showered, and then the rest of the cleaning began. They finished the upstairs, then carried up their sleeping bags and blankets. Harper gave Ivy a choice: sleep with her, or sleep in the room that would become her office when she got her things delivered. Ivy choose the office but asked if they could leave the doors open, which was perfectly fine with Harper.

They were just about ready to go downstairs to clean when someone came in the front door with a "Hello?"

She knew by the way her body reacted that it was Bodie, which was more than a little annoying. Because since when were her body and brain not aligned?

"Harper?"

"Coming!" She jogged down the stairs, Ham on her heels, also expecting Ivy to follow as well, but she didn't.

"Hey," Bodie said when she came around the corner to the front room. He smiled at the sight of her, prompting her to look down.

Yep, covered in dust. "Better than popcorn, right?"

His smile turned into a grin that was made all the sexier for that slash on the left side of his mouth. Why was that dimple so damn irresistible?

"Just wanted to let you know, when you're ready to hit the hardware store, you can find me at the bar or in the warehouse behind it."

"Is tomorrow morning okay?" she asked, still a little stunned by the heart-stopping grin. "We should finish cleaning by tonight."

"We?"

She could almost hear Ivy's suspended breathing from the apartment above. For whatever reason, the teen wanted anonymity, and for now at least, Harper was willing to give it to her. "Ham and I."

Bodie crouched down to give Ham a good rubdown, which had her boy dropping to the floor with an earth-rattling thud, tail swishing back and forth, sweeping the floor. "Morning works for me." Bodie gave Ham one last rub behind the ears and left.

Ham whined in sorrow at his departure.

And Harper nearly did the same.

CHAPTER 6

Several hours later, Harper and Ivy stood at the bottom of the interior staircase that led to her apartment, staring up at the dead bulbs in the light fixtures on the ceiling. Harper had considered climbing onto the hand railing to get to them, but there was a reason she'd never made it in gymnastics. Her balance wasn't great. Her middle school coach had attributed it to her inability to concentrate. Harper attributed it to her love of eating her own baked goods. She was smarter about her choices these days, at least mostly, and she'd added yoga and walking to her daily routine.

Okay, not daily.

But she did her best, choosing not to put too much brain power behind how she looked, preferring to concentrate on how she felt. And she could honestly say, even with the wolf spiders, raccoons, and bears, oh my, she'd never felt more excited or happy.

"I could probably climb up there," Ivy said.

"Yeah, it's the 'probably' part that's problematic. I just need to borrow a ladder."

"Or tell Landlord Dude to fix this."

Harper opened her mouth, but Ivy beat her to it. "Let me guess," the teen said. "Strong, independent women don't ask for help."

"See? Learning already. I'll be right back, I'm just going to borrow a ladder." She grabbed her tin of cookies, her friendship bribe that she knew made her irresistible. She headed outside, surprised by the warmth of the day, a stark, shocking contrast to the night before. The Swiss Alps–style buildings were just as beautiful in the daylight as they'd been at night. The snow was completely gone, like it'd never even been there in the first place.

She headed next door to The Book Spot. When she opened the door, a chime to the tune of the *Addams Family* theme song went off, making her laugh. The charming, quaint store wasn't any bigger than hers, and it was stuffed to the gills with books in the warmest, most welcoming way possible. There were little nooks and overstuffed chairs everywhere, and beautiful, thriving plants on top of shelves and hanging in corners.

Shay sat behind the counter on a laptop. There were two jars on the counter. One labeled "Swear Jar," the other labeled "Telling People About Books When I Wasn't Asked." It was that jar that was filled nearly to the top with coins, making Harper smile.

"What?" Shay asked without looking up.

Harper was startled both by the annoyed tone and also the fact that without Velma's red wig and makeup, Shay was dark-haired, dark-eyed, and stunning. "Are you always this friendly?"

"It's called sarcasm. It's how I hug. I save the cheery hellos for customers."

"Maybe I'm a customer," Harper said.

"Are you?"

"Okay, no."

Shay sighed and pushed away her laptop. "Look, I was late to work and got chewed out by my abuela, *twice*. I can't remember the password to get into the system, but I also can't answer the secret questions correctly."

"So, it's like you don't even know yourself?" Harper asked dryly.

Shay slid her an unamused look.

Harper smiled a hopefully irresistible smile and set the tin of cookies on the counter. "You could try setting an alarm so you're not late."

"I have an alarm set. It's internally wired and called anxiety."

"Well, everyone has that one," Harper said, unimpressed. "So . . ."

"*What?*"

"I kinda need some help," Harper admitted.

"No."

"Shay Rylie Anna Ramirez, what kind of way is that to talk to someone?" This was asked by an older woman who was the spitting image of Shay, with the exception being that her hair was pure white and billowing wildly around her shoulders like the bulbous clouds in the day's sky. She turned her sharp, dark eyes on Harper and said something in rapid Spanish to Shay.

Shay didn't respond.

"I'm Rosa," the older woman said to Harper. She jabbed a finger in Shay's direction. "I'm this one's abuela, though with her horrible manners, I don't often admit it."

Shay rolled her eyes.

"I saw that," her abuela said without taking her eyes off Harper. "And you can call me Abuela. How can we help you?"

"My name's Harper Shaw, and I'm leasing the building next door for my bakery." She opened her tin. "I brought my homemade chocolate and mint chip cookies." She waited until both women had taken one and bitten into it before saying, "I was wondering if you had a ladder I might borrow."

Shay's abuela said something in Spanish to Shay.

"What did she say?" Harper asked.

"She said if I'd ever apply myself, I *still* couldn't make cookies this good."

"You could," Harper said. "I could show you how."

Shay blinked, like she didn't know how to take the random act of kindness.

"It's really not that hard," Harper said.

"I call it strategic incompetence." Shay's lips curved. "The art of avoiding certain tasks by pretending you don't know how to do them."

Harper laughed. "Something to remember."

"Good luck baking this good here at altitude," Abuela said. "As for a ladder, we just borrow the Campbells' tools whenever we need something." A cell phone rang from somewhere behind them. "I'm going to get that." She grabbed two more cookies, one for each hand, then narrowed her eyes at Shay. "Behave."

Shay finished her cookie and looked at Harper, eyes unreadable, silent until her abuela was out of hearing range. "When you go over there for a ladder, steer clear of Mace. He just got out of a longtime serious relationship, so he's not interested."

Harper knew that devastated, just-broken-up look. She'd worn that look. "Let me guess. You're the serious relationship he just got out of, right?"

"Your second day here and already you're the expert on all things Campbell?"

"Oh, trust me," Harper said on a laugh. "I'm an expert on exactly nothing. Well, except cookies. I'm definitely an expert on those." She pointed at Shay. "You almost just smiled, I can tell."

This got her another eye roll.

"Okay, I'm going," Harper said, putting the lid back on her tin and picking it up.

Shay sighed. "Bodie's probably in the warehouse behind the bar, restoring his dad's old boat. He's a sucker for anything neglected or forgotten. If you look particularly helpless, he'll come fix whatever it is that needs fixing."

"Doesn't that throw girl power back about fifty years?" Harper asked.

"Not if it gets you the tools you need."

True enough. "I don't do helpless."

Shay shrugged. "Then I hope you know how to solve all your own problems."

Shay's abuela stuck her head out from the back. "So we're not making any damn money today?" she yelled. "We're just going to stand around and wring our damn hands? Is that it?

Mi madre did not fight for damn women's rights for you two to stand around and quack quack quack."

"Abuela, you stand around plenty when you're on the beach with your metal detector every morning for hours," Shay yelled back.

"I'll have you know I made ten bucks this morning!"

Well, that escalated quickly. Harper motioned toward the door. "Okay, so I'll just—"

"Good!" Shay said to her abuela. "You can put the entire ten bucks in the swear jar!"

Abuela surprised Harper by cackling. "Ms. Smarty Pants with the razor tongue."

"I'm told I get both from you," Shay said.

Abuela cackled again.

Harper escaped outside. She didn't have a sister. Or a grandma, for that matter. She did have a dad who didn't take much notice of her and an ex who'd turned out to be not anything close to the man she'd thought he was. So while both Shay and her abuela were scary as hell, she wouldn't mind sharing a relationship like they had with someone who loved and accepted her as she was.

Since that was a place she didn't want to visit right now, she went to the bar first. No Campbells working, but she placed an order for two burgers, two orders of fries, and two lemonades to go. She said she'd be back in a few and made her way to the old-time metal warehouse. The windows and double doors were all open to the sunny day. Harper moved to the open doorway and found Bodie next to a huge wooden boat, a little sweaty, covered in sawdust, sanding away on the hull in a long-sleeved T-shirt, those faded, ripped jeans, and beat-up work boots.

Flicking off the power, he straightened, the sander in his hand at his side. His tousled brown hair looked to be past due for a trim, and he clearly hadn't touched a razor in a few days. The rough-and-tumble look made her swallow hard. "I need, um . . ." She was trying to remember why she'd come while keeping her eyes on his, but holy cow. No, really, *holy cow* . . . "Hi."

"Hi." His eyes were warm. Curious. "What's up? You want to go to the store today instead?"

"No." She drew a deep breath. "I'm here because it's the last place I was really happy," she said, answering his question from earlier.

He raised a brow. "This warehouse?"

"Sunrise Cove."

He smiled. He'd been just teasing her. "And are you feeling happy yet?"

She took in his sexiness and smiled back. "Getting there." She stepped closer and met his gaze straight on. "And . . . ?" she asked pointedly.

It was his turn to take in a deep breath. "I was hurt on the job."

"Bartending?"

"No." His gaze tracked over her head, like he was trying to make a decision. "I was an ATF agent. A case went sideways. Long story."

Being ATF was a sharp turn from being a bartender. "I like long stories," she said.

Their gazes met and held, and she felt a zing go through her that felt alarmingly . . . real.

"Maybe another time," he finally said.

"Okay." But it took her mind a beat to get off the idea of him working a dangerous job such as being an ATF agent, to him getting hurt, to . . . what had she come here for again? "I was hoping to borrow a ladder. Oh, and a lightbulb." Her feet took her even closer, to the frame of the boat. "It's beautiful. Is this yours?"

He didn't answer, so she looked at him again, which was a whole lot like looking into a solar eclipse for the fact that it left her speechless in the face of its beauty.

"It was my dad's," he finally said.

It was clear by his tone that his dad had passed, and she ached for him because she knew what losing a parent felt like. "I'm sorry."

He shrugged that off. "Sometimes I find myself redoing something on the boat that doesn't need to be redone, just so I won't finish it. Because if I do, it means his last project is done and I'll lose that connection to him."

She held his gaze. "When I lost my mom, I got the pocket watch she always kept on her because it was her grandpa's." She pulled it out of her pocket and showed it to him. "Now *I* always carry it. It's broken, always has been, but she never fixed it. She used to say if she fixed it then time would start again and she was afraid she'd forget him. Now it's mine, still broken, and I can't fix it for the same reason—because it would mean I might forget her."

"Ah, Harper."

And then it was her turn to nod, because she was almost undone by the understanding in his gaze.

"Who raised you after your mom passed?" he asked.

She managed a smile. "It's a long story. Maybe another time."

He smiled too. "For another time then." He ran a hand over the wood hull. "My dad worked on this thing for years whenever he had spare time. But with four boys, spare time was a luxury he didn't have very often." He shook his head. "The real irony is that when he was alive, I never wanted to do this with him, and now all I want is a second chance to do just that."

Harper's tummy fluttered. She told herself it was indigestion from the breakfast burrito, but that was a lie. It was something much more dangerous, something she refused to acknowledge. "He was a good guy?"

"The best. We had it good. Certainly better than I thought while growing up, that's for sure." His smile was wry. "How about you? You close to your dad?"

"He's remarried and has kids."

"Aren't you his kid too?" he asked.

"Yeah." She turned from him, and under the guise of staring at the boat, she ran a finger along the hull. "But I think it's more that I'm a painful reminder and possibly hard to look at, so . . ." She craned her neck to flash him one of her patented "I'm fine" smiles, but there was a genuine empathy in his expression, and she found she couldn't speak.

"I'm sorry, Harper."

She shrugged. "Water under the bridge. So . . . the ladder?"

"I'll bring it over for you."

"No, you're busy. Just point me in the right direction, I've got this."

His mouth—and that dimple—quirked. "You should get that printed on a T-shirt."

She unzipped her sweatshirt and revealed her T-shirt, which read: CHOCOLATE IS MY LOVE LANGUAGE. "I've already got all the shirts."

He let out a soft laugh that, if it'd been any more potent, she'd have gotten pregnant from it. Which meant . . . ah hell . . . he really did spark joy. "Okey dokey, well . . . I've gotta go," she said, and did an about-face and headed toward the door.

"The ladder—"

"Forget it. I'm good." Forget the lightbulb too. She didn't need light. "*Don't come over!*" She shut the doors behind her and leaned against them for a moment, shaking her head at herself. *Okey dokey?* What, was she twelve? She wasn't here to hop in the sack with the first good-looking guy she met. She had goals. Such as fulfilling her own dream instead of helping someone else fulfill theirs. To have her own bakery, to be her own boss, and most definitely *not* to fall in love.

Although apparently she wasn't opposed to a little lust . . .

Stopping at the bar, she grabbed the food she'd ordered and headed back to her building, where she found Ivy teaching Ham how to shake. "Oh, he's not good at tricks—"

Ivy gave him a hand signal, and Ham sat.

Ivy gave another hand signal, and Ham lay down. Sure, he hit the floor hard enough to shake the foundation and rattle the windows, but he lay there panting up at them happily.

Harper stared in shock. "Jeez, how long was I gone?"

Ivy gave another hand signal, and Ham rolled over.

Harper was beyond impressed. "Okay, who are you, and what have you done with my Hambone?"

Ham smiled proudly.

"He's a good boy," Ivy said.

Harper handed Ivy the bag of food and one of the lemonades.

Ivy looked down at it all. "You bought me food?"

"I bought *us* food."

"You didn't have to do that."

"And neither did you this morning. Plus, you worked your butt off for me today. Not that this is in payment for that. I'm keeping track of your hours and will pay you for those too." Harper smiled, but Ivy didn't. She looked . . . worried. "Okay, what's wrong?"

Ivy let out a deep breath. "Nothing," she said softly. "Thank you."

Harper was sure the girl had been about to say something else but had changed her mind. Not wanting to push and scare her off, she watched Ham lean up against Ivy, knocking her back a step. The teen laughed, steadied herself, and then encouraged Ham to lean on her some more.

"You're good with him," Harper said. "Do you have a dog?"

"No."

"Any pets?"

"No."

"Your parents not into animals?"

Ivy took a big bite of the burger and took her time chewing. "We moved a lot."

"That's hard," Harper said quietly. "Are you an only child?"

"Sort of." She slurped some lemonade and hunched into herself.

Harper took a few bites herself, wanting to tread carefully and not intrude too much, but also needing to know more, because she couldn't just let Ivy hide out here if there were people who were worrying about her somewhere. And there had to be. Or so she hoped. "It really is okay if you don't want to talk about yourself. Again, you can just tell me you don't want to."

Ivy looked up, doubt on her face. "And that's it?"

"With me it is. But if we're going to be roomies, I need to know that those who care about you aren't worried about you. And for that reason alone, I need to know a little bit more about you. Is that okay?"

Ivy bit her lower lip.

"How about I start?" Harper said. "I grew up in San Diego. My mom passed away when I was twelve and I don't have any siblings, so it's just me and my dad. We're not close." An understatement, but it was getting easier to admit.

Ivy was concentrating on dipping her French fries in ketchup. "Why?"

Harper would've really liked to evade this question, but Ivy clearly needed more if she was going to open up, so she went with the truth. "He remarried and got a new family."

Ivy looked up at this. Paused. Then finally said, "I don't know my biological dad, but if you count all my mom's marriages, I've got four stepsiblings. I don't know any of them very well, except my stepsister Kylie." She hesitated. "I was, um, staying with her before I came here because my mom's on a cruise on her fourth honeymoon and can't be reached."

"Where was that?"

"Chicago."

Harper tried to tamp down on her horror. Chicago was a *long* way from Tahoe. "Did Kylie come with you?"

"No. But she isn't going to be worried about me because she thinks I'm staying with a friend. But . . ." She looked away. "I texted the other day. I haven't heard anything. It's because she thinks she knows where I am and that I'm fine."

"Hold up. You came this far by yourself?"

Ivy shrugged, like it was no big deal.

Harper's first instinct was to hug her, but that wouldn't be appropriate or welcome. So instead, she'd do her best to protect her, because just thinking about all the things that could have happened to Ivy on that trip made her feel sick.

Ivy's expression was challenging, like, *Go ahead, ask me more.*

So instead Harper said, "I was in Chicago once. With my ex, when he went on a job interview after college."

"You were married?"

"No, longtime boyfriend and sort of fiancé." Sort of, because Daniel had kept promising to ask her to marry him but never actually had. Mostly because his parents had found out and had convinced him that Harper was beneath him. "It took me way too long to figure out that he was a ratfink bastard—" She grimaced. "Er, jerk. After we broke up, I started making plans to come here to Tahoe." Okay, so he'd kicked her to the curb like trash, and it'd taken her nearly a year to get her shit together and move, but that was too humiliating to admit. "Sugar Pine Bakery's going to be my do-over."

"My mom dates a lot of ratfink bastards too." Looking sorry she'd said anything, Ivy shoved another bite into her mouth.

Leaving it alone for now, Harper finished her burger, then stood. The kitchen sink was dripping, just as Bodie had said it would. Dusting off her hands, she crawled under the sink to take a look. "Do we have a wrench in that toolbox?"

Ivy handed her a tool that was big and heavy.

Harper looked at it. "Wait, that's a wrench?"

Ivy laughed, and it was a sweet sound. "Yes. There's also a smaller one. Here . . ." She replaced it. "This will work better." At Harper's raised brow, the girl added, "My third stepdad was a plumber. He was pretty cool. He used to take me on jobs with him."

"Are you still close with him?" Harper asked hopefully.

"Nah. When my mom's done with a guy, that's it. She doesn't look back."

Harper thought that sucked big-time. "So why Tahoe?"

Ivy dug around in the toolbox for a minute, and Harper held her breath.

"I decided it was time to finally meet my sperm donor," Ivy finally said.

Harper was surprised, to say the least. "Do you know much about him?"

Ivy shook her head. "Nothing except he never contacts me and he's never paid anything in child support either."

Wow, what a bag of dicks. "I take it he lives near here?"

"Yes."

"Oh, Ivy," Harper breathed. "That's . . ."

"Stupid? Childish? Crazy?" Ivy challenged.

Harper ignored the tension and defiance in the teen's voice. "*Brave*," she said. "Incredibly brave. Why now?"

"I guess I just want to see if I'm like him. Because maybe . . . he'll want me more than my mom does."

Harper's heart squeezed for this girl she hardly knew but could identify with on a core level.

"I've never fit in," Ivy said quietly. "Not ever. And I've always been a handful. A problem to be dealt with."

Those weren't Ivy's own words. Nope, she'd heard them, probably flung at her, and an anger for Ivy's mom burned deep inside Harper. "You're not a problem."

Ivy lifted a shoulder. "Maybe my dad's as stubborn and as much trouble as I am."

Harper gave up on figuring out what to do with the wrench and got up. "Listen to me. I've been around you for a day, and I think you're pretty amazing." She waited until Ivy met her gaze. "Just because you've never felt like you fit in doesn't mean anything's wrong with you. It means you haven't found your place yet. Also, being a 'handful' really means you're assertive and you know your mind. That's what makes you such an incredible woman."

Ivy shook her head, either not willing or unable to believe her. Which Harper got. Even though she'd done everything she could to please her dad, including getting a degree in international business instead of going to a baking arts institute like she wanted, he never smiled at her the same way he did when her mom had been alive. Not that she could blame him. He'd lost his soul mate. Harper smiled at Ivy, faking her own bravery because she knew one had to fake it to make it. "I hope you find what you're looking for, Ivy. I hope we both do."

CHAPTER 7

Bodie had never unlearned the waking-before-dawn thing that had been ingrained in him in the military, so he'd long ago stopped fighting it. Rolling out of bed, he showered and headed to the warehouse. Then he opened all the doors and stood watching the sliver of a molten red disk perched on the mountaintop slowly transform itself into the sun. Rain had threatened in the night, but no longer. The sky was now a riot of pinks and oranges, with just a hint of purple icing a few scattered clouds while a soft mellow summer wind caressed his skin. It was perhaps the most peaceful he'd felt in a long time.

He worked on the boat until 9:00 a.m., then pulled his truck around from behind the bar to the front of the bakery to pick up Harper for the hardware store run. Before he could get out to go get her, she was hopping into his passenger seat. Her hair was loose this morning, still damp from a shower, the curls wild and crazy beautiful.

"Morning," she said, and handed him a to-go mug of coffee.

"Thanks." He took a sip and moaned out loud. "Wow."

She beamed, her eyes as happy as her hair seemed. "It's my own special blend."

Her smile was more potent than her coffee, and he had to laugh. "You're going to make buckets of money in this town."

She toasted him with her coffee. "Here's hoping."

From in his pocket, his phone vibrated. And then again in quick succession. "Sorry," he said as he pulled out his phone. It was the Campbell brothers text thread. Which was different than the Campbell family text thread, because this one didn't have his mom on it. In fact, she didn't even know this one existed and that was a good thing.

Campbell brothers ongoing text thread

MACE: I can see you. Her too. She's pretty cute.
Does this mean you're off your sex embargo?

ZEKE: Wait, who we talking about? Who's
pretty cute?

BODIE: No one.

MACE: The new baker. Yesterday Bodie chased a
bear from her car, and today he's taking her out.

ZEKE: So he IS off his sex embargo. About time. I'm
telling Mom.

BODIE: We're going to get paint, you idiots, and if you tell Mom, I'll tell Serena you're only pretending to be off caffeine and sugar, that you come to the bar and drink five mugs of coffee and eat all our desserts.

ZEKE: Wow.

BODIE PUT HIS phone on silent and shoved it back into his pocket.

Harper looked at him. "Problem?"

"Other than my brothers are nosy busybodies who need a life? Nope."

She smiled a little wistfully. "I always wanted a sibling."

"I can lend you one of my brothers. In fact, keep him." He pulled out of the lot and onto Lake Drive in tune to her laugh. Her face was glued to the window, eyes on the deep azure lake that seemed to span for days. He loved it here, so he knew what she was feeling—the same awe he'd experienced every single day.

"How did you ever leave this place?" she asked. "Or is that a long story to be told later?"

He smiled. She was catching on.

She looked out the window some more. "It's just so beautiful," she said softly, with a hint of longing and grief.

He fought with himself to not be moved but lost the battle. "Leaving wasn't hard. I was eighteen, full of myself, and over small-town living. I went to college in Los Angeles."

"But you eventually came back."

He nodded. "You can leave Tahoe, but Tahoe never leaves you. At least, that's what my mom always says."

"That's sweet," she said.

He glanced over at her. "You ever going to tell me what prompted you to walk away from your life?"

"I did tell you. I came to the last place that sparked joy for me."

He gave her another look.

She lifted her shoulder. "Sometimes you just need a new start, you know?"

Oh yeah, he knew. "Have you seen much of the area yet?"

"Not yet."

No doubt because she'd been cleaning since she'd arrived, which was his family's fault. So in spite of a packed day, he took a detour and drove to Sugar Pine Point, where she'd told him she'd camped with her mom years before. The campgrounds were wooded and private, and as he slowly drove the narrow, winding road through the place, Harper was quiet, reflective, taking it all in.

"There," she said, pointing to one of the last campsites. "We came every summer for four years, starting when I was eight, and that's the last spot where we camped. We had a tent trailer but slept outside beneath a blanket of stars and the brightest moon I've ever seen."

He nodded. "Nothing like a summer-night Tahoe sky."

They came to a clearing and a large cabin structure that was an old-time museum, and she gasped. "I remember this place! My mom used to take me here."

He turned off the engine.

"We're going in?" she asked with a hopeful smile, making him want to keep doing stuff like this so she'd keep looking at him like that.

"The owner's a friend of mine." Inside, he asked for Joey, one of Zeke's longtime best friends. A few minutes later, he came out of an office off the front reception area with a smile for Bodie.

"Well, look who decided to remember where he came from."

Bodie rolled his eyes and held out a hand, which Joey bypassed to wrap him in a bear hug and lift him up off the ground, no easy feat since Bodie was six foot two. But then again, Joey had four inches and at least fifty pounds on him. When Joey opened his arms and dropped Bodie to his feet, he then slapped him gleefully on the back and nearly sent him flying.

"Good to see you, man." Joey turned to smile at Harper as he jerked a thumb at Bodie. "This guy. Better hold on tight to him or he'll vanish on you and never look back."

"Oh," Harper said. "We're not . . ." She looked at Bodie as if seeking help.

"Joey, this is Harper," Bodie said. "And she's the owner of Sugar Pine Bakery. Harper, Joey, our resident nosy grandpa, so don't tell him anything you don't want shouted to the moon and back."

"He wounds me," Joey told Harper. "All because one time me and his oldest brother, Zeke, embarrassed him after a basketball game that he lost. Did I mention it was the state championship?"

"If by 'embarrassed' you mean when you and Zeke took my

clothes while I was in the shower, and I had to run out to my car in nothing but a towel . . ."

Joey tossed his head back and laughed. "Hey, man, a whole bunch of girls chased you for weeks afterward. You're welcome."

"*And* I hardly lost that game on my own," Bodie said, feeling like the stupid little brother all over again.

"True," Joey said, giving credit where it was due. "The refs took that game from you. Well, that and your team's collective hangover from partying the night before." He smiled at Harper. "Enjoy the museum." He gestured to the huge wood arch that led into the cavernous building. "Bodie made that," he said. "Which I'm telling you because he won't. The guy is a whole bunch of things, starting with being tighter-lipped than my granny is tight-wadded and ending with more stubborn than the devil himself, but he's also too humble." He clapped Bodie on the back again. "Don't continue to be a stranger, man." Then he tipped an imaginary cap to Harper and headed back to his office.

"The arch is beautiful," Harper said as they walked beneath it. "You're good with your hands."

He grinned, and she sighed. "I did not mean that the way it sounded."

"Too bad," he said. "Because it's true." He flashed another teasing grin and was awarded by a sweet laugh.

They walked through the museum, stopping at the thirty-foot model of the Truckee River, which had a working water feature where guests could "mine for gold" with makeshift pans and gold flecks seated at the river bottom.

"I remember doing this," Harper said.

"Me too." He handed her a pan and took one for himself, and they spent the next half an hour mining and splashing each other.

Later, back in the car, heading to the hardware store, she was still smiling. "I haven't done anything like that in forever." She turned to him. "Thank you."

He glanced over at her and realized just how much he liked the way she looked at him.

She drew a deep breath. "Earlier, you asked me why I came back here now. I guess the simple truth is that I was . . . lonely. I really had nothing to keep me in San Diego except a job that gave me a daily stomachache."

He nodded. "Then I'm really glad you're here."

She smiled. "Me too. I'm so excited about the business. My mom always wanted to do this, open a bakery."

"So, you're following your mom's dream?"

She looked at him, brows raised, and he smiled because he knew this game. He'd have to give her something of himself before she'd return the favor. "It was my dad's dream for me to leave the ATF and come home. He wanted me to run the bar and work on boats with him. So when I didn't do that until after he was gone . . . well, I was pretty messed up. My first night back, me and my brothers got crazy-ass drunk and went to the grocery store to buy my dad's favorite cake. It was midnight and there was only one cake left. We got into a bidding war with some guy who'd forgotten to buy his girl a birthday cake. We had to give him two hundred bucks to go away, and then me and Zeke and

Mace got in a cake fight in the parking lot." He smiled at the memory of standing on the sticky asphalt, the cake massacred all around them, the frosting glowing by the parking lot lights, the three of them covered head to toe in raspberry cream cake. "It was awesome." He paused, remembering. "I still think about that night when I get sad."

Looking incredibly moved, she nodded, quiet for a few minutes. "I'm not just following my mom's dream," she finally said. "It's also mine. A new start here means a freedom I haven't had, where I'm my own boss and responsible to no one but myself." She said this casually, but there was nothing casual about the emotion in her eyes.

And here was the thing. She had a history of assholes in her life, and while he couldn't stop thinking about her, he never wanted to be another asshole in a revolving door of assholes. But he wasn't a keeper.

Which meant he needed to resist her, something he was pretty sure would prove to be one of the hardest things he'd ever done. Still, she'd opened up to him, and he owed her. So he turned on a side street and pulled to the side of the road.

She glanced at him, a question in her eyes.

"Across the street and down four houses . . ." He nudged his chin in the right direction. "That's where I grew up."

She took in the modest gingerbread home that fit right in on the street filled with other similar houses. The yards were unstructured, unfenced, and heavily wooded. The houses were kept-up middle-class. Nothing fancy.

"It's a three-bedroom, two-bathroom place," he said. "Six of us lived there together, bursting at the seams. Attendance at dinner was required, complete with talks, hard or easy. And there was plenty of both. My family loves hard, but we fight just as hard."

Her gaze swiveled from the house back to him. "I think that sounds amazing," she said.

He snorted. "My mom might use a different word. As she tells it, having four wild, crazy, rough-and-tumble boys in her house nearly put her and my dad in early graves."

She smiled. "You were all wild?"

"Feral," he said. "But actually, Zeke, the firstborn, spoiled Mom and Dad. Appearances only, of course. He was just really good at hiding shit. I came next, and I broke them both in pretty good."

She laughed. "Troublemaker?"

"Of the highest magnitude. But nothing illegal. Not for Mace either. That was Austin's specialty." He paused. "He overdosed his sophomore year in high school. It still haunts my mom." Hell, it haunted all of them.

He felt a hand on his. She squeezed gently until he looked at her. "Of course it haunts you," she said. "A close family like yours? Something tragic like that just makes it all the more devastating."

He gave a single nod, swallowed the ball of emotion in his throat, and spit the rest out. "So I left after high school. Did two years of college but ended up enlisting to follow Zeke into the army. Zeke came home after his four years. I wasn't ready to come back, I needed something more. That's when I ended up with the ATF."

"Which is where you got hurt."

"Yes."

"Are you ever going back?"

"No," he said. "Not ever." He heard himself tell her what he hadn't even told his own family and felt shell-shocked. Drawing a deep breath, he started his truck again. "Let's do this."

"Um . . . this?" Her eyes were suddenly a little wide, and she sounded flustered.

"The hardware store." He took in her flash of disappointment and found a smile. "But good to know where you're at."

Her mouth opened in automatic denial. "I didn't mean—"

"Didn't you?"

When she closed her eyes and blushed, he laughed softly and pulled into the street, feeling lighter than he had in a long time. Which meant that continuing to resist her adorable sexiness was going to be even harder than he'd thought.

CHAPTER 8

ZEKE: Campbell business meeting in twenty. Be there.

Bodie grinded his teeth at the demand. He was in the office at Olde Tahoe Tap working on billing. He'd planned on gathering his brothers and heading over to Harper's to paint once he'd finished anyway, but the bossy tone of Zeke's text knocked paperwork from its top position of things he hated. If such a thing existed as reincarnation, he hoped Zeke came back as a younger brother of an anal control freak.

Luckily Zeke's office was on the top floor of the art gallery, so Bodie's commute took him two minutes. He headed directly upstairs and walked into Zeke's office without knocking. Hey, if Zeke could be annoying, then Bodie could be too. "You can't just command-text me to get my ass over here."

Zeke shrugged. "Worked, didn't it?"

Bodie threw himself into one of the two chairs in front of Zeke's desk and slid a look at Mace, who was already slouched in the other chair. "You too?"

"Yeah. We need to talk."

Those four words had never once led to anything good. And since both his brothers were looking at *him*, he knew he was the subject of today's little impromptu meeting. Great. "No, thanks."

"Too bad," Zeke said. "We think you're working too hard and . . ."

Bodie stopped listening. He was too busy for this shit. Too busy for a lot of things. Like contemplating what Harper might feel like warm and naked and writhing beneath him—

"He's not listening to a single word you're saying," Mace said, eyes on Bodie. "If I didn't know better, I'd say he's daydreaming."

True story.

"Bodie doesn't daydream," Zeke said. "On his previous job, daydreaming would've gotten him killed."

Mace studied Bodie like he was a bug on a slide. "He's definitely let his guard down now that he's not in constant danger."

Also true. Bodie had started to let his guard down. At least on the job. As for with people, that was a different story altogether, though he suspected Harper was sneaking her way in past his walls. And she was a danger of a whole different magnitude. She threatened his common sense and peace of mind.

"He's still on his silent mysterio thing," Zeke said. "Has been ever since he got home."

"Yep." Mace crossed his arms. "Thinks he's an island of one."

"It's a fucking insult," Zeke said.

"Big-time," Mace agreed.

Bodie tossed up his hands. "Sitting right here."

"But are you *here*?" Zeke asked, touching a finger to his temple.

Bodie did as he'd been taught in the hospital by the shrink he'd been required to see. He breathed. In and out. In and out. In and out.

Because okay, yes, after his crazy past, after losing Austin, Tyler, and then his dad, he'd realized he just needed to be for a change, without the weight of an entire undercover op on his shoulders. Without the unrealistic expectations of his mom to produce her some grandchildren. Without anyone needing anything from him except their next drink.

The only con to this plan was living in close proximity to his hot mess of a family.

No, that was a lie he told himself to keep his emotions in check. He *wanted* to be here. This way, if something happened, he could show up for those he cared about.

"I'm here now," he said.

"Because you want to be?" Zeke asked. "Or because you had no other choice?"

"Does it matter?"

"Hell yeah, it matters."

Bodie tipped his head back and stared at the ceiling. He had no idea what he was waiting on. A sudden abundance of patience? He'd always been low on that.

Zeke opened his mouth, but Mace shook his head at him before turning to Bodie. "Look, we just want you to be okay. You came home three months ago, but sometimes it still doesn't feel like you're all the way here. Let us in, man. You're going through some shit. No one could have survived what you did without some mental trauma. We're on your side. Let us help."

Bodie scoffed. "Like you 'helped' when you told Mom I'm working too hard and not eating enough? Trust me, compared to where I've been and what I've done, being here is a walk in the park." He shook his head. "I don't need help. And the next time you get Mom all worried, I'm going to tell her that you"—he pointed to Zeke—"are cheating on Serena. And you"—he pointed to Mace—"ate all the lasagna she left for me."

"*I'm* cheating?" Zeke repeated in shocked disbelief. "But this asshole just ate some lasagna? What the actual f—"

"I mean it."

Zeke and Mace exchanged a look.

"What now?" Bodie demanded.

"At least I never lie," Mace said. "Cuz last I heard, Mom still thinks that you retired, not that you're still on the payroll, just taking leave. When are you going to tell her you're not sticking around, but eventually going back to the job?"

Never. Because both were lies. And both were better than the truth.

"Look," Zeke said carefully. "Here's what we know. An op went bad. So bad, the ATF notified us that you were MIA and presumed dead. Tyler was dead. Dad had a heart attack at the news. A week later, you surfaced in a hospital in Virginia, close to where you'd been working. You had four holes in your body and nearly lost your leg. You had to stay in the hospital for weeks, and it was so touch-and-go that we didn't tell you we'd lost Dad until you were released."

Bodie was definitely not going to have back molars left after this conversation. "Why are you telling me shit I already know?"

"Because we think you blame yourself for Tyler's death," Mace said. "Which is stupid because you're not Superman. We also think you blame yourself for Dad's heart attack—also stupid. What happened wasn't your fault." Mace drew a deep breath. "Plus, you're mad at us. No, don't deny it," he said when Bodie started to speak. "And that's equally stupid to being mad at yourself, by the way."

Bodie shoved his brother's hand away from his face, pushed to his feet, and strode the length of the office and back until he could speak calmly. Although, since his leg ached like a son of a bitch, it was more like careful walking than striding. "Why would I be mad at my family?"

"You tell us."

He shoved his fingers into his hair and took another lap. "You should've told me."

"About Dad?" Zeke asked.

"No, about the fucking Easter Bunny! Yes, about Dad! I missed his funeral. I missed—" Christ. He had to clamp his jaw together and bite his own tongue to get his emotions under control. Everything. He'd missed everything. And now his family had moved on, like it hadn't happened. Meanwhile, Bodie felt like he'd lost his foothold on his world, leaving him hesitant to attach to anything that he could possibly lose again, including his own brothers and mom.

"You couldn't have gotten out of the hospital in time for the funeral," Mace said, voice low. Very serious. "And your doctors felt you were in a dangerous headspace. So yeah, we held the info. It wasn't like you could change anything. We *all* miss him, man," he said, ignoring Bodie's brewing bad temper. "But we're dealing with it. You're not. Instead, you're hiding out in the bar."

"I'm not hiding out in the bar. I'm working, same as you both."

Zeke was clearly not buying what Bodie was selling. "You're telling us that being a bartender is doing it for you? Seriously? After the adrenaline-fueled life you've led? Or are you just here waiting out your leave and then taking off again for another decade?"

"I'm not a fucking fortune-teller," Bodie snapped. "So I don't know what I'll feel tomorrow, or six months from now, or six damn years." Currently, he was feeling exactly nothing.

No, that was a lie. He was feeling far too much. He needed to get a grip on that. "And you guys don't have any idea how long you'll be happy here either. We all know the hard way that the future isn't guaranteed. But I'm here because I wanted . . ."

"What?" Mace pushed. "You wanted what?"

The three of them were standing close, hackles up like the pack of feral wolves they'd once been. But Bodie didn't want to fight. And suddenly he also didn't want to let any more time go by without saying what was on his mind. "I wanted to be here. With you guys."

Mace blinked in surprise.

Zeke gave a rare smile. "You had me at hello," he said, wrapping a beefy arm around Bodie's neck, giving him a noogie, grinding his knuckles against Bodie's skull—his version of a hug.

And here was the thing. Yes, his asshat brother was six four to Bodie's six two, but Zeke also had seventy pounds on him—his new dad bod. Bodie was a trained, lean, mean fighting machine and could've easily taken him. But brawling wasn't nearly as fun as it used to be, so he turned the tables and wrapped his arms tight around Zeke at mid-chest, completely immobilizing him. For added measure, Bodie squeezed him extra tight and then gave him a smacking kiss on the side of his head before dropping him.

Zeke slipped all the way to the floor, where Mace was already, because laughing his ass off had apparently melted his knees.

Bodie settled into the chair again, idly picking up a pen and doodling on the pad that had been left there. "So. Anything else we need to discuss?"

"Yeah," Zeke said. Then hesitated.

"Shit," Bodie said, imagining the worst. "Now what?"

"It's about Harper."

"No." Bodie shook his head. "Next."

"What do you mean, 'no'?" Zeke asked.

"We're not talking about her."

"Translation," Mace said, "he's into her."

Zeke paused, then continued. "I was just going to say that I'm sorry I dropped the ball on Harper's lease, and I'm available to help clean and paint. It should only take a few days tops, but now I want to hear what Bodie meant by 'no.'"

Bodie ignored this. "I already bought everything we need to paint. I'll call you guys when I'm ready for your help."

Again his brothers exchanged glances, and Mace cackled like an old woman.

"You need a life," Bodie said. "Or to get back with Shay. You ever going to tell us what happened?"

"Deflecting," Mace said to Zeke, who nodded.

"I'm not deflecting shit." Bodie looked down at his notepad, where he'd been idly doodling while thinking. *Harper* was written plain as day. What the hell was wrong with him? Brain aneurysm? Impending stroke?

Zeke barked out a laugh as Bodie crumpled the page and threw it at Mace's head. First plan of action: secure both of his brothers' big, fat mouths before they talked to Mom. "How about we pretend we're not in middle school for a second? Harper Shaw's a tenant. We keep this professional."

"You mean as opposed to the time you took out that woman who works at the art gallery? And when you didn't ask her on a second date, she posted a list of your faults on Instagram, Facebook, *and* TikTok?"

"She still walks her dog over to the front steps of his warehouse to shit every single morning," Mace said. "It's a Great Dane."

Zeke laughed so hard he was bent over, hands on his knees. Bodie was thinking about kicking him when the office door opened.

In bounded two feral wolf cubs/kids. Ian and Xander, three

and seven, respectively, followed by Serena, Zeke's wife, who was holding feral cub number three—two-year-old Max.

Serena looked her usual mom-in-charge self, but there was an unmistakable harried look in her eyes.

The boys were heading straight toward Zeke's computer.

"One!" Zeke yelled.

Not one of the devils slowed.

"Two!"

Bodie looked at Mace. "What happens when he gets to three?"

Mace shrugged.

Zeke sighed. "I've been a parent for almost eight years and still don't have a clue what happens after I get to three." But he stood there and expertly intercepted the boys, scooping up one under each of his arms. He tossed Ian to Mace, and Xander to Bodie before leaning in and kissing his wife. "How's my baby?"

"He just spit up."

Zeke laughed softly in sympathy. "I meant my other baby." He kissed her again. "You."

"Oh." Serena smiled and looked flustered. "Well, I just spent the last thirty minutes pretending to help Ian look for a toy I threw out weeks ago. Mom of the Year, right?"

"You're Mom of the Universe," Zeke said, making her smile.

Xander grinned up at Bodie. "Toss me!" he demanded, referring to the game where Bodie tossed the kids to the closest couch or relatively soft surface and tickled them until they cried "Uncle!"

Since there wasn't a soft enough surface, Bodie hung Xander off his back, holding him by his feet.

Ian yelled, "Me too, me too!"

Bodie scooped him up and let him hang off his front.

Meanwhile, Max was sitting on Bodie's foot, holding on to his leg as he pretended to stagger about the room like Frankenstein's monster, much to their screams of delight.

"You're just in time," Mace told Serena. "Bodie was about to tell us why he's insisting on helping Harper, our new tenant, all by himself."

Serena eyed Bodie with her attorney eyes, then smiled. "Maybe he's finally found someone to hold his interest and take him out of his own head and doesn't want you two bozos to mess it up."

"You do realize I just met her," Bodie said dryly.

"These things happen in an instant," Serena said. "Mace fell for Shay the second she beaned him in the head with a kickball in high school. You know, way back when, before he messed it all up. And you," she said to her grinning husband, "you fell for me the second I told you to eff off in Law 101, freshman year at UC Berkeley."

Zeke's smug grin faded as both his brothers laughed at *him*.

"Tell me about her," Serena said to Bodie.

No one, absolutely no one, ever denied or crossed Serena. "She's our tenant," he said.

"And . . . ?"

"Might as well give in, bro," Zeke said.

Bodie sighed. "She's a baker from San Diego."

"And . . . ?"

"She's kind. Smart. Funny."

Serena smiled. "So you'll go out with her. Come back to the land of the living."

Bodie shook his head, careful not to dislodge any kidlets. "Why did I think coming back to this family was a good idea again?"

"Because we love you and accept you and get you," Serena said. "Make this happen for yourself, Bodie. You deserve it. Yeah?" She kissed him on the cheek, did the same to Mace, then gave her husband a longer kiss, gathered up her children, and headed to the door. "We'll be running around outside until Daddy comes to take us out to eat."

Bodie's mind was racing. Go out with Harper. He liked the thought. And hell, if it got her out of his system, that was a bonus, right? Listen to the crap he was shoveling himself. Clearly, he wasn't getting enough oxygen to the brain, because no way that one night with Harper would be enough. "Look, it's a bad idea, all right? I'm not going to let myself get emotionally attached when I've got nothing to offer her. That's not fair."

"You have plenty to offer," Mace said. "You make a mean mai tai."

"Wow, you're right. I'm certain that would be enough."

Mace shook his head. "You've got a chance to be happy. Why not take it?"

"Says the guy who let the love of his life walk away."

Mace slouched in his chair. "You don't know shit."

"She's loved you for years," Bodie said. "How did you even let this happen?"

Mace's expression was tellingly and carefully blank. "It turned out, we wanted different things."

Bodie shook his head. "How different can those things be when the woman comes to the bar whenever you're there, waiting for you to notice her?"

"Not talking about it," Mace said.

"Perfect. So we get each other." Bodie's phone buzzed with a text from Harper.

Can you come over?

"Meeting adjourned," he said, and left.

Two minutes later, he knocked on the front door of the soon-to-be Sugar Pine Bakery. It took a few minutes for Harper to unlock the door. Ham bounced out, doing his happy dog dance, wiggling his butt on his way to kiss Bodie to death.

Harper was much more muted. She wore jeans, a long-sleeved fitted tee the same color as her eyes, and a distracted expression. "Hey."

"Hey." He scratched Ham behind the ears, and the dog leaned into him for more. "You okay?"

"Yeah. Come in."

He followed her inside. "The labor can arrive whenever works for you."

"The labor?"

"My brothers."

"Oh, I don't want to put anyone out. I told you, I could paint—"

"Not leaving it all on your plate. Besides, this way we can get it done before your pod arrives."

"That's sweet, thanks. But as it turns out, first I need a handyman."

"As you've already noted, I'm good with my hands."

She laughed. "Don't worry, I haven't forgotten. I've got a light fixture in the kitchen that needs fixing. It keeps flickering, and it's giving me an eye twitch. I think something chewed through the wiring. I'd tell you the second thing that needs to be handled, but that'd imply I have a list. Which I don't. What I do have is a problem."

"What is it?"

"Some things are best seen for yourself." On that cryptic statement, she headed into the kitchen, her ass perfection in her jeans.

"You coming?" she asked.

"Yep." He caught up to her, followed by Ham, both stopping short when Harper did. The back door was opened, screen in place. "There," she said, pointing upward to a decent-size spider in the ceiling corner, while completely ignoring the family of raccoons parked outside the screen door, lined up and staring at them.

"You think a spider chewed through the wiring?" he asked.

"Have you seen its fangs?" she asked.

"Have *you*?"

"Yes, in last night's nightmares."

He couldn't help smiling as he pulled out his phone. "Hate to break it to you, but the raccoons are probably your culprit.

Whenever it gets cold, they come looking for warmth. They're cute but destructive." Listen to him saying random shit just to keep her talking to him. Clearly, she interfered with his mental processes. "Looks like Roxie brought her entire family. Normally, she'd only do that if someone was silly enough to feed her."

Harper bit her lower lip.

He laughed. "Stop feeding them. They'll stop showing up."

She sighed and nodded.

"To be clear though, you do want me to kill the spider?"

"*Duh.*"

He had to laugh. It was the craziest thing, but the more unreasonable she got, the more attracted to her he became. Which only reconfirmed the fact that he'd lost it. He had a feeling she could get anyone to do just about anything with a single smile. It was the way she looked at a person, like they were special to her. It gave him ideas. Hell, he'd already had the ideas, but her smile certainly brought them to the forefront of his brain, making it a challenge to think about anything else. It drove him crazy, but he loved everything he'd learned about her so far.

The sound of screeching tires echoed in his head. He loved everything he'd learned about her so far? He sat with that for a second and came to a single conclusion.

He was screwed.

He took care of the spider, flushing the evidence down the upstairs toilet.

She'd followed him into the bathroom, and since it was smaller than his front doormat, it meant her chest was up against his back and he could feel the soft puff of her warm breath on his arm. He glanced over his shoulder to find her *not* lusting after his bod as he'd hoped, but staring at the water swirling down the toilet.

"I read somewhere that spiders can hold their breath for like two weeks," she said. "So if you flush them, they can just come back with their friends and family."

"That story was invented by some evil-minded exterminator so that he could come back in two weeks and charge for another service."

That tugged a laugh out of her, and he smiled, enjoying the light of good humor in her gaze. "The spider's gone for good."

She sagged in relief, then straightened and gave him a spontaneous hug that was so exuberant, she nearly knocked him into her shower. "*Thank you.*"

He grinned. "You barely acknowledged me when I scared off a bear for you, but I get a hug for murdering a spider?"

"Once again, did you see his fangs? And . . ." She hesitated. "I did notice when you took care of the bear. I just tried not to."

He smiled, but his brows went up in surprise when a young woman came up the stairs. The one he'd fed a few nights back and had worried about ever since. She was wearing jeans and a sweatshirt that read, C IS FOR COOKIE AND THAT'S GOOD ENOUGH FOR ME, which he was guessing belonged to Harper. He wondered if the girl did as well. They didn't look like sisters. Plus, the teen still had runaway all over her, and a recent one who hadn't yet been eaten up by the streets.

She took one look at him and froze.

"Ivy, this is Bodie Campbell," Harper said. "He runs the Olde Tahoe Tap."

The girl sucked in a breath. "You own the bar?"

"It's a family thing," he said. "And since we're sharing information, what's your name? What can I call you besides Dine-and-Dasher?"

"Wait." Harper divided a gaze between them. "You two know each other?"

"Nope," Ivy said.

"Okaaaaay," Harper said slowly. "Well then, Bodie, meet Ivy. She's staying with me right now."

Ivy lifted her chin. "And it's not dine-and-dash when you say it's on the house."

"It was absolutely on the house," Bodie said. "It's just that usually, people say thank you before vanishing into the night."

"Thank you," Ivy said, and he doubted she could've fit another drop of dry sarcasm into the two words if she'd tried.

He looked at Harper. "How long have you two known each other?"

Harper smiled. "Two whole days. Almost three."

Ah, hell. The girl *was* homeless, and Harper had taken her in. He opened his mouth to ask more questions, but Harper turned to Ivy. "Why don't you go get us some food from the deli down the street?" She reached into her pocket and pulled out some cash.

Ivy stared down at the money. "That's too much."

"Not for both of us. Get whatever you want, but if at least some of it could be a quarter healthy, that'd be great. Surprise me."

When Ivy vanished out the door, Bodie looked at Harper. "How do you know she'll be back?"

"How do you know she won't?"

"Can I be frank?"

"Sure, but I like the name Bodie better."

This got a rough laugh out of him. "I'm serious. How well do you know her?"

"She's my first employee."

"Which doesn't answer my question."

"I know," she said. "But her story isn't mine to tell."

"What *can* you tell me?"

Harper sighed. "I found her trying to break in on my first night here. To *sleep*," she said when he opened his mouth.

In the military, and then the ATF, he'd seen the worst side of humanity. He'd become numb to it. He'd come across a lot of girls in Ivy's situation, but none of them had affected him like when he'd turned around the other night and found her gone, knowing how cold it'd been forecasted to be. "You know she's a runaway, right?"

"She says she's emancipated."

"I've got a friend who's a cop," he said. "I could have him run her—"

"No." She shook her head and pressed a finger to his chest. "We're not going to run her. I'm not going to betray her trust that way. She's a good kid."

He looked into her pretty eyes and wrapped his fingers around the one she was still poking him with. "I hope you're not wrong."

"I'm not."

"Still. You're going to be careful."

She rolled her eyes.

He gently wriggled her finger. "You're going to be careful."

"Hey, careful is my middle name. I was super careful leasing this place, and look what a gem it got me."

He let out a low laugh. "We'll start painting. And when your stuff comes, we'll help you move in. Along with that, we're going to give you a credit on your first month's lease. It's the least we can do for being so behind."

She smiled as if he'd just awarded her a million dollars. "Thank you. Maybe I'll even take back half the things I thought about you."

"Just half?"

"Well." She looked at a spot over his shoulder as if it was the most fascinating thing she'd ever seen. "Just the bad half."

He grinned. "Ditto."

CHAPTER 9

Several days later, Harper woke up just before dawn, wearing a smile and enjoying the feeling of a warm body in her bed. It took her a few moments to wake up enough to realize it was Ham.

And not Bodie.

She closed her eyes again, but they popped open when she heard a soft cry. She tossed off her covers, and her bare feet hit the floor at a run. Skidding to a stop in the office doorway, she found Ivy thrashing around in her sleeping bag, having a bad dream, if the soft whimpering was anything to go by. "Ivy," she said softly, not wanting to scare her. "Ivy, wake up. You're okay, you're safe here."

Ivy jerked upright, hair rioted around her head, looking much, much younger than her sixteen years. "Wha—"

"You were having a bad dream."

Harper watched as Ivy pulled the covers protectively to her chin. "I wasn't," she said. "I'm fine."

Harper drew a deep breath. In the past, she'd skimmed through all her relationships, including the one with her father, never going much past the surface, since doing so always seemed to get her hurt. But she was starting a new life, and that meant doing things differently this time, and opening herself up. And if she could help Ivy by doing so, she would. "I used to have bad dreams."

Ivy met her gaze. "Why?"

Open a vein and bleed? Or keep it together? Harper drew a deep breath. "I told you it was just me and my dad, right?"

"Yes. Your mom died when you were twelve."

Harper nodded. "That year, a teacher tried to get me taken away from my dad for neglect. She thought she was doing the right thing. She'd been helping me . . ." She broke off for a minute because it turned out opening a vein hurt like hell. "She found out my dad was staying at his girlfriend's a lot while I was at home alone. She always made sure I had food and that I got rides to and from school, stuff like that. But when my dad and his girlfriend went on a trip without making arrangements for me, she called Child Services."

Ivy made a small sound. "What happened?"

"They'd just lined up a foster home for me when my dad came back. He had to fight to keep me, and in my nightmares, he didn't. Fight for me."

Ivy's face said she knew the feeling all too well. "He doesn't sound like a good dad."

"I mean, at the time I would've agreed with you, but in retrospect, I think he did the best he could with what he had."

Ivy shook her head but didn't say anything other than, "Parents suck."

"Not all of them," Harper said. "My mom, she was everything. And in his own way, my dad loves me." She had to believe that.

"Then you're lucky." Ivy bit her lip, clearly holding something back.

"What?"

"So you lived with him and the girlfriend? For how long?"

"I left when I turned eighteen." The *minute* she'd turned eighteen. It'd been . . . okay, but she'd definitely been hardly even an afterthought to either of them. She'd hated the feeling.

Ivy hesitated again.

"It's okay," Harper told her. "You can ask me anything."

"I didn't realize how hard it would be to get food and a safe place to sleep."

Looking at Ivy was like looking at her own past self, and it hurt her heart. "And you want to know how I got by?"

Ivy nodded.

"I was lucky. I had a car. A total POS, but it ran okay. My dad paid for my college tuition, but he didn't have the money for anything else. So I lived in my car."

Ivy's head came up, and she stared at Harper, her surprise evident. "You did?"

"For the longest month of my life, yeah. I worked at a deli and also nannied. I borrowed the books I needed and ate a lot of peanut butter and ramen. Once I had enough saved, I shared a one-room apartment with four other students." She gave a little laugh. "Honestly? I had more room in my car than I did in that apartment. This place seems like a mansion."

Ivy smiled. "To me too. I have more room here than I've ever had anywhere, thanks to you. I'm going to pay you rent for my time here, I promise."

"Your money isn't good here."

"Because you feel sorry for me?"

"Because I've been you. I believe in paying it forward."

Ivy took that in and nodded. "Someday I want to be able to do the same for someone." She lay back down and pulled the covers over her head. "Tell me when you're out of the bathroom and I'll get up."

Subject closed. "You can sleep longer," Harper said.

"I want to work."

And earn money. And oh, how Harper got that. Money for people like herself and Ivy meant freedom. She went and took a shower in the deliciously hot water without seeing a single spider.

Or a raccoon.

She dressed and tried not to notice that her hair was big enough to qualify for its own zip code. She went downstairs with a pep in her step. Her pod was due to arrive today, and she couldn't wait to unpack.

And start baking.

She made coffee and stumbled around a bit until her caffeine kicked in. Bodie and his brothers had finished painting yesterday. After, Ivy had helped her clean out the cabinets and cupboards and lined them with cheerful shelf liners that she'd bought at a cute kitchen supply store down the street. Of course she hadn't made a list, so she'd forgotten stuff and had to go back twice . . .

She'd found an old box of kitchen stuff in her kitchen closet. She'd called Bodie, who'd told her it'd come from the pizzeria that had been there before and that she was welcome to whatever was in the box. She hadn't had time until now, so she started to open up the box, only to be interrupted by a knock at her back door.

It was Bodie, carrying a bag that smelled amazing. He was in his usual uniform of jeans and a T-shirt. He hadn't shaved, and he looked dangerous and sexy. Or sexily dangerous . . .

Ham apparently thought so too, because he wiggled his way over to his new boyfriend and flopped to his back for a belly rub.

Bodie handed Harper the bag and crouched to love up on her dog.

She opened the bag and found two huge foil-wrapped bacon, egg, and cheese on sourdough sandwiches. "Wow, thank you. Did you make these?"

"Depends on if you like them." He helped himself to some of her coffee and gave a sexy masculine groan. "Good God, woman. This is the best coffee I've ever had."

"Compared to yours, yes," she said on a laugh. "Coffee isn't your strong suit."

"Don't worry, I have other strong suits."

"Hmm." She'd have to limit her time staring at him. It made her ache for things she'd told herself she no longer wanted. "I guess you get pretty good at flirting when you work at a bar."

"You think I'm good at flirting?"

She thought he was probably good at a lot of things. "Yes."

"I'm not." He shook his head. "And I don't flirt at the bar. I don't like mixing business with pleasure, and I've been all business for a long time. Keeps life easy. I don't have what it takes to go deeper. Apparently I'm not particularly expressive or nurturing enough."

Nothing in her life had been easy. Daniel had been charming and funny, but expressive or nurturing? Definitely not. She hadn't really realized how badly she'd needed more until she'd taken a step back. Now here was another man, one who outright admitted he wasn't capable of those things or going deeper.

The problem was, his actions didn't match his words. He'd made her breakfast. And he had no problem letting her know that he wanted her. He'd even opened up a little about his past . . . more than she had done.

"What about you?" he asked.

"Well, I'm not very good at flirting. Or asking enough of the people in my life. My last relationship, the one I'd been in since my freshman year of college, was . . . toxic. It's part of why I needed a new start, far away from San Diego."

"Brave," he said softly, his eyes letting her know he meant it as a compliment.

"No, not brave at all," she said on a rough laugh. "I stayed with Daniel for years and didn't even know he was unhappy. Everyone else knew; our mutual friends, his family, my dad, *everyone* but me knew that he was bored and needed something new and shiny. I was so blinded by loyalty and commitment that I didn't see there was a problem until I came home one day and all his stuff was gone."

Bodie shook his head. "If he was unhappy and you didn't see it, it was because he didn't let you see it. You can't fix something you don't even know is broken."

She'd never looked at it like that. Not once.

"Is that why you moved?" he asked.

"First I flailed around for a year feeling sorry for myself," she admitted. "Then I got over myself and decided to start over. Here."

"Brave," he repeated softly.

Because his admission felt too good, she brushed it off. "No more than you, moving from the other side of the country to start a new career."

"That wasn't bravery. I came back home to a safety net. You did the opposite." He looked away, then met her gaze. "You know things went FUBAR. But what I didn't tell you was that our CI turned and gave us bad intel. My partner was killed."

"Oh my God. I'm so sorry." She watched him absently rub up and down his thigh, hating what he'd been through. Putting her hand over his, she felt the knotted muscles. He'd had a whole big, huge badass life before this one. He was only a few years older than her, but going off of life experiences, he was light-years ahead. He'd seen and done things that had changed him in ways she'd never understand. "And you were left for dead too."

"Yeah, and before I recovered, I lost my dad."

She sucked in air. "Oh, Bodie." She didn't take her eyes from his. Couldn't. He'd come so close to not making it himself, and then to lose his partner and dad in one fell swoop . . . her heart ached for him. "And you're still not sure how to come back from that."

"I'm working on it." He gave a small smile as he tugged on one of her wild curls. "Looks good in here. You've done a lot of work."

He clearly wanted to move on from that conversation, which was something she understood. "With help." She unwrapped one of the sandwiches. It was so big it could've fed her for a week. So she cut it in half and rewrapped the other half for Ivy, pushing the still-whole one his way. "You eat yet?"

"No, but that's for the kid."

"We've got plenty here," she said. "Eat." And then she took a bite.

"I wasn't sure if you liked bacon or sausage—" he started, but stopped when she held up a hand, much like he'd done when he'd first tasted her cookies.

"Dear. God." She couldn't say more because her mouth was in heaven. "I think I'm having a sexual experience, just me and this sandwich."

He tipped his head back and laughed softly.

"I'm serious. I want to marry this sandwich and have its babies." She took another bite and moaned. "Why aren't you selling these?"

"Because they're made with love and you can't put a price on that." He laughed again when she choked on a bite. "That's what my mom tells me anyway. And I can cook, I'm just not that into it, so . . ."

"But you're into being a bartender?"

His smile faded some, and he shrugged.

"You're not into being a bartender?" When he just took

another bite, she nodded. "Let me guess. A conversation for another time?"

He smiled, tapped a finger to his nose, and nodded to the old box on the counter. "What did you find?"

"Haven't looked yet." Reaching into the box, she pulled out some cute old wooden signs.

YOU HAD ME AT PIZZA.

HAVE A SLICE DAY.

I WONDER IF PIZZA THINKS ABOUT ME TOO.

She laughed out loud. They even got a smile out of Bodie. That was, until she pulled out a stack of photos, including one of a lanky-lean teenage Bodie wearing an apron behind the front counter. She snorted.

"Yuk it up," he said. "But I was employee of the month nine months running between my sophomore and junior years of high school. I'll have you know I was a heartbreaker in the hairnet and uniform."

She laughed. "I worked at Taco Bell in high school. Our manager always threatened to fire whoever was on last shift if there was food left over. Not knowing he couldn't really do that, I'd always eat whatever hadn't sold. Good thing I loved their food. I finally had to quit or buy new clothes."

He grinned. "What were you like in high school?"

She hadn't thought back that far in a long time. "Lonely."

With their hands full of their food, he nudged his shoulder gently to hers in commiseration. "Is your dad upset you moved so far?"

"He's pretty busy with his new family."

He studied her face, seemed to read her mind, and shook his head. "His loss."

She made a show of looking at him as a teenager and smiled.

He tried to take it. "I should burn that."

"No way. I'm keeping it. It's going up on my wall of fame."

"Wall of fame?"

She smiled. "Customers. Employees." She nearly said "friends" but didn't want to seem presumptuous. "Stuff like that." She looked at the pic again. "You clearly didn't have an evil manager who made you eat the leftovers. You were so skinny."

"I was a late bloomer. Took me a while to fill out."

She eyed his tall, muscled form, thinking he'd filled out perfectly, and he laughed softly, sexily.

"Just making sure you can handle helping me unload all my earthly possessions when they arrive," she lied.

"I can handle anything you throw my way, don't you worry."

And if that didn't give her a secret little thrill . . . "Great, because I need help putting together two shelving kits I had delivered."

"I'm all yours."

Flustered at that, she took another bite of her sandwich. "This really is so good. Thank you."

"You're welcome."

"Did you make the pizzas?"

He smiled, letting her change the subject with no comment. "Nope. I wasn't trusted in the kitchen. I was allowed to clean up and serve customers. My dad wouldn't hire me as a server or a busboy at the bar until I learned the ropes somewhere else. Said

I had a bad attitude and needed someone as a boss who'd kick my ass."

She clapped a hand over her mouth to hold in her laughter and failed. "And did you? Have a bad attitude?"

"I really did. My mom would say I still do."

"This, I believe," she said, enjoying the peek into his past. She was so curious about him. "So . . . did the owner of the pizzeria kick your ass?"

"More than once." He smiled though, as if getting a kick out of the memory. "Toughest boss I've ever had."

"Why did he close up shop?"

"She," he said. "My grandma. She retired. Lives in Palm Springs now and keeps busy terrorizing the seniors in the assisted-living home."

On another laugh, she pulled out a second pic, this one of teenage Bodie and a teenage girl, both wearing aprons behind the bakery counter. Grinning at each other. The girl was Shay, she realized, looking younger and definitely happier.

"We both worked here," Bodie said. "Tried my charm on her, but she wasn't having it. It was always Mace for her."

"She break your heart?"

"Nah." He grinned. "I had a short attention span back then."

"You were a player," she said, not all that surprised.

"I was Trouble. Capital T."

She smiled. "I bet. Always in love?"

"Lust? Yes. Love?" He shook his head. "No."

She studied his face. "Never?"

He shrugged. "I've given it a shot a couple of times. Didn't work out. Love isn't for me."

"Same," she said, and stood, walking to the sink to look out the window, feeling a damper on her current happy, with no idea why. "I don't want anything serious ever again." Because what kind of a person went into a relationship when they knew they weren't whole? Still, there was a flash of disappointment knowing they'd never give this attraction between them a real shot.

Bodie came up behind her. "And what is it you *do* want?" he asked softly.

She turned, and they stared at each other for a long, charged beat, the moment having gone from joking to serious. Finally, she drew a breath. "I thought I knew, but apparently my brain and my body haven't come to terms."

He ran the tip of a finger along her temple, tucking a loose strand behind her ear. "But nothing serious."

Her gaze was locked on his mouth. "I'm allergic to serious."

"Understood." He took the last step between them, moving with clear intent but also slowly, giving her the chance to back away. And she should back away. Instead, she met him halfway, went up on her tiptoes to brush her lips across his. When she felt his tiny start of surprise, she kissed him again. He let her lead, giving a rough groan when she touched her tongue to his. Then she stopped thinking as things detonated.

By the time he pulled back an inch, she'd forgotten where they were and possibly also her name. He searched her eyes—

for what, she had no idea. Her heart was thundering at heart-attack level, and she was hot all over, in some places more than others.

He looked at her for a second longer before lowering his mouth to hers again, just as a sound came from upstairs. *Ivy.* Good God. Harper had completely forgotten they weren't alone, and she jumped back from Bodie like he was a hot potato. "Ivy's upstairs," she whispered.

He nodded, still much slower to pull back. Eyes on hers, his smile faded. "You okay?"

No. No, she wasn't. This wasn't supposed to happen. She wasn't ready to feel. "That was stupid. I'm sorry."

"It was something," he said slowly. "But not stupid."

She shook her head. "Look, that was probably inevitable. But we got it out of the way, so now we can just forget it ever happened and move on."

"Going to be hard to forget."

Damn. Didn't she know it.

"Sorry," Ivy yelled down. "Fell back to sleep! I'm just getting dressed, I'll be right there."

Harper had to clear her voice to answer. "No rush!"

"My gut still says she's a runaway," Bodie said quietly. "Which means you're putting yourself at risk here."

"I know, but she texted her stepsister, who she was supposed to be staying with. So she's not a missing person. Still, the more I talk to her, the more I think her situation is bad." She leaned in close, not wanting Ivy to overhear them. "If she's staying here with me, she's not on the streets facing other dangers."

"Have you asked her to call her parents? If anyone could convince her, it'd be you."

"I'm not sure I can convince her to do anything. She's stubborn. And scared, though she won't show it. And . . . she's on a mission."

"Mission." He frowned. "What kind of mission?"

She couldn't break Ivy's confidence, at least not unless she thought the girl was in actual danger.

"Fine," he said. "Maybe I could offer to drive her home."

"Unless you're willing to drive her to Chicago, it's a no-go."

He opened his mouth, but Ivy came clomping down the stairs. "What smells good?"

Harper pushed half of the sandwich toward her.

Ivy pounced on it just as Shay walked in the back door, followed by her abuela, whose sharp black eyes took in the room before she said something to Shay in Spanish.

Shay handed Harper a list.

"What's this?" she asked.

"Things Abuela wants to see in your bakery. She insisted on me telling you what will and won't sell."

Harper tried to hand the list back to Shay. "You know how I feel about lists."

Shay arched a brow. "You want to tell her that?"

Harper looked at Abuela and took the list.

"I've got my own list going as well, if you're interested," Shay said. "Things I'm out of. You know, in case you happen to see them while you're out and about."

"Okay," Harper said, exasperated. "What are you out of?"

"Wine, patience, fucks."

Ivy snorted and left the room to start mopping. When she was gone, Harper looked over the list and almost but not quite missed Shay giving Bodie a meaningful look. "Bad idea," Shay said.

Bodie just looked at her.

Shay rolled her eyes and left.

Abuela smiled at Bodie. *Smiled*. And then she gently patted him on the cheek and walked out as well.

Harper looked at him. "What was that?"

He shrugged. "Abuela likes me."

"I meant from Shay. What did she mean by 'bad idea'?"

"I believe it was a warning."

"For what?" she asked, eyes narrowed.

"For me not to hurt you."

Harper blinked, then laughed. "You've got that backward. She doesn't even like me."

"Probably not," Bodie said. "She doesn't like anyone right now. But she could use a friend. She's good at pretending nothing hurts her, but she is most definitely hurting."

Harper tried to imagine having the prickly, perpetually irritated Shay as a friend and shook her head. She'd been in too many relationships with people who made her feel bad.

"And hey," Bodie said. "You just got advice from Abuela, which means she likes you. Shay will come around. They're good people."

A week before, Harper had been all alone. And here she was now with a handful of "good people." It was exciting, but also terrifying, because what if she messed this up and once again ended up with no one?

CHAPTER 10

vy had Ham on a leash at her side, and she didn't know what was more exciting: feeling like she had a pet for the first time in her life, or that she was walking along Lake Tahoe and she'd never felt so happy.

Well, except for her secret, which got heavier to carry every single day.

On the bright side, the weather had done a 180 from her first week here. The sun was out, high and bright at their altitude of 6,100 feet. The air warmed her skin, and the water, a color of blue she hadn't even known existed, warmed her soul. So did the 360-degree view of the neck-craning Sierras dotted with granite and pines.

One time a step-grandma had taken her to church, a huge, beautiful stone building where they'd sung songs, and she'd loved it. And this . . . being here felt like that day in church. Reverent. Awe-inspiring. She just felt so . . . lucky—a very new feeling for her. That night she'd tried to sneak into the bakery building felt like a year ago. She'd been desperate for a safe place to sleep—or at least as safe as she could get. She'd figured she'd sleep the best she could while gathering enough courage to follow plan A—getting a new life.

Step One had been checking out Sunrise Cove and getting a lay of the land. She'd always heard Tahoe could be the coldest place in the country, winter or summer, but she'd never believed it. Not until that night, when she'd nearly frozen her toes off—in July.

Being from Chicago, she was plenty used to cold, but not at this time of year. That night she'd been a frozen Popsicle, regretting not taking the offer of a free jacket from Bartender Dude.

Aka Bodie Campbell.

Aka . . . Sperm Donor.

That was what she called him in her head, the father who'd never once paid child support to her mom, not even a single penny. But Ivy wanted those pennies, all of them. After all, they should've come to her over the past sixteen years. But she'd be happy to have them now. The money would fund her new life. On her own.

Which brought her to Step Two of her plan: march up to him and say, "I'm your daughter, and you owe me sixteen years of child support."

But she'd hit a problem: she'd chickened out. Mostly because Sperm Donor had surprised her by being kind and nothing like her mom had always said. Which meant that now she didn't know what to believe. And because of that, she felt more than a little lost.

Ivy knew she was smart. But so was Sperm Donor. He was

watchful and careful. So she had to be more watchful and more careful. She couldn't risk him finding her out before she'd decided what to do. She didn't want to get caught unaware and vulnerable.

Two things she didn't have the luxury of being.

But she still hadn't decided how to tell him who she was, because how did one even broach the subject? Hey, thanks for all the fries, and oh, by the way, sixteen years ago you got my mom pregnant. Surprise, it was a girl!

The thing was, she'd been here for ten days now and she hadn't said a word. She told herself it was because it'd been busy. Harper's stuff had all arrived, including a futon bed for the office—which was now Ivy's to sleep on. Sperm Donor and Sperm Donor's brothers had unloaded everything, and she and Harper had been working on setting up for business.

Last night, Harper had started baking.

And baking.

And she'd let Ivy help, which she'd loved.

Then Harper had decided to have a tasting party with the guys, Shay, her scary abuela, and Ivy. Cookies, cupcakes, croissants, breads . . . it'd all been amazing. Even Shay's abuela had loved everything. And today, Harper had what she'd called a "soft opening," which meant they were open to foot traffic for takeout only.

And people were actually buying stuff. Ivy realized the new feeling in her chest was pride. Harper was teaching Ivy baking basics, and she felt like she'd died and gone to heaven. No one had ever taken the time to teach her something like that, but also . . . spending time with Harper made her feel good about herself. She had responsibilities, and go figure, those made her feel good too. She cleaned. She helped at the front counter when needed. And she babysat Ham—hence this walk. After Ham had eaten a fresh loaf of cinnamon bread, Harper had asked her to take an overly "exuberant" Ham for a very, *very* long walk.

Her days felt full of purpose, also new, and also great. Sometimes she slipped into Olde Tahoe Tap just to steal glimpses of Sperm Donor, who'd continued to be kind. A part of her, a big part, kept reminding herself not to fall for it. It couldn't be real. It just couldn't. And anyway, if he had any idea who she was, that kindness would certainly change. But she was actually smiling while thinking about life here, and she was *not* a smiler. In fact, her mom said she'd been born with a scowl on her face.

She couldn't explain even to herself why she hadn't confronted her birth father yet. Or why she hadn't gone with plan B, put into place in case he turned out to be a complete asswipe—of simply stealing what was rightfully hers.

Sometimes late at night, when she knew Harper was sleeping, she told herself to get up and go, that there was nothing for her here. She clearly didn't have the guts required for either plan.

And yet here she still was.

She could ask herself why all day long, but the truth was, she knew why. It was that secret, desperate need she had to belong somewhere and to someone. Pathetic. She'd had no idea how deep it went until she'd seen Sperm Donor and her uncles talking and laughing. But it was her truth—she had a terrible longing for that same sense of connection, even though she knew she lacked whatever that thing was that allowed people to love and want her. This depressing thought had her tripping over her own two feet, and Ham gently nudged her thigh with his wet nose, reminding her to be careful.

And he was right. She needed to be much more careful. Not with her feet, but with her heart. The plan she'd made as she'd crossed the country had seemed so much simpler before she'd gotten here. But she knew these people now. She liked them. And she wasn't sure how to confront or steal from someone she liked.

But if she didn't do plan A or plan B, her only option would be to go home.

Which was no option at all.

She wanted a new life. She *needed* a new life. And while a little part of her wished this could be it, she knew it couldn't. She was a stray dog, a nearly full-grown one, not a cute puppy who'd be easily adopted.

Her feet stopped her in front of the secondhand store she liked, the one that had a cute window display. Maybe Harper didn't do lists anymore, but Ivy, who'd never made a list in her life, had started one. A mental list of people she owed, and Harper was at the top. She'd shared her personal space with Ivy. She'd shared her dog with Ivy. She'd shared her clothes with Ivy, and as a matter of fact, Ivy was currently wearing a pair of jeans and a sweater, both Harper's, both a size too big for her, but they were warm and comfy.

She wanted to do something to make Harper feel special, the way Harper made Ivy feel.

The wall behind the store's display was completely covered in magnets. And something Harper had said when they'd cleaned out the bakery's huge refrigerator stuck in her mind. Her boss had stared at the fridge for a long moment, then had softly said, "My mom always covered ours with magnets from top to bottom. I wish my dad had kept them so I could have them in my shop."

Ivy's pockets held some cash. Harper had done what she'd said she would, paying Ivy for her hours. She looked down at Ham, then at the huge water bowl next to the store's door, which she'd learned was a sign that dogs were welcome inside. The most amazing thing she'd discovered about Tahoe was that dogs were welcome almost anywhere. So she and Ham entered.

There was a customer inside, a guy who took his concentration off a rack of T-shirts for sale to stare at Ivy and Ham for a solid thirty seconds.

Ivy started to turn to go before he could give her shit or something, but then he pulled a chihuahua out of his sweatshirt.

"I didn't know we could have dogs in here," he said simply.

Ivy was so relieved she giggled. She hated to giggle. But the chihuahua was super cute and Ham wanted to be BFFs, which meant he wanted to lick him to death, so she dragged him to the back wall, where she picked out the perfect magnet for Harper.

BALANCED EATING IS A COOKIE IN EACH HAND.

After, she and Ham crossed the street and walked through the state park to the beach. Kicking off her beat-up sneaks, she dug her toes into the sand. The top layer was dry and sugary, but she dug down and found the underlayer cool and damp. At the water, Ham whined to be free to swim, so she unhooked him from his leash. Sure enough, he raced into the water and bounced through it like a bunny. A hundred-pound-plus bunny.

Then suddenly there was another oversize animal in the water with him, a black behemoth that looked like a . . . bear? "Oh crap. *Ham! Come!*"

But did Ham listen? No. Instead, he pounced on the bear, and they both went under for a second. "*Ohmigod, Ham!*"

They surfaced, and she nearly collapsed in relief when she realized the bear was a huge dog. Still, she rushed into the water, which hit her knees and had her stopping to suck in a breath. What kind of lake was so icy cold? Before she could go any farther, someone called to her from behind.

"It's okay, Dakota's friendly!"

She turned to find a guy around her age, also holding an empty leash. He stood next to a girl who looked very much like him, both tall, lanky-lean to the point of being too thin, dark hair, dark eyes, laughing as the dogs continued to pounce on each other in sheer joy.

Ivy clasped a hand to her heart, which was racing more than any time in recent memory, including the time a few weeks earlier when she'd had to switch buses in Chicago to get to the train station and some weirdo had followed her into the bathroom. She'd escaped out the window and had sat near some exhausted-looking dad with six kids, who hadn't even noticed her pretending to be the seventh.

She was rustled from that memory when the guy on the beach whistled sharply and both dogs came running out of the water.

"Watch out!" the guy warned, but Ivy didn't move in time to escape both Ham and Dakota shaking off what felt like a thousand gallons of lake water . . . all over her.

She scrunched her eyes tight during the dousing but opened them to find both dogs sitting politely, panting happily up at the guy, who pulled something from his pocket and gave it to them.

"Treats," he said with an easy smile tossed Ivy's way. "It's the only way to control Dakota. You okay?"

"Yes. You're . . . siblings," Ivy said inanely.

"Twins," the girl said. "Jessie and James." She shrugged. "Mom had a sense of humor."

"I'm Ivy." She wanted to be friendly, but it was hard to think about anything other than her soaked jeans and sneakers, which were making her shiver. "I should go. It's a long walk back."

"Where to?" James asked.

"Sugar Pine Bakery, right next to Olde Tahoe Tap. I work there." Wow, Pride surge #2. A record for her.

James's smile faded a little bit. "That's a long walk. And thanks to us, you're all wet. We can give you a ride."

Jessie nodded her agreement.

They walked across the beach toward the parking lot. Well, the humans walked. Ham and Dakota ran like wild banshees. "Please be good," Ivy called out to Ham. "Remember, the geese are evil. And that if you poop, I've gotta—"

Ham stopped short, turned in a circle, and, tail up, hunched his shoulders.

"Clean it up," she finished on a sigh.

Jessie laughed.

James did too, but also looked sympathetic.

Resigned, Ivy fished a poop bag from her pocket. Once in science class she'd learned that if you could smell something, it meant you had particles of that something in your nose. Not wanting poop particles anywhere near her face, she pulled the neckline of her sweatshirt over her mouth and nose before bending to pick up the *mountain* of poop. "What the hell are we feeding you?"

Ham panted happily, ran a few more feet away, and damn. Hunched again.

Jessie laughed until James pointed at Dakota, also producing her own mountain of poop.

"It's your turn," Jessie told her brother.

"Shit," James said. "Literally." He looked at Ivy. "Can I borrow a bag?"

"Borrow? No. Keep? *Yes*," she said, knowing Harper wouldn't mind. "Here."

Five minutes later they were in the beach parking lot, standing in front of a beat-up, old Subaru. At one point it had probably been green, but it was currently mostly rust.

"Home sweet home," Jessie said, the words cheerier than her quiet voice.

James gently tugged on a strand of his sister's hair. "Better than a street corner, right?"

Ivy's heart squeezed. "How old are you guys?"

"Eighteen," Jessie said.

James looked at her.

"Fine," his sister said. "Seventeen."

"I'll be seventeen in the winter," Ivy said quietly.

James unlocked and opened the back hatch.

"Hold on a sec," he said. The cargo area was packed with stuff—blankets, clothes, etc.—but only half of it. The other half was wide open, and Dakota jumped into it. Ham followed. Ivy took the back seat, which was crowded with more stuff, and shut the door. Then she realized Jessie and James hadn't gotten in yet. They were outside, arguing in hushed tones that she could still hear.

"What if she tells someone about us?" Jessie asked.

"I don't think she will."

"It's unlike you to trust anyone," Jessie said. "Why her? It's a stupid risk—"

"Jess, I promised to take care of you, and I'm doing the best I can. But I have a feeling she's like us, and she needs a ride. We help people like us, right?"

Jessie looked away.

"Jess."

"Right. Whatever." And she stalked away from him and slid behind the wheel, locking the door.

"Hey. Real mature." James knocked on the driver's-side window. "Open up."

His sister shook her head. "Sorry, can't hear you."

James rolled his eyes, but apparently he was easygoing, because he simply ambled around the car and slid into the passenger seat before glancing over at Jessie. "Try not to get us another ticket."

"Wow," she said. "A girl takes out a parking meter one time and it's like she's a bad driver or something."

A few minutes later, she pulled into the parking lot in front of the bakery.

Ivy got out, and James met her at the back of the Subaru, where he opened the door for Ham to jump down. "What are you off to do?" he asked.

"I'm hungry," she admitted. "I'll probably hunt up some food." She met his gaze. He hadn't changed his laid-back smile or said anything, so maybe it was her imagination that he seemed hungry too. "You guys want to eat with me?"

"Jess?" he called through the open hatch. "You want to eat something?"

Jessie turned, looking interested for the first time since Ivy had met her. "Always."

James grinned at Ivy. "We're in."

Ivy smiled before realizing she'd just talked herself into a corner. She couldn't bring them into the bakery and just assume Harper would feed them all. She knew she was welcome to eat anything in the fridge there, Harper had told her that only a zillion times a day, but it wasn't fair of her to extend that invite to the twins. Not after all Harper had done for Ivy. She didn't want to be a burden.

She wanted to be self-sufficient.

But that was turning out to be harder than she'd ever

imagined. "We could go to Olde Tahoe Tap and order some-thing," she suggested.

James looked over at the bar and grill, then gave a slow shake of his head. "Thanks, but I just remembered, we've got to go."

They didn't have money, she realized. They were clearly living out of their car, on their own, and Ivy knew more than anyone how tough it was to survive. And yet still, they'd gone out of their way to give her a ride. "No, I owe you for the ride."

James looked at her for a long beat, seeming a little uncertain. "We can't let you do that."

"It's okay. I've got it." Or so she hoped. She wasn't actually sure the money she had left was enough. She'd earn more, she reminded herself.

Jessie parked in the cool shade and rolled down the windows for Dakota. She'd be okay since the high today was maybe seventy degrees. The rest of them, including Ham, walked to the bar. She told herself she was hungry for French fries and a root beer, but really she was hungriest for another look at Sperm Donor.

She led them to an open table, where Ham immediately plopped underneath for a snooze.

"You sure about this?" Jessie asked quietly. "It's a really nice place."

Actually, no, Ivy wasn't sure. In fact, she was having regrets about offering at all because she was worried Bodie wouldn't take her money for Jessie's and James's meals. She managed a smile. "Yeah. I'm sure."

She saw Mace busy at the bar and a flash of Bodie just inside the kitchen. A woman on a barstool near her uncle was sobbing her heart out to the woman sitting next to her. Mace set a drink in front of her. "On the house," he said. "And whoever he is, he isn't worth it."

The woman glared at him and yelled, "I'm crying about finishing the best book ever! And now it's over, you moron!"

Mace blinked and turned to his brother, who was laughing at him. Mace discreetly flipped him the bird, then came over to Ivy's table. "Hey, sweetheart."

She'd never had an uncle before. Her mom was an only child, and so was Ivy herself. And he probably called every female "sweetheart," so why it felt special, she had no idea. "Hey." She hesitated. "Is it okay if we get some food?"

"Of course."

Bodie ambled over as well. "I've got this," he said to Mace, tossing Ham a doggy biscuit, which he snatched out of midair from a dead sleep. Bodie then smiled at Ivy. "Hey, Kit Kat. Who're your friends?"

"Jessie and James." She warmed inside at the familiar nickname, but she was also starting to feel sick with worry, wishing she hadn't promised them food.

"Ready to order?" Bodie looked at Ivy first. "Let me guess. For you, a burger, two slices of cheddar, extra pickles, my secret house sauce, and a side of curly fries with Dr Pepper."

Ivy was speechless. Her mom never remembered what she liked, but he had. "Do you remember everyone's order?"

"Grandpa here never remembers anything," Mace said as he walked by with another table's order.

Bodie ignored this and looked at Jessie and James. "And you two?"

When they both hesitated, Ivy piped up with, "They'll have what I'm having."

"Ours to go, please," Jessie said quietly. "If that's okay. And thank you."

To go? They weren't going to stay and eat? Ivy looked at them, realizing they both looked truly a little uncomfortable. They didn't think they fit in. Little did they know, she was the same.

When Bodie moved back to the kitchen, James drew a slow, deep breath. "Thank you," he said quietly, with sincere gratitude.

"Sure." Her initial hesitation gone, replaced by the warmth in her gut that came from helping them, Ivy tried to make small talk. "So, where are you guys from?"

Jessie bit her lower lip and looked at her brother.

"Albuquerque," James said.

"I came from Chicago," she admitted. "Took days to get here. It feels like an old nightmare now."

Jessie seemed to take her first deep breath, then nodded. "Same, but at least I wasn't alone."

James didn't say much. Didn't have to. The dark shadows in his eyes told Ivy what she needed to know.

They were all runaways.

Then, as if each of them needed a lighter topic, they talked about Tahoe and what there was to do for fun.

"We try to get whatever odd jobs we can," James said. "But we like to hang out on the beach. And a friend of ours has a relative who's got property in Hidden Falls and has parties." He smiled, and she realized that beyond the easygoing affability lurked something more—worry.

Something else she knew a little bit about.

"You could come with us sometime," Jessie said.

"Okay," Ivy said, wondering if she'd still be here when that happened. But she had to admit, it felt good to make new friends. Friends who understood her.

Ten minutes later, Bodie came back with the twins' food bagged up and a steaming-hot plate for Ivy. When he was gone again, Jessie and James were already on their feet, with James pulling out his wallet.

"No," Ivy said. "It's okay."

James looked at her, and she nodded, hoping she looked confident. "Thank you," he finally said. "And now we owe you."

Jessie nodded with a warm smile. "We'll text you."

They exchanged numbers, and then they were gone. Ivy ate her food, then pulled her twenty from her pocket. Definitely not enough, but she'd pay the rest back as soon as she could.

A strange thought, considering why she was here.

Just as she set the twenty on the table, Bodie's hand settled on top of hers, stopping her. She closed her eyes briefly, but when he didn't speak, she opened them again and looked at him. This was the first time she'd had physical contact with the guy she knew to be her dad, and in that moment, soaking up his face, she saw . . . *her own eyes looking back at her.* It completely robbed her of thought and the ability to speak.

She really was his. She'd known that, but what she hadn't realized was that she'd *needed* to see something of herself in him. Or something of him in her. But she'd just gotten both, leaving her startled, and also unbearably moved and fighting with surprising tears.

"Do you know what it means when I say your money isn't good here?" he asked patiently. "It means that any time you're hungry, you come here and eat a hot meal on the house."

"But not my friends."

"I don't mind."

He didn't mind? Was he made of money? Her mouth opened, speaking before her brain could catch up. "I'm not a freeloader or a charity case."

"Never said you were," he said lightly. "Consider this part of your payment for all the hours you're working next door, saving me time and labor."

"Harper's already paying me."

"For the stuff you do for her, which is great. But I'm no freeloader either, and I always pay my debts. And when you work on the building itself, that's a debt I owe you."

She considered that, decided she could live with it, and nodded. "Early this morning me and Harper pulled up the gross linoleum in that back storage closet, so probably you owe me a *double* serving of fries."

He smiled. "Bottomless fries it is. And my mom just made her famous lasagna. She makes it weekly and stuffs it into my fridge. I'll set a piece aside for you to take back and eat whenever."

She froze. "Your mom?"

"Yeah, I wasn't born thirty-four years old, you know."

He was teasing her, so she managed a smile, but her mind was spinning. *I have a grandma . . .*

"Kid, you just hit the lottery," Mace said as he passed by again. "Not only is Mom's lasagna notorious, Bodie's never given up a slice voluntarily. I had to fight him for some last time."

Bodie narrowed his eyes at his brother. "Go anywhere near it and consider it game on."

To Ivy's surprise, Mace lifted his hands in surrender.

"I didn't mean to cause a fight." Sudden nerves had Ivy's tummy quivering like it did when she ate too much chocolate. Because how would Bodie act when he was angry? What if when he got mad, he was like one of her stepdads, the Yeller. Or the Thrower. "Please don't fight because of something stupid I said," she said shakily.

"Hey." Bodie squeezed her hand. "First, you didn't do anything wrong. And second, we don't fight. Not really. Mostly we just talk over each other. Mace here has the loudest voice, and he tries to use it to get his way." He took a French fry and popped it in his mouth. "We don't physically fight in our family."

"Well, not anymore anyway," Mace said. "The last time was when Zeke was seventeen and decided to 'borrow' Dad's Blazer. Austin insisted on a turn driving and crashed into our mailbox at the end of our road, remember?" he asked Bodie.

"Hard to forget. We started the blame game and got into a fight right there in the road in the middle of the night."

Mace smiled. "We came home carrying the Blazer's side mirrors and various scrapes and black eyes. Shit, Dad was furious."

"Signed us up for karate lessons the next day," Bodie said with a smile in his voice. "So we could beat the shit out of each other on someone else's watch."

"Yeah, he loved that," Mace said. "I miss him. Austin too."

"Every day," Bodie said.

They'd lost a brother. And a dad. And they'd stuck together. Watching these two grown men show such easy emotion and affection for each other, Ivy really wanted to believe it was all some kind of act. But she knew it wasn't. Bodie seemed like a good guy . . . and yet he'd walked away from her and her mom. So how good of a guy could he really be? "None of you fight, *ever?*" she asked in disbelief. "Even with your own kids? Like, what if they're jerks, or do something stupid?"

Bodie and Mace looked at each other. "The only one of us who has kids is Zeke," Bodie said.

Ivy, who'd been avoiding eye contact, lifted her head, shocked. Startled. Why would he say he didn't have a kid? Was he lying, or . . .

Or was her mom?

"Do you . . . do you want kids?" she asked over the thunder of her heart beating in her ears.

"Sure." This from Mace. "I've made a lot of mistakes, but I'd like to think I could come back from them and have a family someday."

Ivy looked at Bodie and held her breath.

"Not *that* many mistakes," he said to his brother, who gave him a shadow of a smile. Bodie turned to Ivy, and she wondered if he'd answer the question, as he was definitely the more closed off of the two. "Maybe someday," he said.

Her heart sort of died on the "maybe."

"But if you ask one of the nephews," he went on, "he'd tell you that I'm the best uncle on the planet."

Mace snorted as he walked off. "In your dreams, man. That title is mine."

Bodie turned to the counter between the bar and kitchen, grabbed another plate of French fries, and set it in front of Ivy. "How about you? You close to your family?"

She swallowed a fry that felt like a block of wood suddenly. "No."

Bodie gave her a "gimme more" gesture, and she sighed. "My mom's too busy with her new husband."

"And your dad?"

That one was easy. "I'm not sure he knows I exist."

Bodie didn't try to give her any empty platitudes, like most adults did. He simply nodded. "You deserve better."

She wanted that to be true, but she wasn't sure it was.

"Have you called anyone to check in and let them know you're okay?" Bodie asked.

"Harper asks me that every single day."

"And?"

She shrugged. "My mom's out of the country right now, but I'll call when she's home." *Maybe.*

He surprised her by accepting this. Not a nag in sight. It gave her courage to ask him the question she'd been dying to ask. "So . . . have you made mistakes too? Like Mace?"

He was quiet for a long moment, and she wasn't at all sure he intended to answer. But then he did. "In another job, in another life," he said. "I got distracted and made a bad call. And because of it, someone who was like family to me ended up dead, leaving behind a family. And no man should have to leave behind his family."

Ivy could see the pain and regret in his eyes, and she absolutely believed him. What scared her was that she'd never been so confused. All her life, he'd been the Big Bad in her history bank. The dad who'd walked away and never looked back.

But this didn't match up with anything that she'd learned about him. "I'm really sorry for your friend and his family," she said. "And that you had to go through that."

"Thanks. Me too. I'm damn sorry for all of it."

She poked a French fry into some ketchup and swirled it around. "Do you think people can come back from their mistakes?"

"I sure as hell hope so."

She popped the French fry in her mouth and nudged the plate toward him so he'd help himself. "Me too," she said softly. She wished that with all her might.

CHAPTER 11

Harper stood in her brand-spanking-new-to-her bakery kitchen, beaming from ear to ear. She'd only been here two weeks, but she already had something that had been missing from her life for a long time.

Hope.

Yesterday's soft opening had gone well, takeout only. Wanting to get all the kinks out, she hadn't yet placed ads, put up signs, contacted any local restaurants about purchasing her desserts, or let any local wedding planners know she was available for wedding cakes.

She'd get there. She'd ordered four tables and cute mismatched chairs for seating as well. She couldn't wait to see people enjoying and lingering over her goods. Just the thought made her smile.

As did the memory of her first customer that morning. A little girl who'd walked straight up to the counter—a good foot taller than her. She'd opened her hand, revealing a pretty blue rock sitting in her palm. "Can I buy a chocolate chip cookie with this?" she'd asked.

Harper was now one blue rock richer.

The girl's older brother had come running in to get her and apologize, but Harper had no regrets.

Since it was officially the quiet hours—past lunch, nearly closing time—she had no customers at the moment. So she was baking to her heart's content for tomorrow while Ivy had Ham out on a long walk. She was baking more of her chocolate and mint chip cookies, smiling at Bodie, who was sitting on her counter eating one. He'd showed up a few minutes earlier, offering to be her quality taster. But since he'd also tried to quality taste her lips, she wasn't taking him all that seriously.

He sucked some chocolate off his thumb, the sound making her feel a little wobbly on the inside. "You've never said why you stopped coming to Tahoe when you were twelve."

She managed to lift her gaze from his mouth to his eyes. "And?"

He smiled, like he enjoyed her sass. Which was a good thing, since it was a part of her to her very soul. "And you've never said why you aren't going back to the ATF," she said.

He smiled again. "And?"

With a snort, she went back to dropping balls of dough onto a cookie sheet. Not easy because he was making some seriously sexy yummy "mmm" noises, and she wouldn't mind getting him to make those noises for another reason entirely.

Looking amused at them both, he crooked a finger at her. "Come here."

"If I come over there, we both know I'll never finish these."

His laugh was low and rough and scraped at all her good parts. And damn, her feet seceded from her brain and took her right to him. She wasn't sure who kissed who, but she was sure that he tasted amazing, and suddenly she was making her own "mmm" noises.

When they pulled back for air, he ran a hand up her arm, settling his palm at the nape of her neck, his thumb slowly grazing her while holding her gaze. "My mom thinks I'm retired. My brothers think I'm on leave. Neither is the truth."

"Okay," she said. "What is the truth?"

He hesitated. "I've not told anyone."

Startled by the serious intensity in his eyes and the fact that he was telling her what he hadn't shared with his family, she nodded. "Understood."

"The ATF dumped me."

"What?" She straightened with righteous indignity on his behalf. "*Why?*"

He looked away and shrugged a broad shoulder. "I'm damaged goods, and no longer worth a damn."

She sucked in a breath, emotions colliding. Sorrow for him, but mostly fury at the people who'd made him feel like the years he'd spent keeping the world safe meant nothing. Cupping his face, she brought it back to hers. "That couldn't be further from the truth."

He said nothing.

"It couldn't," she said softly.

He touched his forehead to hers.

She wrapped her arms around him, and to her surprise, he did the same. "What does everyone else think happened?"

He drew a deep breath. "My brothers think I took unpaid leave because I needed some time. My mom thinks I retired. I haven't been able to tell them."

She knew he didn't want her sympathy, so she tried to bury it. "I stopped coming here when I was twelve because my mom died. After that, my dad had no interest in Tahoe. I did, but that didn't matter."

They looked at each other for a long, charged beat. Bodie's hands came up to her face, gently tipping it to his.

She put her hands to his chest, leaned in, and—

The back door opened, and in stepped Abuela. "I'm ready to start tomorrow," she announced.

Harper looked at her in surprise. "Start what?"

"Work. Six a.m. is no good for me. I'll give you seven to ten a.m."

Harper had been looking all week for a part-time employee willing to work six to eleven just to help her get the baking all done. She'd been thinking of a teen looking for a summer job— anyone other than the woman she was pretty much petrified of. "You run the bookstore."

"No, Shay runs the bookstore for me. I want to bake."

"Okay, but . . ." Harper attempted to tread lightly. "You should know the pay isn't that great, and we'll be using only recipes I've approved, not to mention *I'd* be the boss. You'd have to at least pretend to respect me and follow my directions."

"We can share the position," Abuela said confidently.

Behind her, Bodie choked out what sounded like a laugh, but when Harper craned her neck his way, he coughed, eyes innocent. "'Scuse me."

She narrowed her eyes at him before turning back to Abuela. "We're not sharing my position. I'm the boss, no exceptions."

Abuela considered this. "Well, maybe you have to go to the bathroom. Or for a supply run. Or to kiss a Campbell boy. I could be, what do you call it, interim boss."

Bodie choked again, this time for real.

"Well?" Abuela said to Harper.

"No on *any* sort of boss, interim or otherwise," she said firmly, since gentleness wasn't cutting it. "But if you can agree to those terms, you're hired."

Abuela beamed. "Great. I'll start tomorrow."

"How about now?" Harper asked.

Abuela smiled. "Tomorrow is better for me." And then she was gone.

Harper let out a breath. "Why do I feel like I've just been bamboozled?"

"Because you have been." Bodie reached for another cookie.

She smacked his hand away just as Ivy came into the kitchen. "Question," she said, stumbling a bit at the sight of Bodie in the kitchen.

Harper knew Ivy was uncomfortable with men, but she had hoped being around the Campbell brothers, who were nothing but easygoing and gentle with her, would help. "I'm all ears," Harper said.

Ivy tore her gaze off Bodie. "Um, I just got back and Ham's

leashed out front, enjoying a sunspot, but a guy came in when I did. He's looking for a special cake for his mom. He doesn't care what flavor or what it looks like, he just wants it to read 'fuck cancer'—his words," she said quickly. "And he's willing to pay extra if you'll use the, um, f-word on his cake. Apparently, the last bakery refused him, and he needs the cake today."

Harper set down her spoon. "Don't take his money."

Looking disappointed, Ivy nodded. "Yeah, okay."

"Just give him his choice of the three cakes in the display and I'll add the wording—no charge. Tell him to use his cake money to get flowers to go with."

Ivy beamed at her. "'K!"

Five minutes later, the guy left happy with his personalized cake. Ivy locked up the front for her and went over to the bookstore.

Which left Harper alone with Bodie.

He slid off the counter and came to her, hands going to her hips, his gaze locked on hers. "You're amazing, you know that?"

Uncomfortable with the praise, she pushed him away with a laugh. "Shoo. You're distracting me."

His back was against the wall now, but he snagged her by the waist and pulled her in. "No, *this* would be me distracting you." He covered her mouth with his, making a little indistinct sound as he angled to get the best fit, deepening the kiss until they were both goners. "Later," he finally murmured against her lips.

"You sure?" She flicked her eyes south to the hardest part of him pressed against her.

"Yeah." He gave her one last kiss below her ear. "I don't feel real stable backed up to the wall."

"You seem stable. Or should I say solid—as a rock."

He laughed, looking inordinately pleased at the description. *Men . . .*

HARPER AND IVY had full days for the rest of the week, and shockingly, Abuela fit right in with them. And though foot traffic had been light, they'd had more than a few repeat customers. Mostly Shay, but hey, a customer was a customer, and Harper felt giddy and hopeful as she cleaned her kitchen at the end of each long day.

Ivy was upstairs, probably on her phone, which seemed to be her favorite hobby. And now that Harper felt somewhat settled, her angst had quieted down and she realized . . . she herself didn't have a favorite hobby.

Or any hobby.

She tried to remember what she used to do with her time before she was with Daniel. She'd briefly taken up running in college, but she'd hated it. She did love to read and was also always up for a good TV marathon, but suddenly being alone didn't appeal.

She wanted to do something grown-up, like . . . kiss Bodie again.

No. That was the wrong body part doing her thinking for her. But damn, the brief flashes of how his hands—and mouth—had made her feel were her undoing.

She drew a deep breath. What she wanted was to go for a drink instead of pouring a glass of wine into a water tumbler because her wineglasses had remained behind with Daniel.

So to that end, she was going to do something really stupid. She was going to Olde Tahoe Tap for that drink. And okay, maybe also for the possibility of other adult things, because the truth was, she wanted to celebrate with someone. Someone of age. Someone tall and leanly built and sexy, who kissed like heaven and tasted like her chocolate and mint chip cookies.

She headed upstairs to change, first peeking in on Ivy, who was, sure enough, on the futon with her phone, ignoring the rest of the world as only a teenager could.

Harper showered, then looked through her closet for something suitable to wear. Something that maybe said this was just a casual drink, nothing more. Something that might also say she was pretty and open to new things.

Tall order for the woman who had only two suitcases of clothes, most of them work clothes. She pulled on a sundress, then remembered that even though it was August now, the nights could still be quite chilly. She tore off the dress and changed into washed-out jeans and a strappy tank top with a sweater that had a chocolate stain on it.

Dammit.

She kept going through the closet until she'd rejected her entire wardrobe and everything she owned was strewn across the bed and fully covering a snoring Ham. Like, seriously snoring. She could hardly hear herself think. She was in leggings and a cami tank, with an oversize sweater that hung nearly to her knees. She added flats, put her hair up into a ponytail, added a swipe of mascara and lip gloss, the end. She grabbed a leftover cookie from the tin on her dresser.

At the sound of the tin opening, Ham's head popped up, ears perked. He could hear food from ten miles away.

"It's my dinner," she said.

He licked his chops.

"Sorry, buddy, but dogs can't have chocolate."

He didn't even blink. Probably because he didn't recognize himself as a dog. He thought he was a person.

Ivy appeared in the doorway. "Did I hear chocolate?"

Harper laughed and held out the tin for her to grab a few cookies.

"You going back downstairs to bake some more?" Ivy asked.

"No, I'm going for a drink."

Ivy's brows raised. "Like a get-laid drink?"

Harper gasped. "No!" At least not that she wanted to admit to a sixteen-year-old.

Ivy rolled her eyes and started shifting through the piles of clothes strewn everywhere, exposing the rest of Ham. "Hambone," the teen murmured affectionally, and gave him a kiss on the snout. "You should've told her to go with her skinny jeans and these boots." She tossed the slightly too-tight jeans and the only pair of sexy boots Harper owned her way. Then stood there waiting while Harper replaced her leggings with the jeans and boots.

"You're still going to wear that sweater?" Ivy asked.

Harper slid her a glance.

"I'll rephrase," Ivy said. "You're *not* wearing that sweater."

"What's wrong with it?"

"Nothing, if you want to never date again. Lose it."

"But I'm not wearing a bra."

"You don't need one."

Harper pulled off the sweater.

"Yes." Ivy walked around Harper and then nodded her approval. "You look great."

"I wasn't going for great. I was going for a drink."

"Uh-huh," Ivy said with a smirk. "Is that why you're wearing mascara when you hate mascara?"

"Hey, the mascara is armor, okay?" Harper eyed herself in the mirror and had to admit, she looked pretty okay. "It's been a long time since I've . . . had a drink."

"Old people are so weird about sex."

"I'm not old! And go get into trouble on the internet, would you?"

"I'd be tempted by that, but the internet up here in the boondocks is complete shit."

"We need a swear jar." Harper sighed. "Why do I get the feeling you're sixteen going on sixty?"

"Because I am," Ivy said. "I was born old as dirt."

Harper laughed. "I'm glad you have new friends your age. Do you know their story? Where are their parents?"

"Out of the picture. Their parents died." Ivy shrugged. "I get the feeling that foster care didn't work out for them because they didn't like being separated. So they're on their own."

Harper nodded, hating that for them. She'd met the twins several times now, mostly when she fed them whenever they came to pick up Ivy to go to the lake. And Dakota. Harper loved that Ham had a new friend too. Or, given how he looked at Dakota, maybe she should say girlfriend. "You enjoy their company."

Ivy shrugged. "Better than being alone."

Harper hugged her. "You're never alone."

That got a rare smile out of the girl. "Thanks." She studied Harper in her outfit. "You know, you're really pretty."

Harper shrugged that off. "It's the mascara."

"No, it's not. Except . . ." Ivy moved close and pulled out Harper's ponytail, then fluffed her hair. "Okay, *now* you're ready to impress."

"I'm not trying to impress anyone."

"Liar. Go have a good time. Don't do anything I wouldn't do."

Harper stopped. Pointed at her. "That better be a lot."

"Hey, this isn't about me. And don't worry—if you don't come home, I can feed Hambone breakfast."

"Oh my God! I'm coming right back!"

Ivy grinned. "You're cute when you get all flustered and embarrassed. Maybe we should have the birds and the bees talk."

Harper went hands-on-hips. "You about done?"

"I'm not sure," Ivy said on a laugh. "This is fun. Look, just have a good time, okay? Oh, and whoever buys you a drink—make him work for it, because then he knows you respect yourself."

Harper stopped and felt herself smile stupidly. "Aw, you *have* been listening!"

"Well, I wouldn't go that far, but I *have* been reading your latest *Cosmo*."

Harper hugged her, touched by this teen who'd wormed her way into her heart in a blink of an eye. "Don't ruin this for me. I feel like a proud mama."

Ivy pretended to be choking on the hug and Harper gave up, pulling back on a laugh. She knew Ivy wasn't someone accustomed to physical affection, but hell, neither was she. They were two lost souls who'd somehow found each other. "Lock up behind me. And don't talk to strangers."

"Yes, ma'am."

Harper eyed her. "Your use of sarcasm to cover your discomfort with emotion has been noted."

"The only reason you recognize that is because we're two peas in a pod. Now go," Ivy said.

Outside, Harper drew a deep breath and walked the cobblestone sidewalk, taking in the quaint buildings lit by so many twinkle lights it felt like Christmas in August.

Except tonight it was raining, not snowing. She stuck close to the buildings' overhangs, and two minutes later, she stood at the front of the bar, trying to gather her courage. Turning, she looked into the dark, wet night sky, wondering why she was being such a chicken. *You're better than this. You're a strong, independent woman—*

At a rustle behind her, she froze for a beat, because oh God, it was probably a bear. Quickly, she whirled, hands up in a defensive pose, making herself bigger than she was, only to freeze again. Because not a bear, just someone every bit as grumpy as one.

Shay.

CHAPTER 12

Shay stopped short at the sight of Harper's aggressive stance. "What the . . ."

"I thought you were a bear."

"Huh," Shay said, but didn't offer anything further, snarky or sarcastic or otherwise.

That was when Harper realized Shay had more than just rain on her face. It was tears, streaming down her cheeks. "Hey. Are you okay?"

"Do I look okay?"

"No, you look like you're crying."

Shay swiped at her tears. "That's because my life status is currently holding it all together with one bobby pin."

Harper hesitated. Any other woman, she'd have reached out with a hug or sympathetic words. But this was Shay. "Do you want to talk about it?" she asked cautiously.

"No." But more tears fell.

Harper grimaced, then waded in. "Is this about Mace?"

"We're not talking about him."

"Okaaaay. So why are you still standing in the rain with me?"

"I'm not with you." Shay turned back to the bar. "I'm trying to build up the courage to go back inside."

"I know the feeling."

"Oh, do you really?" Shay asked, angrily swiping at her tears. "Were you stupid enough to pick a fight with the man you love, acting like a total asshole, leaving him no choice but to walk away from you?"

Harper's laugh was mirthless. "Well, actually, the man I loved turned out to be the asshole *and* he walked away from me, so . . ."

Shay tipped her head back and stared up at the sky. She let out a softly muttered "dammit" and then looked at Harper again. "I'm sorry that happened to you." She pulled out a flask. "It's Abuela's, and if you tell her I have it, I'll put her favorite curse on you."

"What does the curse do?"

Shay shrugged. "She's a bit vague on that. And I can't believe you hired her."

"Hey, she scared me into it. But she's great in the kitchen."

Shay snorted and took a long pull from the flask before offering it to Harper, who took a sip, swallowed, then proceeded to nearly cough up a lung. Eyes streaming, she swiped her mouth. It took her a full two minutes to be able to do anything other than wheeze. "Dear God, what is that?"

"Moonshine. Abuela's brother and uncle make it for their cronies in the old folks' home. They claim it's better than any depression or anxiety med." Shay held the flask up in a mock toast. "To . . . all the men we love to hate and hate to love." She took a shot and then gasped, eyes watering as she pounded her own chest. "Okay, so this batch is a bit stronger than most."

"You picked a fight with Mace, the king of easygoing, laid-back, effortless charm? That must've been difficult to even do," Harper said, knowing she was taking her own life into her hands for wanting to know.

"I had my reasons."

Harper studied her. "Is he a closeted dickwad? Was he mean to you? He didn't hurt you, did he?"

"No, nothing like that." Shay sighed. "The Campbell guys . . . they're exactly what they seem, no hidden agenda, not a mean bone in their bodies. I mean, they can be badass, Bodie especially, but they're good men to the bone. It's me who's got the mean bones." She eyed Harper. "You were engaged to an ass-hole?"

"Not quite, but close."

"What made him an asshole?"

"Well, he wasn't always one," Harper said.

"More words," Shay said.

Harper gave her a look. "Goes both ways."

"You first."

"Fine. We met freshman year in college. I was young, shy, lonely, and pretty much on my own. Daniel came from a large, prominent family that loved him. He was confident, funny, and had a lot of friends, and drew me out of my shell with embar-rassing ease. But when we got serious, his parents started to get in his head. I wasn't good enough, I was a nobody who worked at a bakery, I was using him . . . And then he suddenly started not including me in things, telling me *I* was the one pulling away from *him*, saying I was difficult to care about because I was insecure about him and his family, stuff like that."

Shay looked pissed-off. "He gaslit you."

Harper shrugged.

"No, he gaslit you," Shay repeated. "Because believe me, I've tried not to care about you, and I've tried *really* hard too, but here's the thing, Harper—you are *very* easy to care about. Which, for the record, I hate."

"Um, thanks?"

Shay sighed. "Look at it this way: you dodged a bullet. Not all men are created equal."

"Okay, so if Mace is your person, why did you let him walk away?"

Shay lifted a shoulder. "I panicked."

"More words," Harper said dryly.

Shay sighed. "Look, I came from a shitty upbringing. My parents separated when I was young, and neither wanted to keep me. So my abuela took me in. You probably haven't noticed, but it left me with some serious trust issues."

"Hmm," Harper said.

Shay tossed up her hands. "Mace came out of nowhere and . . . just loved me, which was ridiculous of him. I've told him a million times relationships *never* work in the long run. So then what does he do? He asks me to marry him."

"Wow, what an asshole," Harper said.

"No, you don't get it. When we were in high school, we agreed to just be and have fun. No marriage, no white picket fence. He knew how I felt about . . . love, and where I'd come from. And now he wants to change the rules and label it? No." She shook her head. "It's a foul on the play. And when I told him so, he tried to talk to me about it. And that's when I picked a fight, and he proved me right by walking." She looked away. "Once people put a label on things, it ruins everything."

"Maybe," Harper said. "But what I know for sure is that relationships scared the hell out of me too."

Shay nodded. "Did you really drive away from everything just to come to a place that made you happy when you were a kid?"

"I know it sounds dumb." Harper shook her head. "But everything just added up. I felt . . . broken. I finally took a good look at my life and realized I wasn't happy."

"So you got in the car and drove until you felt happy?"

"Sort of. I drove to the last place that I remembered being happy. My family used to camp at Sugar Pine Point when I was little, back when my mom was still alive."

Shay sighed and knocked the back of her head against the wall of the bar a few times.

"What?"

"I'm not nearly as good a person as you. You realized your life wasn't what you wanted, so you made changes. When I realized my life wasn't what I wanted, I detonated it." She took another sip from the flask and offered it to Harper again.

"So are we drinking buddies now?" Harper asked.

"Look, I'm not a good friend. You should know that by now."

Harper shrugged. "You seem pretty solid to me. You shared your alcohol, your abuela—"

"Uh, she should probably go in the negative column."

"You're honest," Harper said. "That's extremely valuable to me." Ignoring Shay's surprise, she gestured to the door. "Ready to do this?"

She grimaced.

"Am I missing something?"

"I sort of accidentally on purpose dumped a drink on the woman Mace was flirting with."

Harper gaped at her. "You do realize he's a bartender. He's being nice to the patrons, not necessarily flirting."

"The man was born to flirt." Shay shrugged. "But I probably should apologize to Carrie."

"Carrie?"

"My cousin. The one Mace's flirting with."

A laugh escaped Harper. "You dumped a drink on your own cousin?"

"Yeah," Shay said, and smiled. "It was very satisfying."

"Look," Harper said. "I'm not going home until I do this, until I walk in there and be social like a normal person. And you, my wingwoman, are coming with me."

"I'm a terrible wingwoman."

"We're both going to do better at human-ing starting now, right?"

Shay wrinkled her nose.

"Right?"

"Fine. Right."

"Good," Harper said. "So follow me." And with that command, she walked in the door and toward the bar. Her sure footsteps faltered a bit when she saw Bodie.

His gaze locked on her, and she tripped over her own feet.

"Okay, so I was wrong," she whispered out the side of her mouth. "I can't do this." She paused, waiting for Shay to scoff and make fun of her, but Shay said nothing.

Harper whipped around.

Shay said nothing because she was gone, the front door swaying shut in her wake.

Damn. She really was a rotten wingwoman.

Bodie crooked a finger at her in the age old "come here" gesture. After all these days of watching him paint, fix, and repair whatever she'd needed, as well as help unload all her furniture with that hard body moving so effortlessly and efficiently, she was melting down. Or maybe that had been courtesy of Shay's abuela's flask. In any case, she hardly needed another drink, unless it was a glass of ice water.

Or an ice-water shower . . .

Concentrate. You've got three options. One, pretend you accidentally wandered in. Two, go sit in the corner and hope he joins you. Or three, be bold and make it look like this was the purposeful decision it was and you're totally in control.

Her feet made the decision for her, and she headed his way. Only the moment she slid her ass onto a barstool in front of him and he smiled that sexy smile, the one that said he knew one of her favorite places to be kissed was that spot just beneath her ear and that he intended to find more of those places, she knew she wasn't in control at all.

Mace called down from the other end of the bar. "Hey, man, I need two IPAs, a red ale, and a pitcher of Stella ASAP."

Completely ignoring him, Bodie leaned into Harper, his elbows braced on the bar. "What can I get you?" he murmured.

"I'm not sure. I just had a few sips from Abuela's flask and now I feel all . . . discombobulated."

Bodie laughed softly. "That flask is lethal." He paused, holding her gaze. "Trust me?"

She bit her lower lip, her body saying YES, her mind saying the exact opposite. "TBD?"

"Fair," he said, not looking insulted in the least. "Can I come up with a drink for you? It's one of my superpowers."

"One of? What are your other superpowers?"

He flashed a bad-boy grin, and she felt herself flush. Okay, so they were flirting. Isn't that what she'd come for?

"How about something with . . ." Tilting his head, he studied her. ". . . an elegant glass, something a little different, fun, playful . . . with a spectacular finish."

She got a hot flash. "Are we still talking about a drink?"

He just smiled, then turned around and grabbed a martini glass. She could see his hands moving and the muscles in his shoulders shifting and bunching very pleasantly beneath his shirt. He glanced at her over his shoulder. "Decision time. Alcohol or no?"

"No," she said, knowing her limits. She'd made enough poor decisions in her life. Tonight wouldn't be one of them.

Two minutes later he turned back to her with a martini glass that seemed to be filled with liquid chocolate, rimmed in graham crackers, with a skewer across it holding a big marshmallow. Wielding a mini blowtorch, he lit the marshmallow on fire. It went up in a single flame, and when the smoke cleared, it was a perfectly toasted marshmallow. A virgin smor'tini, be still her heart.

"It used to be I had all the moves," Mace muttered, walking by with a tray.

Harper took a sip and sighed in genuine pleasure. "Amazing. How did you know?"

The woman next to her leaned in. "No one knows how he does it, but he always seems to know what a woman wants, even before she does."

Hmm. That was more sobering than thrilling. She'd been with a man who'd known how to please any woman, but she'd also been duped and cruelly dumped.

Bodie was watching her think too hard. "It's hardly a secret," he said quietly. "You love chocolate, and I've seen you drink hot cocoa with marshmallows. And one of the pictures you put up in the balcony is of you and your mom roasting marshmallows on an open fire at Sugar Pine Point."

True. She drew a deep breath. She'd promised herself to not fall into bad habits, and she wasn't. She was using her head and her instincts, not her heart. Even if when it came to Bodie Campbell, her body also had an opinion, she *was* in control.

Mostly.

Still, she played it safe, and when Bodie was called into the back for something, she finished her drink, dropped money to cover it onto the bar, and slid off the stool and out the door.

Thankfully the rain had stopped.

She headed around the back, to the alley that ran behind the buildings, because it was quicker. Except while turning the corner, she ran smack into . . . Bodie, holding a trash bag.

Steadying her with his free hand, he tossed the trash into the dumpster with his other and then looked at her. "You okay?"

"Sure."

He studied her. "Really okay, or not-ready-to-talk-about-it okay?"

She grimaced. "Maybe the second one."

That appeared to pain him, but he didn't push, for which she was eternally grateful. "I'm just heading home," she said, hitching a thumb toward her building, like he didn't know where she lived. "I don't want to leave Ivy alone too long."

"That kid is more capable than most people I know."

She was having a hard time keeping her eyes off his mouth. Clearly, the combo of alcohol and sugar had gone to her head. That, or *this* was what she'd come for, another taste of him, another chance to feel his body against hers. Just the thought made her shiver, in the very best way. Dammit.

"Here." He pulled off his plaid shirt, the one that had been opened over a navy blue T-shirt, and wrapped it around her. "Not that I don't love what you're wearing," he said, "because . . ." His eyes warmed. "I do."

"Ivy's idea," she muttered.

He pulled her in for a hug that held warmth and strength and something she wasn't often on the receiving end of—comfort. "I'm not sure what I'm doing," she said to his chest, then slowly lifted her head and stared at his mouth some more.

The one she wanted back on hers.

"Harper."

"Hmm?"

Letting out a very sexy male sound, he gently cupped her face, tilting it to his so he could study her. He didn't kiss her. Instead, he smiled at her in his sexy way. "On a scale of a sip of booze to drunk, where are you?"

She thought about it. "Tipsy enough to want this. But sober enough to know that it's still a stupid idea." Fisting her hands in his T-shirt, she nudged him back a few steps and up against the brick wall.

His eyes went dark and dilated. "How stupid?"

"*Very* stupid." She rubbed her jaw to his.

He let out a breath. "Harper—"

"Let's not talk." Instead, she danced her lips along his rough jaw before grazing it with her teeth.

Hands tightening on hers, he groaned low and masculine in his throat. "Talking is important."

"It's overrated." She kissed him, nibbling at his lips. With another groan, he pulled her closer and kissed her long and deep, one hand holding her tight to him, the other burying itself in the hair at the back of her neck.

And kept kissing her. Her toes curled, and some other reactions were setting off charges along her entire body, but then he broke off to stare into her eyes, as if making sure she was as in it as he was. Though how he could doubt her when she'd wrapped herself around him like a pretzel, she had no idea. "Why are you stopping?"

"Temp check," he said. "Where's your head at?"

"I don't know, but my body's at hot-and-bothered."

He let out a half laugh, half groan and smiled at her in a way that made her ache for more. "Same," he said.

She uncurled her fingers, smoothing his shirt out before letting her hands do as they'd wanted since she'd first walked into the bar, run up his chest. And the south . . .

Covering her hands with his, he kissed one palm and then the other before meeting her gaze. "While I'd really, really like to take this further . . ."

"Oh boy," she whispered. "The brush-off."

He pressed his forehead to hers. "No. Not even close. But we're outside, in an alley, and I not only want better for our first time, I'd like to actually take you out first."

"I'm not dating right now." *Or ever.*

He gave her that smile that never failed to fry her brain cells. "If this is your idea of not dating, I'm not going to complain." He squeezed her hand. "Just hoping to get to know you a little better. Is that okay?"

Feeling a little pouty that he wasn't just giving in to her, she said, "You know everything you need to know about me."

"I've got the feeling I've barely scraped the surface." His free hand came up, his thumb gently gliding over the base of her throat where she knew her pulse was racing. "But I'll make you a promise. We go at your speed."

She liked the idea of that. A lot.

"Can you make me a promise in return?" he asked.

She hesitated.

His mouth curved like her suspicion amused him—she was so glad it amused someone—and he cupped her face. "Maybe you could just promise to let whatever this thing is between us have its way for a bit. Just a bit."

"Maybe." She drew a deep breath and stared up into his eyes, those light brown eyes streaked with gold that were at once warm and unfathomable. And something else.

Familiar?

Dear God, she thought. It wasn't just the color, it was the shape of them, and the prominence of his cheekbones. And . . . the dimple. "Um . . . I gotta go," she whispered, and took off.

She ran straight to the back door of her shop and up the stairs. Out of breath, she opened the office door and looked at Ivy, sitting on the futon with her phone.

Ham was asleep next to her, his head on the teen's lap, mouth open, lips flapping with each exhale.

"What's up?" Ivy asked.

"That dad you're looking for. You find him yet?"

"Uh . . ."

"It's Bodie, isn't it?"

CHAPTER 13

The next morning Ivy was downstairs, prepping for the day. She was cutting individual brownies from a pan while trying to avoid Harper, which wasn't easy in a few hundred square feet of kitchen.

Last night when Harper had casually tossed her bomb about figuring out Bodie was Ivy's dad, she'd nearly swallowed her own tongue. What she had for certain swallowed was the very last of her doubts. There'd been that teeny-tiny chance she'd been wrong about Bodie Campbell being her sperm donor, but she knew she wasn't.

And now Harper knew it too.

"Ivy," Harper said softly when she'd slid her sourdough bread in the oven.

"Not talking about it." That had been what Ivy had said last night, and she was sticking to it. Denial was a way of life.

"Okay." Harper nodded agreeably. "What *do* you want to talk about? The weather?"

"No." Ivy let out a reluctant smile at Harper's sarcasm. "But I do want to be a baker like you someday."

Harper blinked. "You're not just saying that because I want to talk about . . . that thing we're not talking about?"

"No, I really do want to be a baker. I want to be as good as you."

Harper smiled almost reluctantly, it seemed. "I can teach you everything I know, and when it's time, I can help you apply to all the best schools to learn even more."

Harper could have no idea how much that meant to her. But . . . "Still not talking about it."

Harper didn't look deterred. "You should know that I once out-silenced my dad for two and a half months." She smiled and shrugged, like *bring it.*

Ivy had grown up with the queen of passive-aggressive. Her mom could out-tough, out-mean, out-lie the pope himself if he stood between her and what she needed. The only person better than her mom was Ivy. But she was starting to see that Harper's persuasive techniques, based on genuine interest and kindness, were far superior. Something to think about. But she had skills too. "You promised me if something was too personal, I didn't have to talk about it."

"That was before I knew that this whole time you've been using me as a ruse to feel out if Bodie was your dad."

Ivy felt herself go pale. "No, honest. I'm . . ." How to say that being here with Harper was . . . *everything?* And here she was messing it up without even trying. "I'm sorry I didn't tell you," she said. "But it's not like it even matters."

Harper gaped at her. "Are you kidding? If he knew—"

"What if he does know, has known for sixteen years, and just didn't want me?"

Harper hesitated, because in truth she barely knew him, but then shook her head. "I've seen how he treats his family, Ivy. Like they're more valuable than all the gold in the world."

Ivy wanted to believe it, but . . . "You're just saying that because you kissed him last night." At Harper's wide eyes, she nodded. "Yeah, I saw you. I got worried you'd be too cold in that shirt I made you wear. I started to bring you a jacket, but when you backed him up against the wall and kissed him, I figured you were plenty warm."

Harper drew a deep breath. "Oh my God. You saw us." She ran a hand over her eyes, then met Ivy's straight on. "I'm sorry. Obviously, I didn't know you were there and had no idea he was your dad at the time."

"You wouldn't have known if a comet landed at your feet." Ivy shrugged. "It doesn't matter."

"It *does* matter." Harper held her gaze. "It matters because *you* matter to me. And regardless of what you saw, I know Bodie Campbell's a good man who—"

"Look, *everyone* says they're not that person—until they are. I mean, just look at you and your ex. You didn't even know he was an asswipe." The second the words were out of Ivy's mouth and she saw the flash of hurt on Harper's face, she felt awful and wished she could take them back. "I'm sorry. I didn't mean that."

"Yes, you did, and that's okay. I get it." Harper turned to her workstation and pulled down a bowl and some more ingredients. Who knew for what, the woman was a food magician.

"You feel like you're backed into a corner," Harper said. "And you're scared. I get that too. I can't tell you I know how he'll react to the news. I can't even promise you'll get the reaction you want, but I can promise you that if you don't say anything, you'll never know."

Ivy closed her eyes rather than let any tears escape. "You're right about one thing: I'm scared." She hated that the words escaped, but the truth was, it felt good to finally admit this to someone who would understand.

"Oh, Ivy." Harper set down her whisk. "Listen, whatever happens, I'll be right here. Okay? Whatever you need."

Ivy's heart suddenly ached. "I wasn't using you," she managed, having to say this, needing Harper to believe her. "You . . . you matter to me."

Harper smiled. "And you matter to me. A lot."

Unable to talk, Ivy nodded her thanks. She breathed for a few seconds, then released her greatest fear. "What if I tell him and he says he never wants to see me again?"

"Or he could welcome you with open arms, excited you're his."

Ivy shook her head in automatic denial, unable to fathom a happy ending to this venture. "You're not close to your dad. What makes you think this could have a happy ending?"

"Well, I was *very* close to my mom. And it's true, when she passed, my dad was sort of . . . MIA. And yeah, we're not close and we might never be. But, Ivy, that doesn't mean *your* story will end that way."

"I left home because my mom didn't want me around." Just admitting that out loud hurt so much she put a hand to her chest.

Harper's eyes were soft, her voice warm and caring. "I could go with you to talk to him."

She'd never had someone in her life like Harper. It almost felt too good to be true, but even though she had a wall around her heart, something deep, deep down told her Harper was the real deal. The last thing she wanted to do was put her in the middle between Ivy and Bodie. That wouldn't be fair. But more than that, she also didn't want Harper to see him reject her. She wouldn't be able to handle the pity. "It's okay. I've come this far on my own, I need to see it through."

Harper looked like she wanted to argue that but nodded instead. "I understand. But please know that I'm here, right here, if you need me."

Now *that* Ivy believed, which somehow, in some way, took a little tiny bit of the anxiety away.

MIDDAY USUALLY SAW Bodie either in the warehouse working on his dad's boat, paddleboarding at the lake, or rock climbing at the summit. Anything that cleared his mind from thinking too much.

But today he was at the bar because they were short-staffed. When Mace and Zeke showed up wearing shit-eating grins, he narrowed his eyes, wary. The last time they'd looked at him like that had been on his seventeenth birthday. They'd stolen a bottle of tequila from this very spot and had gone to the lake to drink, and when they were good and drunk, they'd dumped him off the dock.

In January.

Miraculously he hadn't frozen to death, but no one could blame him for taking a step backward. "What?"

"Follow me," Zeke said, then led the way to the small office in the back. He went straight to the laptop on Bodie's desk and brought up the security footage.

"What are you doing?" Bodie asked.

"The trash company tried to tell me they dumped our bin a few weeks back, when I know they didn't. So I was flipping through the footage to prove it and found something interesting."

Mace snorted.

Bodie glanced at Mace's shit-eating grin. "What?"

Zeke turned the laptop to face them. It was nighttime, and all Bodie could see was the brick wall, the bar's back door, and their dumpster at the far end of the alley.

"Wait for it," Zeke said.

A minute later, Bodie watched as he came out the back door, big black trash bag in hand. He tossed the bag into the bin—at the same time a woman appeared from the other end of the alley.

Harper.

The him on camera let loose a dopey-ass smile. Harper beamed at him in return. And since he knew what came next, he lunged for the laptop, but not before on the screen Harper pushed him up against the brick wall and kissed him.

"Bakers do it better," Zeke said with a straight face.

"If she bakes it, you will come," Mace said.

Bodie gave them both deadpan looks. "You done?"

"Whip it, whip it real good," Zeke said.

"What's under *your* apron?" Mace asked.

"Seriously, dough," Zeke said, and they both lost it.

"Assholes." He deleted the footage and then turned and walked out of the office.

"Don't go baking my heart!" Mace yelled after him.

He served a few customers, then found a smile when he saw Ivy sitting at a high-top table. He made her usual lunch of burger and fries and brought it to her.

When she didn't immediately dive in, he paused and took in her expression. More closed off than usual. And nervous. And . . . damn.

Scared.

He'd come to care about this kid. Something about her reminded him of . . . well, himself. "What's wrong?"

Ivy shrugged.

"Come on, Kit Kat. Talk to me. Is the burger too well done for you? Or maybe you're getting sick of burgers. I've got plenty of other stuff on the menu."

She shifted. "It's not that."

"She speaks," he teased.

She rolled her eyes, but he could tell her heart wasn't in it. Concerned, he kicked out a chair and sat across from her. "You and Harper okay?"

"Yes." She bit her lower lip. "Well, mostly. Did you know Harper's ex was a Richard?"

"A Richard?"

"Yeah, you know, a dick."

That almost made him laugh. Almost, because the idea of Harper being with a "Richard" made his gut hurt. "I've guessed."

"He made her feel like she wasn't worth the risk, that she was unlovable. I want to pound on him."

Bodie felt the same, but he drew a deep breath. "I've got a better idea."

"You're right. I'll help you bury the body."

At that, he did give a short laugh. "I was going to say that since she isn't with him anymore, we work extra hard at letting her know how much we care about her and how we'd never let her feel like she wasn't worth . . . well, everything." He heard his words and realized he was in deeper than he'd even known.

Ivy shrugged. "Yeah. That's the grown-up way to go, I guess." She was working really hard at making zero eye contact and fiddling in her chair, her fingers entwined, showing white knuckles.

"Something else is bugging you," he said quietly.

She hesitated, then looked at him. "Have you ever wanted to tell someone something, something *really* important, but you're too scared of how they're going to react, so it's easier just to not say it at all?"

He let out a rough laugh. "Very much yes." He tugged on a loose strand of her hair. "I'll tell you mine if you tell me yours."

She regarded him carefully. Seriously. "You first."

"Wait here." He went into the kitchen. He'd begun buying all his desserts from Harper. He got the last two pieces of her moose tracks pie and two forks and went back to Ivy's table.

They ate for a few moments in silence, then Bodie set down his fork. "My dad left me this place and I don't feel like I deserve it."

This got her attention. "Why? Because of what happened at your work? You think he'd judge you for that?"

He shook his head. "That's the thing. He wouldn't have. I know all he'd want is for me to be happy, but the truth is that I don't know if I'm there yet."

"Have you told your brothers? Or mom?"

"No. I worry they'd take it personally."

"You mean they feel responsible for your happiness?" she asked, looking like that made no sense to her at all, which made his heart ache in his chest for her.

"My mom takes her sons' happiness *very* personally," he said. "And her sons inherited that."

"So you keep it secret."

He nodded. "Even though I know I shouldn't."

"I've kept a lot of secrets from my mom." Ivy stuffed a big bite into her mouth, clearly to stop herself from saying too much. She was silent for a full minute. Finally she said, "I don't think we're anything like your family though."

"And your dad?" he asked, picking up his fork again.

She stilled for a single beat, then took a big bite, as if to keep her mouth busy.

"Does he know you're here? I could call him for you, let him know you're safe."

Now she set her fork down and started to get up, but he gently put a hand on hers.

"It was just a suggestion. I won't." When she didn't budge or relax, he gently squeezed her hand. "I promise. Finish the pie, it's okay."

She took a few more bites, chewing more slowly as she came to the end of the pie.

"That was the last piece, but would you like something else?" he asked.

"Actually, it's about my dad." She was still doe in the crosshairs, her eyes on his, intense and . . . terrified.

Shit. "Kit Kat, if you're scared of him, I can—"

"No," she said, so softly he could barely hear her. "It's not what you think. The thing is, I'm not sure he knows he has a kid."

What kind of asshole doesn't know he has a kid? "Okay. Well . . . you're pretty incredible. If he knew you, he'd immediately love you."

She blinked, as if this thought had never occurred to her. She was killing him.

"Really?" she whispered.

"*Really.* What do you know about him?"

"Just that he and my mom met in Mexico on college spring break."

Bodie was watching her face, had been the whole time she was talking, trying to figure out what the odd little niggle was in the back of his head that was telling him that he was missing something, something big.

Mexico . . . And then there was the fact that Ivy had come from Chicago. Not to mention her facial expression, including her carefully hooded light brown and gold eyes.

And the merest suggestion of that dimple on the left side of her mouth.

He choked on the bite of crust he'd just put in his mouth, then had to drink an entire glass of water. Ivy was . . . his? Holy shit. *Ivy was his.* Heart pounding loudly in his ears, he leaned forward, his entire being tight with fear that she'd run, which was the last thing he wanted. "You're . . . mine."

Her eyes filled, and she lifted a shoulder. "Seems like it, even if you don't remember being with my mom."

Holding eye contact so she knew just how serious he was, he said, "I remember your mom, Ivy. I remember everything about that night. Jenny and I were at some dumb party, bonding over how irritated we were at our friends. Your mom was beautiful and funny, and I was immediately drawn to her."

"Yeah," Ivy said tightly. "That's her talent. Drawing men in." She met his gaze, her own filled with so much pain it hurt to look at her. "So . . . did you know?"

"No." Bodie's gut clenched as he took in her doubt. "I'm so sorry, Ivy. She never told me, though I really, *really* wish she had."

"Yeah?" She lifted her chin, all feisty sass and heartbreaking vulnerability. "What would've been different?"

He knew that his answer would set the tone for their relationship. And God help him, he wanted a relationship with her. He'd never thought kids would be in his picture. His lifestyle hadn't lent itself to even imagining it. But if this was all true, and he knew in his gut it was, there was no way he was going to let Ivy down. She'd had enough disappointment in her life. "Kit Kat." He waited until she made eye contact, because he needed her to believe him. "If I'd known about you, I'd have done everything in my power to be your dad, in every sense of the word. Every single day of your life."

Her eyes went shiny again, and she swallowed hard, trying so hard to be brave.

"Ivy?"

"Yeah?"

"Can I hug you?"

A single tear slipped down her cheek, but she nodded, and as if she was the most precious piece of china, he scooted his chair close to hers and gently pulled her in, cupping her head with one hand, wrapping his other arm around her shoulders when he felt her trembling. "I'm so sorry I didn't know, Ivy. So, so sorry."

"You said you weren't ready to be a dad." She sniffed against his chest. "At least not right now. And it's not like I'm a baby or anything. There's no cute baby stuff to do." She pulled back, eyes flat. "I'm just a kid who hates to be told what to do, and I get into trouble and ruin everything all the time. Like, *all* the time."

Bodie dipped his head until he could see into her eyes. Which were his eyes. Jesus, what a trip. "I promise you that's not true."

"And I promise you, it is. Every relationship my mom had, I ruined. They all left because of me."

"No," he said. "That was on them. Not you."

"You don't know."

"You're right. I don't know all you've been through." But he vowed to find out. "What I do know is that you're a kid, and any man in your mom's life was the adult. Your mom and her relationships are not on you."

She looked down at her hand, so small in his. "I don't, like, you know, want anything from you or anything."

Damn. A knife to the heart. "Sweetheart, that's the thing. You deserve *everything* from me."

At this, Ivy sagged, as if she was tired of holding herself so stiff, tired of keeping her walls up. And then she burst into tears.

Feeling his own heart crack open for this amazing, resilient, vulnerable kid, *his* kid, he hugged her again, holding her tight as she sobbed against him. And this time her eyes weren't the only wet ones.

CHAPTER 14

Harper was in the kitchen when Ivy came back from Olde Tahoe Tap. The teen's eyes were red-rimmed, but she was visibly relaxed. "How did it go?"

Ivy smiled, and Harper felt her chest cavity fill with relief.

"Okay if we don't talk about it right now?" Ivy asked.

"Of course. Do you want to work the front for me?"

Ivy's face creased in happy surprise. "Really? You trust me with that?"

"Completely." It was the utter truth. Plus, it was their quiet hours, but even if it hadn't been, Harper knew Ivy could handle things.

And she did, right up to closing time. After, she went to the lake with Ham to meet up with Jessie and James.

And Harper went to the bookstore. As she entered, the chime went off—still the *Addams Family* theme song.

Shay was humming along with it as she looked up from her

perch and eyed Harper. But unlike always, she didn't immediately frown.

Progress.

She did, however, look exhausted. "Hey," Harper said. "What's wrong?"

"Oh, nothing. Except I'm twenty-nine and completely burned-out." Shay tossed up her hands. "Like, what am I supposed to do for fifty more years? Get cats? Bitch about summer lake traffic? Keep buying veggies by the ton and watching them die? Get oil changes?"

"Well, cats are great. And yeah, okay, traffic sucks. But you don't have to buy veggies by the ton. I won't tell a soul, I swear."

Shay thought about that. "Sage advice. Which reminds me, I need you to come to yoga with me tomorrow and pretend to be my friend."

"What? Why?"

"It's bring-a-friend week, and if I do, I get twenty percent off next month's fees, so . . . you're up."

"You run out of friends already?"

"You're the first and only person I've asked," Shay said.

"Oh." Harper didn't know what to say to that. "So we *are* friends."

"More like *pretend* friends."

Harper laughed. "I'm not going until you admit you like me and that we're real friends."

Shay narrowed her eyes.

"Twenty percent is a *lot* . . ."

Shay sighed. "Fine. We're real friends. Happy?"

Harper smiled. "Very. Oh, and I thought of something genius that could help us both. To the left of my register, I've got an empty bookshelf."

"Fascinating," Shay said, and yawned. "But I've got bills to worry about, so—"

"I think you should use the shelf to sell books. Like cookbooks, or whatever you'd like, really."

Shay paused. Blinked. "I'm sorry. Did you just offer to help me sell some books?"

"I did. Why, is that weird?"

"Yes." Shay shut her laptop. "What's the catch? What percentage do you want?"

"Zero. I just want some cute books on that shelf and thought you might like the idea."

"I do." Shay looked wary. "Have you always been like this?"

"Like what?"

"Too good to be true."

Harper laughed. She laughed so hard she nearly had to sit down.

"I don't see what's so damn funny," Shay muttered.

"It's just that I thought I was the most screwed-up person I knew, that's all."

"Hmph," Shay said, but looked like this made her feel better.

The front door opened, and the *Addams Family* theme song went off again.

"Shay Rylie Anna Ramirez," Abuela yelled from the other room. "What did I tell you about changing the chime to suit your moods?"

Shay sighed. "I hate when she uses all my names."

"It's a lot of names," Harper said.

Shay shrugged. "My mom's Irish, my dad's Mexican. Each wanted their stamp on me. Then of course they divorced after one week of marriage and gave me to Abuela, so . . ." She shrugged again.

Harper sucked in a breath. "I'm sorry."

"Don't be. My place is here, driving Abuela loca." Which she said loud enough for Abuela to hear her, and they heard the woman's cackle. Shay was smiling a little too, but it faded when she realized her next customer was Mace.

He strolled up to the counter with the same loose-limbed, easy grace his brother had and smiled at Shay.

Who did not smile back.

"I'm looking for a book," he said.

"You haven't read a book in years," Shay said. "Well, other than Serena's copy of *Fifty Shades*."

"Hey, that was for curiosity's sake."

"Uh-huh."

"And I have so read other books," he said. "There was that time in our college English class."

"I took that class for you." Shay pointed at him. "You read zero books in that class."

"I'm going to enroll you both in an English as a second language class!" Abuela yelled from the back.

Harper laughed, but pretended it was a cough instead when both Shay and Mace sent her a look. "I'm just going to . . ." She hitched a thumb over her shoulder and let herself out.

She ended up back in her kitchen, baking to her heart's content. Ivy came home at some point near 10:00 p.m. and went to bed.

Harper stayed in the kitchen. She'd have to be up before dawn, but baking was like putting gasoline in her car. It filled up her tank. Her soul tank.

A soft knock sounded on her kitchen door. Through the window, she could see a tall, leanly built shadow in a sweatshirt and open leather jacket, hoodie up.

Bodie.

Her heart skipped a beat. She'd steered clear today, not wanting to intrude. This was about family, *his*, and she was very aware that she wasn't a part of it. She opened the door, but her smile quickly died because his mouth was grim, his eyes intense.

He looked past her. "You alone?"

"Ivy's upstairs sleeping." She stepped back. "Come in."

He shook his head. "Can we go somewhere? Maybe for a drive?"

"Sure."

At the word *drive*, Ham woke from his bed on the floor. He began tap-dancing at the door, panting with happiness because no one had ever told him he wasn't automatically welcome everywhere.

Bodie crouched down so he was eye to eye with Ham. "You want to come?"

Ham tipped his head back and "woo-woo"ed.

Harper grabbed a sweater and texted Ivy so if she woke up, she wouldn't worry. They walked out to Bodie's truck and loaded up.

"You're going to want to roll down all the windows," she said.

"You sure? It's chilly."

"He gets carsick unless all the windows are down."

Bodie turned in his seat and looked at Ham.

Ham leaned forward and licked his chin.

"He says he won't get sick in my car," Bodie said.

"He's lying."

So Bodie rolled all the windows down. Luckily it wasn't cold, not like it'd been her first week. In fact, the night was warm and gorgeous. "Where are we going?"

"Where would you like to go?"

"Some place with a view?"

"My property in Hidden Hills has a view." He glanced over at her as if to gauge her response. "Only if you'd like."

"I would like. Very much."

He nodded. There was a solemnness to him she hadn't seen before, and something else that she couldn't quite place.

As they drove along the lake, she was moved both by the glow of the moon dancing on the choppy waters and the man next to her, silent but in easy, calm control, handling the narrow, curvy highway like he'd been born to it, shifting smoothly, his body moving with the vehicle. After a few miles, he made a turn from the lake, and they went up. And up. The road went from paved to dirt, and she glanced over at him.

"Almost there."

It was a thrilling ride, and all too soon he made a turn into a clearing with a small cabin in the center of it, backdropped by a semicircle of towering pines behind it.

"I bought this land and the cabin years ago from an old friend who's gone now," he said. "When I'm done with the boat, I'm going to renovate here too."

She could picture him doing just that. "It's beautiful. I bet the inside is too." She tried to remember if she had pretty undies on.

He looked at her face, then closed his eyes and groaned.

"What?"

"We're not going inside."

"We're not?" she asked in surprise.

"I brought you up here to talk. I'm not going to be the guy who lured you up here under false pretenses. And if I bring you inside, I won't be able to resist you."

Well, if that wasn't something to think about . . .

He turned off the engine. "Come on."

Ham hopped out of the back seat and pranced around like he'd been taken to Disneyland, lifting his leg at every tree and bush he could find in the dark. They walked past the cabin to where the clearing ended at a cliff, and thanks to a glowing moon and a myriad of stars, she could see the lake hundreds of feet below.

"Wow," she whispered.

They sat on a bench made from the trunk of a huge tree, which she knew he'd made. Ham was still very busy sniffing . . . everything. Harper didn't speak, because there was clearly something on his mind, and she had no doubt it was Ivy.

He turned to her. "Did you know?" He took one look at her face and swore softly, closing his eyes for a beat, jaw tight, eyes and mouth grim. "How long? Please tell me it wasn't before we kissed."

"No. *No*," she repeated firmly. "I didn't know before that. But . . ." When she hesitated, he surged to his feet and paced.

"That's why you ran off last night outside the bar," he said. "It's why you avoided me today." His body was tense, eyes remote and nowhere near the warmth she was used to. "You agreed to give this thing between us a fair chance. But then you kept a huge secret from me, one that affects my life."

That he was right made this all the harder. "I promised Ivy I wouldn't tell you before she did."

"You told me you couldn't tell me about her because it was her story to tell."

"I didn't know then," she said. "All I knew was that she was looking for her dad. It never occurred to me that you were that dad."

"You figured it out somehow. On your own. How?"

She could tell he was devastated that he hadn't figured it out on his own. "Last night. I was looking up at you . . ." She shook her head. "And it just hit me. I wasn't certain, but Ivy confirmed it. She's got your eyes, and—"

"My cheekbones," he said with a single nod. "It's like I gave her my face."

Harper smiled even as her eyes burned with unshed tears. "Yeah."

Bodie turned away, facing the black night, hands in his pockets, quiet.

"So . . . are we . . . over?" she asked quietly.

He turned to face her, surprise on his face. "Why would you think that?"

She hesitated, but now wasn't the time to hide in plain sight. "People are always afraid to lose things that mean a lot to them."

He dropped to his knees at her side and met her gaze. "I mean a lot to you."

"More than I wanted you to," she admitted.

He gave a soft laugh, then kissed her gently.

"Are you okay with all this?" she asked.

"With Ivy being mine? I couldn't be more okay. But it's bothering me that I didn't see it. All this time I had a kid out there in the world who needed me, and I had no idea. I don't even know why it was kept hidden from me."

"My mom used to say the only thing you should ever hide is presents."

He snorted and stood. "Yeah."

Getting up, she moved to him. "She's a pretty good kid."

That got her a ghost of a smile. "Yeah."

"Were you and Ivy's mom . . . together?"

"No. Jenny and I were complete strangers." He grimaced when she went brows up. "I'm not proud of this, but I went through a dumbass player stage. I was trying to somehow forget Austin's death. Some friends and I were in Cabo on spring break and there was this party. We had a good time. Too good." He paused and shook his head. "Jenny was gone when I woke up the next morning."

"And she never tried to contact you?"

"Not a word. She knew my full name and that I was from Lake Tahoe. My parents wouldn't have been hard to find."

"I'm sorry, Bodie."

"I'm not. We used a condom, so I don't know what happened, but I'll never be sorry about Ivy. I'm . . ." He lifted a hand, palm up, like he was searching for the right words. "Overwhelmed and amazed by her. What she did, coming here, finding me . . . that was so fucking brave."

She smiled. "Sounds like she got some of that from her dad."

He shook his head, seeming marveled by even the thought. "No, she is that all on her own. And I'm so grateful. I didn't even know what I was missing in my life, but now I do. I'm hoping to make things right for her."

"It's never too late. What are you going to do?"

"As much as she'll let me," he said. "I spent the day trying to track Jenny down. I get she's out of the country, but how did Ivy manage to leave her stepsister's house and get all the way across the country with no one noticing? She's *sixteen*. What the hell was Jenny thinking?"

Harper stood and took his hand. "I wouldn't lead with that question. Not if you want her cooperation for what you *really* want to ask."

He studied her face, then let out a long breath. "Yeah. This is all up to Ivy, of course, but if she wants to visit me, I want the right to have her."

"You'll ask for shared custody." She said this as a statement, not a question. Because she already knew the answer.

"Absolutely," he said. "Whatever Ivy wants."

She slid her hands up his chest to wrap around him and felt the knotted, tight line of his injured shoulder. She dug her fingers in a bit, massaging it.

Bodie let out a breath, relaxing under her touch, so she kept at it. "You're hurting," she said.

He shrugged, like he was used to it.

"You know, I can only imagine how scary it'd be to find yourself pregnant at seventeen," she said softly, working at his tense muscles. "Knowing you'd have to share custody with someone you don't know, who lived on the other side of the country . . ."

"I'd have moved. I would've helped her." He shook his head. "I should've tried to find her the next morning instead of just shrugging it off when I woke up alone." He looked Harper straight in the eyes. "I'd like to say that was my one and only time sleeping with someone I didn't know and never saw again. Unfortunately, it took me a while to figure my shit out, to understand that all it ever did was leave me feeling . . . empty." He paused. "I don't, won't, do another one-night stand. I want more. I need you to know that."

She stared at him, her heart picking up speed. "What are you saying?"

"I'm saying that if we pursue this thing between us, I want more than one night." He tilted her face up to his and lowered his head, brushing his mouth across hers in a warm and startlingly intimate kiss. Pulling back, he held her gaze. "Can you tell me what *you* want?"

Did she even know? On the one hand, this amazing, wonderful man was telling her he wanted something with her. On the other hand, she was terrified of opening her heart again, and no longer believed in the promise of love. But she couldn't imagine walking away now. The thing was, she was settling into all the changes in her life, but he hadn't settled into his yet, having just learned about Ivy. Harper would never expect to be a priority over Ivy, but neither did she want to be a distraction.

His thumb stroked her jaw. "You've gone through a lot of changes lately."

"And I'm not the only one."

He let out a half laugh and nodded.

She let her hands fall from him. He'd been so honest with her, she had to give him the same. "I'm just finding myself again, and everything's mixed up inside me right now. But there's one thing I know for sure."

"What's that?"

"I want you."

This got her a smile complete with dimple. "I like the sound of that." His smile faded slowly, though his eyes remained warm and on hers. "I'm not going to rush you, Harper. I think maybe you've had enough of that in your life. I'm a patient man, and I'm not going anywhere. Take your time."

She drew a deep breath. "That's giving me a lot of power."

"Yeah." His smile was back. "Deal with it." He ran his thumb over her bottom lip and her brain checked out and her body took over, moving closer. Cupping her face, he kissed her until warmth pooled in her belly and she couldn't remember why she wanted to move slow with this thing between them.

Ham bounced back to them and flopped down, rolling over to raise all four legs in the air. "Do you want your tummy scratched, is that it?" she cooed, and laughed when Bodie silently raised his hand and nodded.

She was still smiling when he drove her and Ham home. He walked her to her door, kissed her again, unfortunately with a lot less tongue and heat, then whispered, "Sleep well," and was gone, leaving her to her own thoughts and decisions that needed to be made. Was she where she wanted to be? Yes. Was she who she wanted to be? Yes.

Had she found someone worth taking a risk for? She sucked air in between her teeth because . . . maybe?

With a hopeful smile on her face, she checked on Ivy and found her fast asleep. Ham pushed past Harper and jumped up to cuddle next to Ivy.

Deserted by her own dog, she went to bed and fell asleep with that same hopeful smile on her face.

CHAPTER 15

B odie didn't sleep well and ended up hitting the laptop again, doing a deep internet dive to search for a way to contact Jenny. He could've asked Ivy for one, but he also knew she wasn't ready for him to tell Jenny where she was. His life had often depended on a well-thought-out plan. Today that plan meant playing the card he'd never played before—the dad card. Ivy was going to have to understand that he would always act with her well-being in mind and do the right thing for her. Which was often going to be the hard—and unpopular—thing.

Jenny didn't answer her cell or immediately respond to a text or email. No big surprise if she was still on her honeymoon, which Ivy had hinted to being a monthlong endeavor.

But now he needed advice and a plan, so he texted the Campbell family text chat—different from the brothers-only chat—that he needed a meeting ASAP.

Everyone met him at his mom's. His childhood neighborhood was working-class, so homes were older but decently cared for.

His mom's house was a small three-bedroom gingerbread house built in the 1970s, renovated here and there by his dad as time and money had permitted. And three bedrooms was really two bedrooms and a small den turned third bedroom. He and Zeke had shared that closet, living practically on top of each other. Same for Austin and Mace. Bodie had long ago lost track of how many times walls had to be repaired from fists going through them.

Or heads.

He was striding up the front walk when his mom opened the door, alerted by some inner maternal radar that one of hers was home.

"Thank God you're here," she said. "I've got a computer question. How many times do you have to accept the cookies before they show you the cookies?"

Before he could answer, everyone else pulled up at the same time and got out of cars en masse. Mace; Zeke; his wife, Serena; and their three heathens.

Zeke's kids ran circles around all of them in their usual family meeting room—the kitchen. Xander stopped to ask his mom if they could have his birthday party in Grandma's attic because of all the "old" stuff Bodie and his brothers had up there from their growing-up years, like Atari, foosball, and Ping-Pong.

"They're, like, antiques!" Xander exclaimed.

"How old you gonna be, Xan?" Mace asking teasingly. "Cuz you gotta be an antique yourself to play with some of that stuff."

"Well . . ." Xander smiled proudly. "If the good lord sees fit, eight."

Zeke swiveled his eyes in his mom's direction at the odd phrasing.

"What?" she said. "Your nanny's sixty years old, what did you expect?"

"Mom, *you're* the nanny."

Mace snorted.

Zeke eyed him. "You think this is funny? Cuz Mom's busy two of the five days next week and you're our backup nanny."

Mace's smile disappeared.

Serena clapped her hands for everyone's attention. "Nothing personal, but I've got another meeting scheduled in twenty."

"It's a mani/pedi," Zeke said.

"And?" Serena asked.

"Nothing," Zeke said.

Bodie drew a deep breath. "There's something I need to tell you guys."

Everyone fell silent because everyone knew Bodie never wanted to tell them anything. He filled them in on Ivy, and after a beat of stunned silence, everyone jumped in, excited and beyond thrilled for him. Especially his mom, who couldn't stop hugging him. "A girl!" she kept saying. "I finally got a girl in this testosterone-overloaded family!"

"Hey," Zeke said. "What are we, chopped liver?"

His mom waved him off. "I couldn't love you crazy boys more, yadda yadda . . . but a *girl!*"

Mace was watching Bodie. "What are you thinking?"

"I need to do everything in my power to help Ivy, because from my point of view, her situation falls under neglect."

"You mean *we* need to do everything in *our* power," Mace said. "You're not alone in this."

"Not ever," his mom said fiercely.

"What do we want the outcome to be?" Serena asked.

Bodie knew he loved his family, but even he and his cold heart warmed to the unconditional support. "I want fifty-fifty custody."

"And what does Ivy want?" Zeke asked.

Bodie had been afraid to ask. "All I know is that she somehow managed to get two thousand miles across the country to find me. I think we can at least consider the fact she wants me in her life. And she hasn't left, so on some level, she wants to be here, and I want that too."

Serena nodded, but her expression was concerned. "I believe that too, and these days a judge will take into account what a kid Ivy's age wants regarding custody, but, honey, you *could* still have a battle."

Didn't matter. He'd taken down Colombian drug lords, been on raids for firearms and found explosives instead—the hard way—and investigated acts of arson by homegrown terrorists. He could handle this. "I'm her dad. I'm going to fight for her. Especially since I've got the feeling no one ever has."

"Okay." Serena nodded. "So you need to be able to show the court that you acted swiftly and responsibly. You've reached out to Ivy's mom?"

"I've called, texted, emailed."

"Have you talked to Ivy about any of this?" Zeke asked.

He'd been unwilling to push her on day one of being dad. "I

will. I wanted to talk to Serena first. What kind of a home life could she possibly have that she traveled across the country, has been gone three-plus weeks, and no one's even worried? I mean, I get that her stepsister Kylie was told by Ivy herself that she went to a friend's, and I think she's casually checked in via text, but come on."

"That doesn't mean the court will award you custody," Serena warned.

"It's clearly neglect," he repeated.

"Yes, but fair warning, her living with a random stranger above a bakery doesn't look good for *you* either."

"I just found out about her," he said. "And before that, she was basically homeless. Harper took her in, which I'm grateful for. I don't care what looks good, I just want what's best for her. I know she's safe with Harper. She's amazing." He knew his mistake the moment the words left his mouth.

And sure enough, everyone's eyebrows raised in unison.

"So, are you and this 'amazing' Harper . . . *dating?*" his mom asked hopefully.

Shit. He shoved his fingers through his hair and turned away from the mixed looks he was getting from his family. Zeke was grinning, hoping he was "dating" Harper. Serena looked surprised, since as she knew all too well that Bodie hadn't exactly been on the people train. Mace looked torn, which Bodie knew was because he cared about Bodie, but he also cared about Harper, and understood more than anyone just how fucked-up Bodie's head was. His mom though . . . her expression was

all soft maternal expectation, and that just about killed him.
"Mom—"

"Please say it's true." She stepped into him, all five feet zero
inches of her, and cupped his face, having to tilt her head way
back to look up at him. "You've been through so much, baby, I
just want you to have your happy-ever-after."

He knew happy ever after wasn't for him, not that he had the
heart to break it to her, but he took her hands in his. "I'm okay,
Mom. Just as I am."

"Well, of course, but—"

"This is about Ivy," he said. "Not me. Not right now."

"You'll need to talk to her about all of this," his mom said.
"And soon."

Bodie nodded. "I know. I will."

"You know what I found works best with my kids?" Serena
asked. "Especially with Max. It's having an honest, open conversation."

Bodie looked at her. "Max is two. Have you ever even had a
single honest, open conversation with him that didn't involve
poop?"

"Hey, he's the only kid in his playgroup who's fully potty
trained, and that was the result of a direct conversation. No poo-
poo in the potty, no candy reward."

"Poo-poo in the potty!" Max yelled, fist in the air. Then he
raced out of the kitchen, presumably toward the bathroom.

"Someone going after him?" Mace asked.

Serena looked at Zeke.

"Why me?" he asked.

"Because I was in labor for a total of seventy-two hours to bring you these kids. My lady town still isn't the same. It's your turn."

Zeke sighed in defeat, then followed after Max without another word. Five seconds later they heard him say, "Buddy, the toilet lid has to be up first, remember?"

Serena grimaced. "Sorry," she said to Bodie's mom, who shrugged.

"Not my first rodeo," she said. "Zeke could never hit the pot to save his life."

"Thanks, Mom," Zeke said.

Bodie's thoughts were racing, and not about poop. He was more than ready for an honest, open conversation with Ivy, but he was pretty sure the offer of a candy reward wouldn't solve any of their problems. Still, he was willing to try anything. He went outside to call her with some relative privacy. Relative, because he heard his mom open her kitchen window—the better to eavesdrop—but his cell rang in his hand before he could call her.

It was Jenny, and he had to tamp down on the swell of temper that rolled over him at the sound of her voice. "Hi," he said. "You forget to tell me something?"

"Oh, hell."

Bodie pinched the bridge of his nose. "How could you not let me know I have a daughter?"

Jenny's voice went from curious to pissed-off. "Oh, you mean after you left town so fast there was nothing but dust in your wake?"

"You were the one who was gone from my bed the next morning. You knew I had a flight out that day, and when I woke up alone, I figured you had your reasons. But you knew my last name, you knew where I was from. You could have located me fairly easily. Am I even on her birth certificate?"

"You know what? I'm not doing this with you," she said. "We've got bigger problems."

"You think? Your emancipated daughter crossed the country by herself to come find me."

"Emancipated? Is that what she told you?"

Shit.

Jenny snorted. "That girl has always been headstrong, and trust me, she's smarter and tougher than she looks. She's just bent out of shape because I got married again. To a good man, I might add, with a huge family. She was staying with her stepsister Kylie while we honeymooned."

"Which clearly worked out well," he said. "Ivy was gone for at least a week before she texted Kylie."

"First of all, she lied, saying she was going to be at a friend's, so I can't foist her back on Kylie now. You'll have to keep her until I get home. At least it's summer, so she's not missing school."

"Jenny—"

"Look, this is a fourteen-dollar-a-minute conversation from the middle of the Atlantic Ocean, okay? As long as you stock up on Hot Pockets and internet, you'll be fine to keep her."

"Absolutely I'm going to keep her," he said.

But Jenny had already disconnected.

Bodie turned to the kitchen window. His entire family was

face to the screen, unabashedly eavesdropping. "Anyone miss anything?"

No one looked ashamed of themselves. The Campbell mantra was best to do as you wanted and ask for forgiveness after the fact—which none of them ever did.

Serena smiled. "I think you've got a pretty good case."

"Just tell me what my next move is."

ON THE WAY home from his mom's, Bodie called Ivy, who didn't pick up. Two seconds later he got a text that she was with Jessie and James. Bodie would have really liked to talk to her some more, see where her head was at. But he didn't want to push.

He ended up stopping at the grocery store. Most days he ate at the bar, and as busy as he'd been, his cupboards and fridge were bare bones, and he had some secret hope that Ivy might want to stay with him. Or at least spend some time at his place, and he wanted to be able to feed her.

He was surprised when he ran into Zeke in the ice cream aisle, staring into the glass-fronted freezers, looking morose.

"You're usually more of a chips guy," Bodie said.

Zeke sighed. "On the way home, I asked Serena if she wanted some dessert later. You know, with a suggestive wink, cuz dessert's our code word for—"

"Please don't explain it."

"Yeah, well, now the kids want to know what's for dessert, only I know we're out of everything, so here I am. And that, in a nutshell, is everything you need to know about romance when you're married with children."

Bodie laughed, but later, that night alone in bed, he stared at the ceiling, thinking that that kind of romance would be nice.

THE NEXT MORNING, Ivy was alone in the bakery kitchen, playing around with frosting. Harper had set her up to finish off some cupcakes while she went to talk about some recipe with Abuela, who lived above the bookstore.

Ivy loved Harper, always would, but she was glad for the time to think. She'd gotten a call from her mom earlier. They'd had a talk. Actually, her mom had talked and Ivy had listened, grinding her teeth. The gist was that she was in *big trouble, young lady*, and they would discuss it when her mom got home.

Great. Because by "discuss" she really meant yell. And yelling was so much fun.

Her phone buzzed with a text. James. Ivy had met them at the lake last night to let the dogs play. They'd brought her a Slurpee from the local convenience store, and she'd brought a bag of goodies from Harper, which made them all laugh.

"Seriously," James said. "We appreciate you and the food."

"I'm lucky to have Harper," she said, uncomfortable with the gratitude. "If it wasn't for her, I'd be doing what you guys are, camping out. I'm just glad it's been warm at night lately."

"Us too," Jessie said. "Now if only I could figure out a way to go to school."

Her brother looked at her. "It's going to happen. *It will*," he said when Jessie looked worried, his voice serious in a way Ivy had never heard before. He sounded more intense than she imagined he could be. Almost scary.

But then he blinked and he was smiling again. They'd gone on to have a good time, and when they'd dropped her off, Jessie had waited in the car while James walked Ivy to Harper's building.

And kissed her.

She was still trying to decide if she'd liked it, or if it'd been Jessie she would've rather kissed, when a knock came at the back door and scared her into squirting the frosting up in the air.

A big blob of it landed on top of her head, then slid slowly down her face. As it hit the floor, her living vacuum cleaner named Ham rushed to lick it up.

"Need help?"

She whipped around and found Bodie standing in the doorway, laughing at her. No, wait. Not laughing at her. Just smiling, like he was super happy to see her. She sucked in some air. "Hey."

"Hey." He grabbed a few paper towels off the counter, wet them down, and handed them over. "You okay?"

And that was another thing. How did he always seem to ask the question that squeezed her heart so hard it hurt? It didn't make any sense. "Yeah." She tried to get the frosting out of her hair. "Harper's teaching me how to bake, which I love. She doesn't like to admit it, but she's stressed about making this place a success. I know how much she's got riding on this, which is *everything*, you know?"

He went back for more paper towels and squatted down to hand-mop the floor around her. "You're a good friend."

"No." She shook her head. "*She's* the good friend." Just saying it put a lump in her throat. "I want to pull my weight."

Bodie stood up and gently tugged on a strand of hair that had come loose from her ponytail. "You are. And I have a feeling you always will. It's how you're made."

"How do you know?"

He smiled. "You haven't met my mom yet. But trust me, it's in your genes."

Yep, that lump apparently could get bigger, making it impossible to swallow. "Your mom. My . . . grandma?"

"Yes. And she can't wait to meet you. When you're ready, of course." He paused. "You're stressing too. About . . . us?"

"Maybe," she admitted. "A little."

"Please don't. I'm not. Not about that anyway."

It was weird. Even after only a few weeks, with Bodie, everything seemed easier than with her mom. It made her ache for what might have been. "You're also stressing?" she asked.

"Some." He smiled a little bit, warm but . . . unsure. "I want to make sure you always feel like you belong."

And here she'd thought he couldn't surprise her any more. "I told you. I don't need anything from you." Guilt swamped her since this wasn't strictly true.

"You didn't come all the way out here to just take a look at me," he said.

No, she hadn't. She'd come to steal from him. Heat flooded her face, and she hoped like hell he couldn't read minds. "I don't know what I was hoping for," she muttered. "Just to meet you, I guess."

"I think we can do better for you than that."

She looked at him, unable to hold her natural suspicion back. "Like what?"

There was his unsure smile again. "Like a father/daughter relationship," he said.

"With rules and stuff?" Suddenly she was unsure too. "Like you telling me what to do?"

Harper had a wood table in one corner that she sat at sometimes to mix or frost or whatever when her feet needed a rest. Bodie nudged a chair from the table with his foot, spun it around, and sat on it backward, crossing his arms over the back of the chair and leaning on it, gesturing with a hand for her to sit as well.

With a sigh, she did exactly as he'd done, kicked a chair out and sat on it, backward. Wary.

Scared.

Like maybe this wasn't real. Or he'd changed his mind.

"A relationship between us wouldn't have conditions," he said. "But we do need to talk about a couple of things. I spoke to your mom."

"So did I." Then it sunk in what he'd said—and hadn't said. "Wait—you called her?"

"I did."

"You mean you wanted to see if I'm really who I said I am," she said, hearing how flat her voice sounded, unable to stem the hurt.

"No. *No*," he repeated more firmly, looking her straight in the eyes. Which, really, was impressive. It was hard to lie while looking someone right in the eyes. She should know. It'd taken her a long time to learn that skill.

"I wanted to make sure she knew where you were," he said. "And that no one was worried sick looking for you."

"I told you no one was worried at all."

Something flickered in his eyes then. Temper, but not at her, she realized. And regret. But the worst was the pity. She stood up, but he caught her hand. "I had to let her know you were here, Kit Kat. You're a minor—"

"I told you I was emancipated."

"Which wasn't the truth."

Shit. Right. She sat back down. "I didn't want you to call her."

"Why, because you never intended to go back?"

Her gaze jerked to his. "How did you know?"

"I didn't."

God, she was so stupid. "What did she say? That you should keep the brat?"

"She said you could stay."

She knew her mom. She knew that it couldn't possibly have been that easy, which meant Bodie was being kind for her sake.

"Listen," he said quietly, that same vulnerable expression on his face. She'd never seen him anything but calm and confident, so she got more worried, if that was even possible.

"You want me to leave," she said.

"The opposite. I'm hoping you'll consider staying with me. At my place."

She stared at him, sure she'd heard wrong.

"If you're not comfortable with that, you could also live at your grandma's," he said. "She'll of course overwhelm you with food and talk nonstop, but she'll love you unconditionally. Trust me, I've tested that theory." He gave her a small smile. "Repeatedly. And also, Harper's already said you could stay here with her, if that's what you prefer. It's your choice, Ivy. But I'd really like it if you'd at least think about staying with me."

She knew her mouth was probably hanging open, but of all the things she'd thought he might say, this hadn't even been in the realm. "You really want me to live with you?"

"Of course."

Of course . . . She swallowed hard and did what she did: got difficult in order to test people's feelings for her. "I'm all grown up, you know. I don't need a dad anymore." All true, because needing and wanting were two very different things.

"I'm really hoping that's not all the way true," he said. "That we could forge some sort of relationship from this, that you'd let me be a part of your life."

"How do you know you can trust me?"

He shrugged. "I just know."

Seriously. She was . . . shell-shocked. Boggled. Overwhelmed. None of this made any sense. No one *ever* trusted her. "But, like, we're strangers."

"Look, maybe. But we're also blood. And you're a total mini-me. Your eyes, your smile." He gave her a full smile now, warm and sweet. "Your stubbornness. All of us Campbells have it."

She didn't carry his name, but he thought of her as one of them. That should've made her feel panicky, but it didn't. "Doesn't mean we have to do anything about it," she said.

"I told your mom I'd take care of you," he said.

She lifted a chin at this. "I take care of myself."

"I know. So how about this? We start slow, take things at your pace." After he said this, he smiled a bit wryly.

"What?" she asked.

"I realized I just recently said that very thing to Harper as well. Seems you two have some things in common, starting with deep-seated mistrust and an innate suspicion of anything that might be good in your life."

She snorted. "Yeah. I've noticed."

He laughed softly, not irritated, but seemingly proud of her toughness.

"Subject change," he said, and pulled out a credit card. "In case of emergency." Then he also handed over sixty bucks. "For incidentals."

She stared at him. "What?"

"If you ever need more, I've got a cash drawer in my office."

She blinked. "For what?"

"For food that isn't at the bar. For anything you need."

Her first emotion was more guilt. Her second emotion was disbelief. "You're just giving me money?"

"Yes. Though in return, I'd like something."

She sucked in a breath. She *knew* there'd be a catch.

Holding her gaze in his, he said, "You'll always have a place with me, Ivy. I'll fly you back and forth, whatever you want. But you have to promise me two things: One, no lying. And two, if you decide to leave here, which, for the record, won't be because

I want you to, you won't just walk away without saying goodbye. No matter what. Because I'll come for you, always. I need you to know you're safe. That's how family works."

In her experience, family meant her doing all the work and she never got a say in anything. But that wasn't what he was doing. He was allowing her to be a part of the decision-making. This was a brand-new thing for her, and . . . terrifyingly appealing.

"So?" he asked. "Do we have a deal?"

She drew a deep breath. "I won't leave without telling you," she said. "But can I think about the moving-in-with-you thing?"

"Of course. The offer will never expire."

She took that in and realized that the odd sensation inside her was a tentative happiness. "I've got something I want to add to the deal. If that's okay."

"Name it," he said easily.

"The no-lying thing goes both ways." She paused. "You know, in case you get sick of me."

"No lying," he agreed. "But you don't get it. Me lying to you? Never going to happen. That's *definitely* not how family works."

A part of her really wanted to believe that, but the rest of her knew she couldn't. Still, they parted on a hug, and, surrounded by his strong, warm arms, with her head resting on his chest for those few seconds, she never wanted to let go.

Later, when Harper was back and it was just the two of them, Ivy tried to figure out how to talk about it.

"Okay, spit it out," Harper said.

"What?"

"Whatever you're sighing about." Harper was smiling, but when she saw Ivy's face, it vanished. "What's the matter?"

"He asked me to move in with him."

Harper smiled warmly. "Oh, that's so sweet. What did you say?"

Ivy plucked at a nonexistent loose thread on her sweater. "I haven't answered yet."

Harper nodded and let the silence sit a moment, which Ivy loved about her. "For what it's worth," she finally said, "I think the offer's genuine. But you also know you're welcome to stay here as long as you want."

Ivy met her gaze. "Really?"

"Always." Harper hugged her, then pulled back. "I'm not going anywhere. But I think if you don't at least give his offer serious consideration, you're missing out on an opportunity to really get to know your dad."

Knowing she was right, Ivy nodded, relieved that there would be no hard feelings when she left.

Not if. When.

Because if she was being honest, she wanted to move in with Bodie more than she wanted anything on the planet.

CHAPTER 16

B odie had no idea what time it was. Late, for sure. He was in the warehouse, covered in sawdust, working on the boat. Sort of. Mostly he was thinking about his girls. Ivy—and how he could embed himself into her life. And Harper—whose lips he could still feel on his. He wanted another taste, wanted to lose himself in her.

A dangerous prospect.

Earlier, he'd taken Ivy out to dinner, then shown her the warehouse and his dad's boat. She'd been fascinated and had helped him sand for a while before she'd peeked at the texts she'd been getting. She said her friends Jessie and James wanted her to bring Ham to the lake for a dog playdate.

Hard to compete with that. But it was odd how . . . *parental* he suddenly felt. He wanted to say, "I'd like to meet them, especially this James dude," but she'd looked at him like she was daring him to become all weird and possessive, so he'd just nodded.

Note to self: Ask Shay if she carries a parenting book, maybe something like What to Expect When You've Got a Teenager.

Ivy had gone to the doors, then turned back. "About James."

He tensed. "Yeah?"

She bit her lower lip. "I think I might like girls."

He looked into her vulnerable eyes and smiled. "Something we have in common." And he'd known he'd done the right thing without a book when she'd laughed and looked relieved. His heart ached for her, and he was shocked at the murderous urges he felt at the thought of anyone ever hurting her.

Now it was hours later and his mind had moved on to easier subjects. Okay, one subject.

Harper.

His mind did that a lot. His body too. She was a really great distraction. He was in the middle of one of his favorite daydreams about her showing up wearing a trench coat and nothing else when the warehouse door creaked open behind him. He turned and found his greatest fantasy in the flesh. And she was eyeing him with the same look that he knew he wore—hunger. Desire.

"You're all covered in sawdust," she said softly, not looking bothered by that in the least. Wait . . . he took that back. She did seem bothered—as in *hot and bothered*.

"Thirsty?" she asked.

Hell, suddenly he didn't know what he was. She turned him upside down and inside out in her flowery sundress, which showed a lot of smooth pretty skin. Her hair was loose and wild around her face and shoulders. In one hand was a clear box with what looked like four huge pink cupcakes, and from the fingers of her other hand dangled two bottles of beer.

And his stress and worry took a back seat to something else entirely.

She handed him a beer. He opened it and handed it back to her to drink, then took the other for himself. They clinked their bottles together and sipped. They continued to say nothing for a few minutes. The silence was comfortable and . . . cozy. Not a word he used often. Or ever. After a few minutes, she thrust out the box. "Congratulations, it's a girl."

He laughed, then looked into her eyes. They were warm, curious, smiling. "You got me saturated fats and processed sugar? I'm undone."

"Seemed like that kind of day." Her smile faded. "I know it can't be easy, what you're going through. You okay?"

He'd lost track of how many people had asked him that, and his answer had been the same to all of them. Yes, he was fine. Hell, he was great. He was safe for the first time in his adult life, feeding people for a living, which he loved, and best of all, he had a daughter.

And then there were his feelings for this woman in front of him. Feelings he hadn't thought he could feel.

But the truth was, he wasn't all the way fine. He was . . . hell. Scared. Scared to fuck this all up. "Ivy looks at me like she's trying to figure out who I am and what that means for her."

"And you're worried about it?"

"What if she's looking for something I'm not sure I have?"

"You mean love?" She looked surprised that he'd think he couldn't give that to her.

He shook his head. "More than that."

"Like what?"

He struggled to find the words. "The same thing I see in your eyes sometimes," he finally said softly. "Reassurance . . . about what kind of man I am."

She took that in, not denying it.

"Ivy's struggling to define herself," he said. "Her identity as my daughter is affected by my character. You're redefining yourself, and understandably considering what it might mean to let me be a part of that. I want to be the best man I can be, for the both of you, but I'm not sure I know who that man is, except for a deeply flawed individual who's done things I'm not proud of."

"Hey." She shifted closer, looking up into his eyes. "It's called being human."

He smiled at her, and she smiled back, dissipating some of his tension.

"Don't be stressed," she said. "It's all going to work out."

"You're here, so how could it not?" He rubbed his jaw to hers, turning his head to brush his lips to her cheek. Then, because he couldn't help himself, the spot beneath her ear as well, which he knew damn well melted her bones. The air suddenly felt charged, and he wondered which of them was going to get burned. Most likely him.

Willingly walking right into the fire, he pulled her closer, finding himself letting out a pent-up breath he hadn't realized he'd been holding when she came willingly, cuddling herself into him like she belonged in his arms.

"Ivy?" he asked, face pressed in her hair. God, she smelled good.

"Fast asleep with Hambone." She pulled back. "I think she's really considering coming to stay with you. She asked me what I thought, and I said I was all for it. Are you ready for a teenager?"

"Yes."

Her brows raised.

He smiled. "I mean, I feel like I skipped a few steps in this whole parenting thing, but I'll figure it out as I go." He paused. "I hope."

"Teenage girls are aliens." She grinned. "I know because I was one."

"Teenage boys aren't much better. I gave my parents hell, so probably I should just hope she breaks me in gently."

"She's a good kid, Bodie. A really good kid."

"I know. She came over earlier."

"She told me. You showed her how to do some sanding on the hull. It meant a lot to her. I don't think she's had a lot of parental interest."

Yeah, and that pissed him off, big-time.

"You could show *me* how to sand too," she said with a smile. "If you want . . ."

"You'll get dirty."

Her smile widened. "And?"

With a laugh, he took her hand and brought her inside the

boat, showing her around. The galley was all raw beautiful woods he still had to stain.

"It's amazing," she said.

He ran a hand along the galley cabinets. "Would've been more amazing if my dad were still around to be a part of it. I seem to be a day late and a dollar short when it comes to taking care of the people I love."

She leaned back against the counter and looked at him. "It's never too late."

"You think?"

"I think you can turn your life around at any point." She shrugged. "Look at me. I packed and moved five hundred and fifty miles from everything and everyone I've ever known."

She was right. He'd been given a second chance at life. Maybe he should live it. "Haven't eaten down here yet," he said casually.

"Should I go get a few more beers?"

Probably a bad idea. He needed to be in peak mental and physical condition to hold his own against Harper Shaw. "I'm good. You?"

She nodded at the box of cupcakes she'd set down. "Got all I need right here."

He was really hoping that wasn't true. "So did you come over here just to give me your cupcakes?"

"Well, maybe also to find a spark of joy."

"And did you?" He ran a finger along her temple. "Find a spark of joy?"

Her eyes never left his. "I did."

His breath caught. She was looking at him like maybe he was

breakfast, lunch, *and* dinner, and damn, that hadn't happened in a while. She slid her hands into his hair and pulled his face to hers. Then she slowly sank her teeth into his lower lip, and he was done thinking. He'd give this thought, a lot of thought. His plan had been to take his time, showing her the power he could wield over her body to drive her wild. But he was an idiot because only one of them had any such power, and it was her.

It'd been a long time since Harper ached for someone. She and Daniel hadn't been intimate for a while before their breakup. In retrospect, she should have seen it coming for that reason alone. But she'd buried her needs, which bothered her. She enjoyed intimacy, touching someone, being touched, being wanted, if only for the moment.

With Bodie, she knew it would go far deeper than that, a risk because it meant she might accidentally open her heart to him. But she'd already opened her heart to his daughter, so it was probably too late to protect herself against him anyway. In which case, why not let this happen then, maybe even to make the first move and claim this part of her back? Liking that idea, she wrapped herself around him and deepened the kiss, letting her hands roam wherever they ached to roam. Over his shoulders, his chest, his arms.

South . . .

He caught her hands. "Harper."

Instantly, she was alert and all too aware. "Is someone coming?"

"Me, if you don't stop."

She laughed. "And . . . ?"

"And . . . first I want to do this . . ." He let go of her hands so that his were free, one curling around the nape of her neck, the other low on her back, holding her close. Then his mouth closed over hers again. When he touched his tongue to hers, she heard herself moan.

He lifted his head with a hot smile. "My favorite sound." He kissed her jaw, then the base of her throat. "I'm going to make you do that again." Another kiss, to her collarbone this time. "And again . . ."

She shivered in anticipation but managed to say saucily, "Promises, promises," before giving him a nudge to the leather bench seat. Catching her hand, he tugged her down with him. She landed in his lap, where he rearranged her legs so that she was straddling him, her thighs hugged up to the outside of his.

And then smiled wickedly up at her.

So smug. Leaning over him, she kissed him until he made his own helplessly aroused sound. Then she pushed at his shirt until he broke free of the kiss and tore it off over his head, sending it sailing somewhere behind them. Letting herself get lost for a moment, her fingers trailed down his chest and abs, planning on following up with her tongue.

No slouch, he was busy too, encouraging the spaghetti straps of her sundress to slip, where they caught at her elbows. Another little nudge had the bodice falling away, exposing a skimpy bra. Yes, hi, her name was Harper Shaw and she was frugal in all things *except* lingerie. And given the glazed, heated, sensual look on Bodie's face, he appreciated it. His work-roughened fingers skimmed over her see-through-lace-covered breasts. "Pretty," he said in a husky voice, and then unhooked the bra and slowly pulled it off. "And I've found something I want more than your cupcakes." His hands slid down her back to palm her ass, his mouth dropping to reverently tease everything he'd just revealed to the night air.

She looked down at his bowed head, his dark hair dusted in sawdust, the muscles in his bare shoulders and arms bunched as he pleasured her. They were in a warehouse, in a boat, the cavernous space lit only by a few hanging lightbulbs overhead. It should have felt seedy, but instead, the golden light danced over his skin, the air scented with cedar and gorgeous heated male, and she'd never experienced anything so erotic in all her life.

His mouth was driving her mad and she ached for more, so she toyed with the top button of his Levi's, then slipped her fingers under the waistband in search of what she'd been rocking against—

Again, his hand caught hers as he lifted his head and met her gaze, his own rueful.

"Oh." He'd changed his mind. "Okay." Embarrassed, she started to climb off him, but he wrapped his arms around her and pressed his forehead to hers.

"You don't understand. I want you, Harper. And I want you bad too, but I don't have a condom with me."

It'd been a really long time since she'd been with someone other than Daniel. She couldn't remember the etiquette, not in her overheated state, and she was horrified he'd remembered when maybe she might've totally forgotten. "Right." She closed her eyes. "I'm sorry, I—"

"Shh." He cupped her face. "I know you're not on the trust-me program yet, but maybe you could try, just for the next little bit . . . ?"

Her eyes flew open. He gave her the sweetest, hottest smile she'd ever seen, then shifted, laying her back on the bench to kneel between her legs. The light above gilded him, making him look like something out of a movie as he slid his hands up the fronts of her thighs, bringing the hem of her dress with him, slowly exposing her to his heated gaze. "Hold this," he said, and she automatically obeyed, holding her dress up.

He smiled at her matching panties, running a finger over her until she squirmed. Then he hooked his thumbs in the tiny scrap of material and slowly slid them down. When they were gone, sailing through the air, he eased her thighs farther apart for greater access, then proceeded to make good on his promise.

After all, he was a man of his word.

BODIE CAME BACK to himself sometime later, when the tired beauty stirred in his arms. Lying beneath her on the galley bench, holding her close and warm against him, he opened his eyes. "Best damn cupcakes I've ever had."

Laughing breathlessly into his chest, she brushed a kiss to his heated skin and got up.

He watched as she fumbled around for her clothes. "Where are my undies?"

He rose and snatched them from their perch on a low-hanging

light. Coming up behind her, he reached around, her panties dangling from his finger.

She took them with a wry smile. "And my wits? Did you find those too?"

Her hair was wild. He'd done that when she'd returned his trust-me favor, first kissing her way down his body, taking extra time at each of his many scars. He'd fisted his hands in her hair, lost in the feelings she generated in him. "You okay?" he asked softly.

"I think you know that I am, in fact, very okay. But . . ." She bit her lip. "We're still going at my pace, right?"

"Always." He paused. "Does your pace have anything against me asking you and Ivy to go on the Campbell weekly bike ride tomorrow afternoon, and then dinner at my mom's afterward?"

She looked like maybe she was trying hard to think of a reason why she couldn't. "I don't think so?"

He smiled at the way she worded that as a question. "Problem?"

"It's just that I'm a really bad bike rider," she said. "And also, I don't have a bike."

"We'll borrow one for you, and we won't do anything difficult. Dinner will be easy too."

"Are you sure? Meeting your mom . . ." She bit her lower lip.

She was nervous about it, he realized. "Trust me, she's going to adore you. Much more than her own heathens."

She smiled. "She must be pretty tough, raising all boys."

"Tough, but also a big softie."

"I could bring dessert," she said.

He smiled. "I'll never turn down your cupcakes."

THE NEXT MORNING, Harper was pulling her grandma's cinnamon rolls from the oven when the knock came at her door. It was early, 7:00 a.m., and she hadn't opened for business yet. But never one to turn a customer away, she headed to the front. Probably it was Bodie, looking for a cinnamon roll. She was so certain, she opened the door without lifting the shade first to check. "Hey— Oh," she said in surprise to the woman standing there. "I'm so sorry. I'm not quite open yet, but depending on what you want, I can still possibly help you."

"You're so sweet." The woman, sixtyish, clapped a hand to her chest. She looked vaguely familiar, even more so when she smiled. "I can wait. But it sure is chilly out here this morning."

"Come in." Harper shifted aside for her to enter. "I'm still on takeout orders only, but you're welcome."

"Something smells delicious." The woman moved to the counter.

Harper walked behind it. "It's my grandma's cinnamon rolls. What are you looking for today?"

"Actually, you."

Harper looked up in surprise. "Me?"

"I'm Suzie Campbell."

Oh dear God. Had she even brushed her hair earlier before tugging it up on top of her head? "You're Bodie's mom."

"The one and only," she said on a laugh. "I hear he's sweet on you."

Harper choked out a laugh. "I don't know about that." But actually, she sort of did . . . "I'm pretty sweet on him though."

Suzie Campbell clapped a hand to her heart. "You don't know

how wonderful it is to hear that. He's been through so much. I just wanted to get my eyes on the woman who's lightened his heart. He's back to looking happy again. Thank you for that."

The woman's smile was guileless, but Harper suddenly had the realization she was anything but. "I'm not sure I can take credit for all that."

"Sure you can. And I can see why. You're kind enough to let a perfect stranger into your shop simply because it's too chilly to leave her waiting outside. You're also protecting Bodie's privacy. That makes you sweet, smart, and loyal to boot. My favorite qualities in the women who love my boys."

Harper set down her spatula. "Mrs. Campbell—"

"Suzie," she corrected gently.

"Suzie," Harper said. "I think maybe you've misunderstood. Bodie and I, we're not . . . like that. We're not in love." She meant it. Or, more accurately, she wanted to mean it.

"*Yet*," Suzie said confidently.

Harper laughed a little roughly. "I just moved to town. We work next door to each other." *And we did it in the boat he's renovating for your dead husband . . .* "I'm sorry to disappoint you."

"Oh, honey, you're not a disappointment at all. And I'll take that entire batch of cinnamon rolls." She dropped a hundred-dollar bill on the counter.

Harper bagged everything up. "Hold on, I have to run upstairs. I don't have change down here yet."

Suzie just smiled. "No change needed." And then she was gone.

CHAPTER 17

Ivy's stomach was in her throat as her feet swung what felt like a million feet above the ground. She sat on a five-person ski lift, which turned out was also a bike lift, heading to the top of a huge-ass mountain, where apparently some of the best biking trails in the world could be found.

She had Bodie, Harper, and Shay on her left, Mace on her right. Zeke and Serena were on the lift right behind them.

Shay had made it clear when they'd all met at the mountain resort's parking lot; she was only here so her pass didn't go to waste, but she still wasn't speaking to Mace.

Whatever Mace thought of this, he kept to himself, though he did tell Shay that she looked hot in her bike shorts.

Shay had just stared at him, but when she turned away, Ivy caught her smiling. Apparently adults were just as screwed-up as teenagers.

"Hey, Bodie," Shay said. "Can you tell Mace to stop kicking

his feet? He's making the chair swing and I'm getting carsick. If he doesn't stop, I'll puke on him."

"I'm pretty sure he can hear you," Bodie said.

"Hey, Bodie," Mace said. "Can you tell Shay I'd do anything for her, including stopping breathing, but I can't stop swinging my feet because I'm not swinging my feet? The wind is kicking us around, not me. If she'd been on time, we'd have been up here twenty minutes earlier and missed these series of gusts."

"Seriously?" Shay asked him. "Like you know anything about a woman's struggle to get ready in the morning, what with your thirty-second showers and short hair that you don't even brush. I mean, it takes me a solid three minutes just to get my hair all the way wet! And don't even get me started on the rest of it. *You* think sticking your face into the shower spray is washing your face, meanwhile, my skincare routine is a five-step process."

Ivy couldn't help it: she snorted. She was fascinated by their dynamic. They fought but never stopped hanging out with each other. Like, they actually all wanted to be together.

"Point one for the prosecution!" Serena yelled from the lift behind them.

"Is this what we're doing today?" Bodie asked no one. "Really?"

Shay stuck her tongue out at Mace.

Ivy laughed again.

Bodie looked at her and smiled as if he couldn't help it. "How am I stuck between the two of you?" he asked Mace and Shay. "Either stop poking at each other or tell us once and for all why you guys broke up."

His brother looked at his ex-girlfriend, who turned her head and stared at the mountainside.

"Someone needs to speak or someone's getting pushed off," Bodie warned.

"That would be murder one," Mace said.

"No, it'd be manslaughter," Bodie corrected. "And I know a good lawyer."

"Yeah, he does," Serena called out.

Only a few weeks earlier, this conversation would have made Ivy tense and unhappy. But now . . . now she was starting to get it. This was how they showed their affection.

Mace sighed and tipped his head back. "I asked her to marry me," he said to the sky.

All heads swiveled to Shay in shock, including Ivy's.

"Hey," Shay said. "I've always told him, from *day one*, I wasn't going to ever get married. Ever. *Ever* ever. Marriage ruins everything."

"Yeah, it does," Ivy said, in total agreement.

Shay high-fived Ivy.

"Stop that," Bodie said to Shay. "I want my daughter to believe in love."

The "my daughter" warmed Ivy from the inside out, but it didn't change her views.

"*Ever* ever?" Zeke asked Shay.

"No means no."

"Point two for the prosecution," Serena yelled.

"And it's not like I don't have my reasons," Shay said. "My

mom and dad were married, and they hated each other. Like *hated* hated . . ." She drew a deep breath as if she was struggling to control her emotions, and Ivy felt her throat sting in sympathy.

Mace leaned forward to look directly at Shay. "I'm not your dad," he said quietly. "And you're not your mom."

Shay just shook her head and refused to look at him. "I'm not doing this one hundred feet in the air with witnesses. Someone who loves me needs to change the subject now."

There was a single beat of silence. Then Mace said, "How about this weather, huh?"

Shay surprised Ivy by actually smiling at her ex.

Harper outright laughed, and Bodie smiled at her. Since he already had his arm around her, he pulled her in—as if they weren't already plastered up against each other—and brushed a kiss to her temple.

Harper looked at him as if he'd hung the moon or something equally stupid and sappy, and Ivy frowned, startled by the unexpected surge of irritation. It made no sense, but the truth was, when Bodie had invited her today, she'd thought it would be something special, just the two of them. Not that she didn't like his brothers and Shay and Harper. She did. She liked them all, *so much*. She just . . . hell, she had no idea why she suddenly felt irrationally grumpy. Maybe because the math said she was an outsider.

And she was far too used to that.

"Can we call a truce?" Mace asked.

Shay looked undecided.

"Maybe you can agree to start out by being friends," Harper

said. "You could take it from there. Kinda like when you lease-to-buy."

Shay and Mace eyed each other.

"Not a bad idea," Mace said.

Shay looked at him for a long moment. Then shrugged. "Definitely not the worst idea I've heard."

Mace reached out and covered Ivy's ears. "And if you wanted to do the whole friends-with-benefits package, I wouldn't object."

"I can still hear," Ivy said.

Bodie smacked Mace upside the back of his head, but Shay laughed. "Lease-to-buy it is."

They got off the lift at the top and stood in a clump adjusting their helmets and gear. Harper was the only one in the group who wasn't a strong bike rider, but in Chicago, Ivy's most prized possession had been her bike because it'd meant freedom. She'd ridden everywhere. This bike, the one Bodie had borrowed for her, was light-years better than anything she'd ever had, and she was excited to get going.

"Please, I don't want anyone waiting for me," Harper said, looking embarrassed. "Just go as fast as you all want and don't look back. I'll meet you all at the bottom in about five years."

Everyone laughed, and Bodie hugged her. *Again.* "I'll stay with you," he said.

So much for her first father/daughter day. Ivy tried not to let this get to her, she really did. She'd known about their attraction. Hell, the air sizzled whenever they were in the same room, and she'd seen that kiss. But today felt different, like they'd . . . oh crap. They'd done it, they'd slept together. Gross. But also . . . she couldn't shake off her bad mood. She'd trusted Harper, who'd known her history, known that Bodie was her biological father and that Ivy was terrified of messing it all up.

She didn't understand why Harper would do this to her, but she knew one thing—this was how the beginning of the end always started with her mom. She'd bring a good guy around, they'd all get attached, and then her mom would ruin things and they'd be alone again.

"Ready?" Bodie asked her with a smile, and she felt herself smile back. And thankfully as soon as they started down the hill, she forgot to be grumpy because it was . . . magical. The wind in her face. The tall, towering pines on either side of the trail, the gorgeous flashes of the lake far below. The trail was long, which she loved, and she smiled the whole time.

Ivy, Mace, Shay, Serena, and Zeke all got to the mid-mountain lodge. She had a perma-grin on her face. They'd talked smack to one another, laughing the whole way. About ten minutes later, Harper finally came into view, going awkwardly slow, Bodie just behind her.

"Isn't this amazing?" Harper asked when she stopped at Ivy's side.

"It was, before we had to wait forever for you to get down." The second the words left her mouth, she felt like the biggest jerk on the planet. "I'm sorry." She covered her mouth. "I didn't mean that. Teenagers shouldn't talk. My mom always says that, and I never listen."

Harper glanced from Ivy to Bodie, just up ahead and in some sort of joking shoving contest with Mace. "Don't be sorry, I get it," she said softly. "And I'm the sorry one, Ivy."

"No, please." She felt near tears, which she hated. "Forget I said anything. I didn't mean it. Really."

"You did," Harper said, so kindly that Ivy had to bite her tongue, hard. "And you were right." She turned to the others and raised her voice. "Hey, guys. I really need to catch my breath. I'm going to sit this next one out."

Bodie turned from Mace. "You sure? I'm happy to keep biking with you at your pace."

Harper smiled at him, not a hint of irritation with Ivy in her voice. "I'm very sure, I really want to sit and watch while you ride. The view will be great."

Everyone laughed while Ivy's gut churned, but still Harper didn't tattle or give her away. "Harper, you don't have to do this."

"Yes, I do." Harper squeezed her hand. "I shouldn't have crashed your day. I'm sorry."

Ivy hated that she was still far too close to tears. "You didn't crash it. He invited you."

"That doesn't mean you don't get to be upset." Harper's eyes were solemn but genuine. "I'm going to be happy sitting out, trust me. And, Ivy? If you ever want to talk about anything, even if it's about me, or your dad, or me and your dad, I'm always here, okay? Even if it's something you think might hurt my feelings, I'm *always* available to you."

Ivy's stomach felt icky. And heavy. Guilt ate at her, but she didn't know how to deal with it, with any of it. But Harper saved her again by calling to Shay, "You want to join me on the sundeck outside the lodge for a quick break?"

Shay looked undecided.

"I'm buying the snacks," Harper said.

"Should have led with that." Shay craned her neck to Mace. "*Hey.*"

"I didn't do it," he said.

"Do what?"

"Whatever you think I did."

Shay snorted. "Good to know. Come on. Harper's buying. I'm going to share my goodies with you."

Mace made a show of looking around. "Babe, I've already told you I'd do anything for you, but this is a family resort."

Zeke curled his upper lip. "Seriously, man?"

But Shay laughed, and Mace smiled at her laughing and parked his bike.

Zeke rolled his eyes and looked at his wife. "Race you to the bottom?"

"If the winner doesn't have to do laundry for a week," Serena said.

"Or dishes," Zeke said.

Serena took off like a shot, leaving Zeke in her wake.

"Oh, very mature," Zeke yelled after her, doing his best to catch her.

Everyone was laughing, but Ivy couldn't. She knew what Harper had done, coaxing Mace and Shay to stay with her so that Ivy could be alone with Bodie, and she felt like a shithead to the highest magnitude.

"Come on, Kit Kat," Bodie said, and slung an arm around her as they turned back to their bikes. "Back up to the top, or all the way down?" he asked.

"Up," she said, needing a minute to process.

As they waited in line for the lift, she stood quietly, feeling the weight of Bodie's gaze several times, but he didn't speak until they were on the lift again, just the two of them. Which was exactly what she'd secretly wanted, but she now felt ashamed that she'd broken them all up when they were clearly happy to spend the day *together*.

It was like this whole place and all the people in it were completely alien to her, a group she wanted desperately to be a part of, but no idea how to do that.

"I'm sorry," Bodie said.

She turned a startled gaze to him. "What?"

"I should've thought that maybe you'd want today to be just us. I'm . . ." He let out a rough laugh. "Really new to this. I'm afraid I'm going to make mistakes."

Embarrassed that he'd figured out the problem, *her* problem, she said, "Me too. Like . . . a lot of them."

"Ditto." He smiled at her, a sweet, warm smile, and she found herself helplessly smiling back. "I know we're a big, noisy, obnoxious group," he said. "And I know that can feel overwhelming. I should've warned you. We're a lot."

And just like that, she was back to feeling that stupid lump in her throat. Turning her head away, unable to voice her thoughts, she took in the 360 degrees of sharp, majestic mountains blanketed in summer greenery, so stunning it took her breath.

She'd truly never seen anything like it.

"Ivy?" Bodie nudged her gently with his shoulder.

"I like them," she whispered. "Your family."

"Good." He waited until she looked at him again. "You fit right in, you know. With us. I hope you feel that."

How pathetically desperate was she that she wanted to believe him more than anything?

A few minutes later, they got off the lift at the top of the world and he flashed a smile at her. "Race you to the bottom."

She felt a grin split her face and a surge of adrenaline. "You're on."

BODIE FLEW DOWN the trail, the wind in his face, grinning while watching as directly in front of him, his daughter—*his daughter*—kicked serious ass on the trail.

She'd started out slightly hesitant though skilled. But she was used to city biking, which was a whole different beast than mountain biking. But she'd gotten her bearings quickly and he felt pride bursting out of every pore watching her handle herself with confidence and grace.

She was a chip off her old man's block, he thought with pride, as the mid-mountain lodge came into sight, and knowing everyone was watching her, he just couldn't stop grinning, his heart two sizes too big for his chest.

Which was when he hit a rock with his front wheel, and . . .

went sailing over the handlebars. His last thought was, great, he was biffing it right in front of the lodge with an audience that no doubt included his family.

The next thing he knew, he was flat on his back, blinking up at the sky. Nope, scratch that. Five heads, as they popped into his field of vision.

"Good thing he was wearing a helmet," one of the heads said. Mace.

"It's okay, his head is as hard as any of those rocks." Zeke.

"Ohmigod, are you okay?" This was Harper's worried voice and, he assumed, her soft warm hand on his shoulder.

"You should have seen how high you got!" Ivy said, grinning wide with . . . pride?

"You were in the air for *forever* before you went splat," she added.

"Thanks, Kit Kat."

"I mean you literally made the splat noise."

Mace wrapped an arm around Ivy's neck and hugged her to him. "I love you so much. We're going to make a great team."

And given Ivy's quick grin at his brother's words, Bodie couldn't even be mad.

IT WAS AFTERNOON when they called it a day. Harper moved to where Bodie was loading up their bikes. She was proud of herself for making it through the day without dying or embarrassing herself too badly. There *had* been that one time when she'd gotten dizzy. Not from riding, but from Bodie peeling off his sweatshirt, causing his T-shirt to slide up a little, exposing his lower abs, including that sexy-as-hell V-shaped indention that really fit guys had.

Shrugging that delicious memory off, she took a deep breath and told herself to just say it. "I think I'm going to skip dinner at your mom's tonight."

He stopped what he was doing and turned to her, his eyes creased in worry. "Why? Are you feeling okay?"

"I'm not the one who went flying over my handlebars."

He smiled, as she'd intended. "Smart-ass."

She stepped a little closer so no one could overhear them. "Tonight will be Ivy's first time meeting her grandma."

"I don't see the problem."

"I know you don't," she said, putting her hand on his arm. "It's because you're a man, and you probably never once in your life wondered if you were going to be welcomed somewhere."

"Harper." He shook his head and captured her hand in his. "You and Ivy are going to make my mom's night. Do you have any idea how many years she's been after me to get serious about someone? Or bring her a grandchild?"

Her breath caught. "You're . . . serious about me?"

"Very." He grinned. "Even before you let me taste your . . . cupcakes."

She laughed, because he had a way of making her feel so good about herself. Good, and sexy, and . . . like she was cherished. She drew a deep breath and tried to stay on track. "I just think that tonight should be about Ivy."

They looked over at the teen, who was helping Zeke load his bikes, the two of them laughing. Zeke was teasing her, and she was giving it right back. She was a smart-ass. Sharp. Tough. And God, he loved her already, more than he thought possible.

"You're what she needs right now," Harper said.

"You're right," Bodie said quietly. "And I should've thought of it."

She smiled. "That will all come with time. But for now, she needs your undivided attention tonight. She's never had this much loving family around her. She's nervous, scared, and a flight risk. She needs her dad."

Something he knew she knew a whole bunch about.

"Trust me on this, Bodie. You need to choose her."

"I do. And I always will. But, Harper?" He cupped her face. "You're a choice too. A priority. I want you to know that." He dropped a quick kiss on her lips, hoping she could believe it.

ON THE WAY home, Harper watched Bodie and Ivy tease each other with a new level of comfort that thrilled her. She was also hugely amused when Ivy wanted to be dropped off at the lake to spend some time with James and Jessie before dinner at her grandma's—like a regular teen who'd had enough dad time.

So when Bodie pulled up to the bakery, it was just the two of them. "Do you want to come in?" she asked at the same time that he said, "Can I come in?"

She laughed. "You don't have to ask."

He caught her hand before she could slide out. "I do," he said. "You've got some personal-space boundaries and I'm trying to respect them." He was turned to face her in the driver's seat, one hand draped over the wheel, the other on the passenger headrest, his fingers playing with her hair, the look on his face messing with her resting heart rate.

"I appreciate that," she said. "But I don't feel the need for space from you. At least . . ." She smiled. "Not at the moment."

He flashed a grin and walked her up to her apartment. They were accosted by a sleepy but excited Ham, who they walked until he'd pooped his heart out. They all made a quick stop in the bakery kitchen for snacks, and then they were in Harper's small apartment.

Bodie filled that space in the very best of ways. He turned in a circle, taking in the personal touches she'd added. Some pics on the walls. A few plants. Ivy's shoes in the entryway. He smiled. "Feels nice in here. Like how I feel with you. Warm and cozy."

"I make you feel warm and cozy?"

His smile went a little wicked. "Well, not at the moment. Not in those shorts you're wearing. I've been having fantasies about your legs all day long."

She laughed as they settled on the couch with apples, cheese, crackers, and half of a moose tracks pie she had left over. They talked about everyday stuff. How the bakery was shaping up, the things she still needed to do to make it successful but hadn't found the time for. Ads, connecting with caterers, local restaurants, stuff like that. He told her some more about his family, some of his and his brothers' hijinks, and made her laugh so hard she cried. They were on the moose tracks pie when he told her about his brother Austin and how he still missed him every single day, but especially how much Austin would've loved her moose tracks pie, which had been his favorite thing of all things.

They got quiet, and Bodie pulled her close, pressing his forehead to hers. "I know we haven't known each other that long, not yet, but you being here . . ." His eyes held hers, warm and steady. "You already mean so much to a lot of people, Harper."

Not sure she was able to believe that, she shook her head and opened her mouth, but he gently put a finger to her lips. "Like to Ivy," he said. "Shay . . ." He kissed her softly before pulling back, running the pad of his thumb over her bottom lip. "*Me.*"

She drew a deep breath to clear the fog of arousal his touch always had her in. "It does feel like we've known each other a lot longer than we have."

"Agreed." He pulled her onto his lap. "And yet there's still so much more I want to know about you."

"Like?" she asked breathlessly, sliding her fingers into his hair for the sheer pleasure of feeling him rock against her.

"Like . . ." He twisted so that she lay flat, pinned by 180 pounds of highly motivated man. "What sound you'll make when I do this . . ." Leaning down, he kissed the soft, sensitive skin just beneath her ear, then lightly bit her, eliciting a gasp of pleasure from her.

"Mmm, that one," he whispered huskily against her skin as his mouth took itself on a hot, wet, thorough tour to the hollow of her throat, making her moan. "And that . . ."

"Bodie, you have to leave soon to get Ivy to your mom's . . ."

"I've still got enough time to make us both very happy."

She laughed. "I take longer than you to get . . . happy."

"Trust me, Harper. Your happy is my highest priority."

She had her hands inside his clothes now, trying to get him

naked. Luckily, their goals were aligned as he divested her of her clothes. "Love how you taste. I need more." Lowering his head, he kissed everything he'd uncovered before making a home for himself between her thighs. "And I especially love the way you look like this."

"At your mercy, you mean."

"You've got that entirely backward." Thankfully he'd taken to having condoms on him, and he didn't disappoint. They wrestled a little to get into a good position, bumping into each other, laughing and swearing as they tried to line things up on the too-short couch. Finally, he sat up and had her straddle him, slowly letting her sink over him until he was in as deep as he could go. She couldn't speak, couldn't breathe, could only feel. When she rolled her hips to his, he stilled, head back, eyes closed, a look of sheer ecstasy on his face. Then he opened his eyes and looked deep into hers. "I'm at *your* mercy, Harper. Always."

He kissed her then, and the way he held on to her like she was everything sent them both flying.

She'd had good experiences before, even great. But even with Daniel, who'd told her he loved her, whom she'd lived with . . . she'd never felt like they'd made love. The intimacies she'd shared with Bodie had pointed that out for her. He'd made her no promises, had offered nothing but pleasure, and yet she'd felt joined to him in a way she'd never felt with her ex. Something to think about.

"I smell smoke," Bodie said, a quiet rumble in her ear as he gently ran a finger along her temple, pushing a strand of hair behind her ear. "You okay?"

She nodded, her hand rubbing back and forth over his chest. God, she loved his body and the way it made hers feel. "Just reminding myself to keep my head and my heart separated, because that was . . . wow."

He smiled with just a hint of his dimple, but his eyes were warm and serious. "You don't have to keep them separated. I still want more for us. Can you understand that?"

"No," she said honestly.

He was clearly surprised by her answer. "Just out of curiosity, what is it you think we're doing?"

"Fulfilling fantasies. Having fun." She smiled to soften her shrug. "Burning bright."

He exhaled like the air had been kicked from his lungs. "You still think this is just a fling. That maybe I'm going to walk away from you."

"I mean . . . it happens."

He gave a small, disbelieving head shake. "What am I doing wrong?"

She couldn't have possibly cared more for him in that moment. But the funny thing about living with fear of attachment for so long was . . . it didn't just go away. "Nothing. It's the shit from my past. It's the voice in my head. It's not you, it's me."

He choked out a laugh.

"What?"

"I've just never had that line used on me before. Usually . . ."

When he trailed off, she laughed. "Usually you use it?"

He grimaced.

She took his hand and pressed it to her heart. "For me, it's not just a line, Bodie. It's the truth." Then she used his own words. "Can you understand that?"

He looked into her eyes. "After all you've been through, yes."

She'd expected him to be scared off. But he wasn't. She seemed to be the only scared one. Which had her thinking that maybe, for the first time in her life, she should try living without that fear for a change.

If she even could . . .

CHAPTER 18

Bodie parked at his mom's and turned to Ivy, smiling because she looked so serious. "It's just a family dinner," he promised. "With *really* great food."

She gnawed on her lower lip. "What if they figure out . . ." She lowered her voice. "You know, how difficult I am?"

His entire heart cracked wide open. "Look at me." When she did with a slight flash of sass, he smiled at her. "You're amazing, and my mom will love you." When she gave him a doubtful look, he said, "I'm never going to lie to you, Kit Kat, so when I tell you something, you can take it to the bank."

She nodded but still looked like a flight risk. And even though he really did know his mom was going to love her, he was afraid Ivy wasn't going to let herself be loved. "Look, you're her first and only granddaughter. She's going to like you better than all the rest of us put together, I *promise* you."

She nodded bravely, and he reached over to hug her, pressing his jaw to the top of her head, catching Zeke's and Serena's eyes as they, along with Shay—in her own car—and Mace got out of their vehicles.

Everyone smiled reassuringly. It took him a beat to realize that while he was here for Ivy, *they* were here for him. Not that he deserved it. When he'd first come back to Sunrise Cove, he'd been a broody, moody asshole. He hadn't come around much.

Or at all.

He'd holed up in his cabin in Hidden Falls and he'd . . . well, he'd hidden away. He'd had a lot of healing to do, physically and emotionally, and it'd taken him a shamefully long time to get over himself and come back to his family. And actually, he hadn't done it on his own. He might never have, but one day, maybe a month after he'd gotten here, there'd been a knock at his door. He'd ordered food delivery, so assuming it was that, he'd limped painfully to the door, only to be shocked by his family pushing their way past him inside.

Mace. His mom. Zeke. Serena. Their rug rats. Shay. All of them carrying food, and not just for dinner, but for his cupboards and freezer. They'd stocked him up, and after that night, someone had come by every few days with more. Respectfully keeping their distance, taking their cues from him.

It'd happened so slowly, so gradually, he couldn't even pinpoint exactly when he'd gotten comfortable with them all up in his business. Now they'd collectively do that for Ivy, until *she* believed. He knew that without a doubt, and they wouldn't give up until they'd succeeded.

As always, his mom opened her front door before he got up the walk. She'd had a rough year, and it showed, but the pain in her eyes was less visible tonight. "Come in and eat," she demanded. "You're skin and bones, all of you."

Zeke, who wasn't as fit as Bodie and Mace—they liked to tease him about his "dad bod"—snorted. "Well, not *all* of us."

"You're perfect," his mom said, and grabbed him by the face and kissed both cheeks.

She repeated this for Serena, and then Mace—whose face she held a little longer than she had Zeke's and Serena's. "I see the woman who is your far better half standing right behind you. Does this mean you two have come to your senses?"

Mace glanced back at Shay. "We're trying to be friends."

"Ack. *Idiot,*" his mom said fondly, and pushed him past her so she could reach for Shay, whom she hugged hard.

Never comfortable with familial affection, Shay squirmed a bit, but in the end, no one had ever resisted Suzie Campbell's genuine love for all things in her orbit. She was warm, sweet, caring, *and* nosy as hell. She was simply impossible to escape or resist—proven when Shay gave a snort and hugged her back. "Good to see you, Suzie."

"Right back at you, honey." Then those miss-nothing eyes landed on Bodie and . . . filled.

"Ah, Mom," he said, pained. "Please don't cry."

"I can't help it." She pulled him in hard and rocked him to her even though he had over a foot on her. Then she quite literally shoved him aside. "Oh . . . Oh, honey, you're perfect. Come here, I've got sixteen years of hugs to give you."

Ivy, deer in the headlights, tried to duck behind Bodie. He caught her to him and turned to face her, his back to everyone else, blocking her from their view. "I get the fight-or-flight response, trust me," he said quietly. "And if you want to leave right now, we leave. Your decision, always."

"I'm not scared. I was just thinking a burger and curly fries sounds really good about now, that's all."

He smiled. "Trust me, your grandma's five-cheese lasagna is way better than my burgers."

She wasn't blinking, maybe not even breathing, and he tilted her chin up. "I'm serious about it being okay to leave. If you're not okay with this, if you'd rather be anywhere else, we go right now, no questions asked."

Her eyes slid to the right and he knew she was looking at his mom. "She smells like vanilla," she whispered. "And maybe cinnamon."

"I know. I think she does that on purpose to make herself irresistible."

His mom's hand smacked him lightly on the back of his head, and he laughed. "Honestly, Kit Kat, she's the best. In the most terrifying way possible."

"He just forfeited his dessert to you," his mom said to Ivy. "And hi, I'm your grandma. I couldn't be happier to meet you. But, honey, he's right. It's okay if you're not ready. I can be a lot."

Ivy pulled back from Bodie and looked at her in surprise. "So can I."

His mom smiled, her eyes shimmering brilliantly. "Then we're made for each other. Now let me get a look at you." She took Ivy's hands and spread them out. "Oh my goodness, you're so beautiful. And you've got the Campbell eyes. You know we can bat them at anyone and bend them to our will, right?"

"*Mom*," Bodie said.

His mom smiled and ignored him, speaking directly to Ivy. "It's mostly on the female side. You're welcome." Her eyes went even more shiny. "Thanks so much for coming. I know it wasn't easy. Can I hug you?" She looked at Bodie. "Did you tell her I'm a hugger?"

"I think she's getting that, Mom."

"Is it okay?" she asked Ivy.

Ivy nodded and was immediately swallowed up by his mom's arms. She looked at Bodie over her shoulder, eyes still a little wide, and he smiled reassuringly. "You okay? Is she squeezing too hard? Sometimes she does that. She swears it's an accident. Blink twice if you need a rescue."

Ivy laughed, and though it sounded rusty, the sound was music to Bodie's ears and warmed his heart.

Three-year-old Ian tugged on Ivy's hand and pointed to the backyard visible through the house and out the sliding glass doors, and the huge swing set there. "Swing!" he yelled. "*Pweaze?*"

At his side, two-year-old Max nodded hopefully.

Five minutes later, Bodie watched out the window as Ivy played with her three cousins. She was pushing Ian and Xander on the swings and laughing, looking so open and happy it hit him right in the feels. Max was on her hip, his little arms wrapped around her neck. There was a strong physical resemblance between them, but the real reason he couldn't tear his eyes away was because despite the age gap, they clearly had a built-in bond. Ivy hadn't had that. He could only imagine what her life so far had been like, and it made him sick. And damn. He was either getting old or turning into a sap, because it put a lump of heart in his throat.

His mom came up beside him. He expected her to give him grief about taking his sweet time about bringing Ivy here, or maybe something about the fact he hadn't even known he had a daughter. But she didn't. In fact, she didn't speak at all, so he turned his head and looked at her.

"Thank you," she whispered, voice teary.

"For bringing Ivy? Of course."

"For bringing *you*."

"Mom." He hugged her. "I've been back for *months*."

"But today . . ." She cupped his face. "Today is the first day I've had all of you."

Growing up, dinner had been a family affair, attendance required, even if it was on the stands at the baseball or soccer fields, or at the bar because his dad was working. It'd driven him crazy, always having to eat together, but it'd been a staple in his life.

He hadn't appreciated it until he'd been on the other side of the country from his entire family. Yeah, it'd been his choice, and he didn't have regrets, but he also hadn't realized how much he could miss something until it was gone.

And now he had it back again.

His mom went into the kitchen. "Tell everyone five minutes."

Bodie headed to the den, where he heard Zeke's voice say, "Tell me you'll wear it again tonight."

"If you do the bedtime with the heathens," Serena answered.

"Are we making a deal?" Zeke asked.

"Maybe," she said. "We could review the taboo list and see if anything's negotiable."

Zeke laughed. "Baby, we wiped out your taboo list a long time ago."

"Oh yeah." Serena laughed too. "Damn that bottle of whiskey . . ."

Bodie grimaced and entered the kitchen. "TMI."

Zeke grinned. "Jealous?"

"I need brain bleach. Do either of you have any brain bleach?"

A few minutes later, they all gathered in the dining room. When they were seated, as always everyone started talking over everyone. It was loud, boisterous, and messy. He looked at Ivy, who was watching them all like maybe she was at the circus, which basically, she was. "Don't worry, you get used to them."

She laughed, and he decided that it was the best sound he'd ever heard.

His brothers were going on about skiing this coming year and which resorts they planned to get passes from. "Do you know how to ski?" he asked Ivy.

"No."

The table went silent in shock. They'd been skiing since they could stand on two feet. As early as kindergarten, it'd been a part of their PE in school. Zeke often taught skiing to the under-ten set on the weekends, which he loved to do because he could bring his kids. Mace and Bodie had been on the local ski team their entire childhoods, and even now Mace sometimes hired on as ski patrol.

"This must be fixed ASAP," Mace said.

"One hundred percent," Zeke agreed.

"Only if she wants," Bodie said, not even sure she'd come back this winter, and not wanting to push.

"I want," Ivy said.

Zeke high-fived her. "One of the first times Bodie skied, he broke his arm."

"Because I was seven and you pushed me off Dead Man's Bluff," Bodie said. "A diamond run, which means expert," he explained to Ivy. To the room he said, "*I'll* teach Ivy to ski."

"Who taught you?" Ivy asked.

"My dad."

"*Keep your knees bent!*" Zeke said in an imitation of the man they'd all lost.

"Lean into the turns," Bodie said in that same voice. "What are you slowing down for, boy?"

Mace laughed. "Stop dragging your poles like they're a set of brakes! You guys are a bunch of girls. No, scratch that, girls are awesome skiers, you're giving them a bad name!"

"He did not say that," his mom said, laughing in spite of herself.

"Oh yes he did," Bodie said.

"Was he scary?" Ivy asked.

"As a puppy," Bodie's mom said. "He was all bark and no bite. Oh, how he would've loved you, honey. I hate that you're missing out on knowing him."

"But you can still see him." Zeke pulled out his phone, accessed Google Earth, and brought up his mom's house. He zoomed in as far as he could go and showed Ivy the man on his knees in front of a flower bed out front. "He died six months ago, but on Google Earth he's still gardening."

"Which he loved," his mom said softly.

"Hey," Mace said to Zeke. "Remember that time Bodie's back pocket got caught on the lift as he was getting off and it dangled him above all of us for like half an hour before they could get him down? By the seat of his pants? Oh, and his boxers had Disney princesses on them?"

"Hey, I was ten, and that's what Mom had bought me," Bodie said in his defense.

"They were from Walmart," his mom said proudly. "They were on sale."

Ivy was shaking from mirth, a few tears streaming down her face, and Bodie smiled down at her. "You find this amusing?"

"So much." She grinned at him. *Grinned.* He felt like he'd just won the lottery. "Your brothers are so cool."

"True story," Mace said, unabashedly eavesdropping. "Just make sure it's me who teaches you to ski. Your dad sucks at it."

"*I'm* the one who taught *you*," Bodie said.

"Which is why I *used* to ski into trees."

Zeke laughed. "Save yourself some trouble, Ivy. *I'll* teach you to ski. The right way."

"Uh-huh," Serena said dryly. "What about that time you hit a tree because you wouldn't wear your glasses, saying they kept fogging up?"

"Hey, a guy hits a tree one time . . ."

"Skiing's expensive, right?" Ivy asked, a worry frown between her eyes.

"We get a locals discount, and Zeke's buddy has a ski shop where we get gear cheap," Bodie said. "So not as much as you'd think. Don't worry about it." Besides, he'd go broke giving her the moon, he didn't care.

Mace told everyone a story about something that had happened on his job the week before, when he'd been dealing with a plumbing issue—aka an exploding toilet. Zeke one-upped him with one of his short-term renters, who'd let himself into the wrong condo, because too many people left their keys under the front mat, and slept there for two nights before he realized he was in the wrong place—only figuring it out when a large family flipped on his bedroom light one morning, yelling, "Happy birthday, Stan!" taking years off his life.

Ivy was still grinning when she turned to Bodie. "Does anything interesting ever happen at your work?"

"Other than the occasional drunken karaoke night, not really."

Ivy looked a little disappointed, and Mace opened his big fat mouth and said, "Your dad has two jobs, and the other one is the coolest job ever. He's an ATF agent."

"Was," his mom said. "He was an ATF agent. He retired."

Zeke and Bodie both glared at Mace.

"Right," he said, pushing away his wineglass. "Don't talk when you've had alcohol. Ever."

His mom was ashen, her eyes on Bodie's face. "You're not retired?"

"Mom," Zeke said gently, "he's not even thirty-five. It's unrealistic to think he's not going to go back—"

"I'm not." Bodie looked at his mom. "I'm not going back." He then looked at his brothers. "I didn't know how to tell you before. But they released me. Too injured to be effective in the field, and I can't ride a desk."

"Oh, honey." His mom's eyes were fierce. "That just means they're too stupid to know what they've lost."

His brothers nodded.

Ivy was looking at him like he'd hung the sun and the moon in one try. And suddenly he couldn't remember why he'd tried to hide the fact that he was done working a crazy-dangerous job that no longer suited his lifestyle anyway. Not with a daughter. Still, the silence was awkward, at least for him.

Until Mace looked at Ivy. "One time, your dad took down a ring of illegal arms dealers."

Zeke nodded. "And then there was the time he had to hide in a freezer while undercover. He got frostbite on his as—er, behind area."

His mom gasped. "On top of the four bullet holes?"

Ivy's eyes were huge—and impressed—as she looked at Bodie.

"He also still can't fully bend the pinkie finger on his left hand," Zeke said.

"So much for 'these stories stay in the vault,'" Bodie said dryly, but also wanting to hug his family for making this easy for him.

Mace just grinned. "He means the night we plied him with alcohol to tell us why he was so surly and grumpy all the time." He looked at Bodie. "Promises made with alcohol don't count, man."

"Okay, got it," Bodie said, and turned to his mom. "Remember when the vase from your great-grandma vanished? You might want to ask your youngest what happened to it."

Mace choked on a piece of bread and glared at Bodie. "*Wow.*"

Zeke was laughing his fool-ass head off, so Bodie smiled evilly. "And, Mom, Zeke's got a story to tell you about the time the hot tub turned green."

Zeke stopped laughing. "Man, why you gotta be like that?"

Ivy DIDN'T KNOW what she'd expected out of dinner, but it hadn't been to have her cheeks hurt from smiling so much.

"Do you do family dinners back home?" Bodie's mom—*her grandma!*—asked.

"No." Ivy almost laughed at the thought. Her mom didn't cook, much less even *like* dinner. She always said dinner made her fat. "There'd probably be warfare."

Bodie's mom chuckled. "Honey, I raised four boys, I've seen my share of warfare, believe me. And destruction too. One time, the boys decided to sneak into my kitchen at midnight and make brownies. They thought the microwave would be faster. My brand-new microwave. The brownies exploded. I thought we were in the middle of a home invasion."

"Hey, we cleaned it all up," Mace said.

She snorted. "The next day. You were all too . . . 'baked' in the moment."

Zeke choked on his iced tea. "Mom, do you even know what that means?"

"I grew up in the sixties, of course I know what it means. And if I didn't, the fact that you guys ate me out of house and home that night would've clued me in."

Ivy laughed.

His mom smiled at the sound. "Did I mention they thought they were invisible? They kept asking each other in a hushed whisper, 'How is she seeing us?'"

"*Mom*," Bodie said, sounding pained. "You're talking to my teenage daughter."

"About you and your brothers being stupid, yes I am. Maybe she can learn from your stupidity." Her smile faded, her eyes remained warm and caring on Ivy. "For Mace's twin brother, Austin, that sort of harmless play turned out to be a gateway to bigger and far worse things. They played into his demons and changed the course of his life."

"I'm so sorry," Ivy said, meaning it from the bottom of her heart. She hated that Bodie, that all of them, had lost someone they loved so very much.

Bodie's mom gently cupped her face, and even though her eyes were a little wet, she gave a very small smile. "Don't ever be sorry for things that aren't your fault." She hugged her tight, then pulled back. "Does your mom have other children?"

"*Mom*," Bodie said.

"Sorry, honey. It's just that I want to play catch-up more than I want my next breath. I'm told I can be a little pushy."

Bodie held up his hands about three feet apart from each other. Her other sons laughed.

Ivy usually ignored pushy entirely, but she didn't want to ignore her dad's mom. "It's okay, Mrs. Campbell—"

She broke off when the woman's eyebrows vanished into her

pretty white flowing hair. "Mrs. Campbell was my mother-in-law's name, God bless her soul. I'm Mom or Grandma to everyone in this room, you included."

"You could go with Grandma *Nosy*," Bodie suggested.

Everyone snorted. Even his mom, who also threw her napkin at Bodie and hit him smack in the face. Ivy sucked in a breath, but Bodie just pulled the napkin away and rolled his eyes.

"He used to roll those eyes of his so hard I was sure he could see his own brain," his mom said. She stood and grabbed some dishes to clear the table.

Bodie tugged affectionately on Ivy's hair. "Kit Kat?"

"Yeah?"

"I'm so glad you're here."

Something deep inside her tightened in the very best of ways. "Me too," she admitted. "It's been the best day of my life." A little embarrassed that those words had escaped, she stood to help her grandma clear the table.

She heard Bodie speak just as she'd left the room.

"If anyone needs me, I'll be out buying her a pony," he said.

Ivy realized everyone was following her, helping to clear. They all ended up in the kitchen, where Bodie's mom was piling cinnamon rolls on a plate. Harper's grandma's cinnamon rolls, to be exact. Bodie stole one, took a bite, then looked at his mom in surprise. "Mom, where did you get these?"

"In town."

He narrowed his eyes. "In town where?"

"Sugar Pine Bakery."

Oh boy. Ivy almost laughed at the look on Bodie's face.

His mom met his gaze straight on, brows raised high in a dare. "Why?"

"You know why," he said. "What did you do?"

"Just introduced myself to the woman my son's seeing." She gave him a look of pure attitude. "Which *you* should've done yourself."

Zeke, Mace, and Shay were laughing so hard, they were no longer making any sound. Ivy was watching with utter fascination. She couldn't believe that everyone let this tiny old woman boss them around, but then again, they clearly loved and adored her. Hell, Ivy already did, in spite of herself.

"Harper is a lovely woman, by the way," his mom said. "So kind. Courageous too, starting over so far from home. She's intent on making a good life for herself. You know I love me a sweet, courageous, smart woman. Zeke got lucky to land his."

Serena blew her a kiss.

"And sure, Mace somehow messed up with Shay, but he's at least smart enough to know she's his better half," their mom said.

Shay also blew her a kiss.

"But you," Bodie's mom said to him. "You need to let go of the past so you can move on and accept love."

"He's working on it, Mom," Mace said.

"He really is trying," Zeke said. "It's not his fault he's all fucked up in the head—er . . ." He eyed the children. "I mean, messed up over what happened."

Once again, Ivy felt herself surprised. Bodie's brothers gave him some serious shit, like *all* the time, but they also always jumped to defend him. She'd loved to have siblings even half as great.

Her grandma pointed at Zeke. "Let me remind you that you're never too old to have your mouth washed out with soap for swearing." She softened. "But you're both right." They all looked at Bodie. "I believe he's trying too, and . . ." Her voice cracked, and her eyes welled up. "I'm so relieved. For a while there, we thought we were going to lose you, for something that wasn't your fault."

Even Ivy's heart, which was usually a cold lump in her chest, squeezed hard.

Bodie just drew a slow, deep breath. "Mom, we all know that what happened to Dad was directly related to my job, which means it *is* my fault."

His mom came over and cupped his face, though it sounded a little bit like a two-handed slap. "You listen to me." Her head didn't even come quite up to his shoulders. "You were gone a long time—"

"I know," he said, covering her hands with his. "I—"

"Shh. You weren't all that great at keeping in touch, so let me tell you what I've never told any of you before. Your dad had a heart condition."

Bodie froze. So did his brothers. "What?"

"For several years before he died. He didn't want me to tell any of you. He didn't want the fuss."

"Jesus, Mom," Zeke said. "Why didn't you at least tell us after he died?"

"He made me promise I'd never tell you." She tossed up her hands. "You all know how he was. Stubborn as a fool, and as hardheaded as . . . well, as each of you." She'd kept her gaze on Bodie's. "But that secret is no longer serving him, and it certainly isn't serving any of you, so I'm telling you now. So yes, he had a fatal heart attack when he heard what happened to you, but, honey, it was *not* your fault."

Bodie opened his mouth, but she shook her head. "It *wasn't*," she said fiercely.

All of them looked . . . well, stunned, as well as highly emotional, and Ivy stirred, feeling like she was eavesdropping. "I should go—"

"No, Kit Kat, you're all right." Bodie turned to her, reaching out a hand to pull her to his side. "You remember how I told you family should always be there for you?"

"Yes," she said, hearing her voice sound thin and unsure.

His mom smiled and reached out to squeeze her hand. "*Always*," she said. "Even when it's hard."

"If you want to talk about me," Ivy said, "just tell me and I'll give you your privacy."

"Never worry about that," Mace said. "We talk about each other right to each other's faces."

"As for your grandpa," her grandma said, "we keep him alive in our hearts. Come. I'll show you some photo albums, so you can do the same. You've got his eyes. And I think, probably, his ability to out-stubborn even me."

Ivy smiled. "My mom says I was born stubborn."

Everyone started to file out of the kitchen, but Bodie caught Ivy's hand, holding her back, bending a little to look into her eyes. "Hey," he said softly. "You okay?"

She nodded.

He gave her a "come on, let's hear it" gesture.

Her smile faded, and she picked at a nonexistent piece of lint on her jeans. "You know how you asked me to stay with you?"

"Yes." His smile faded too, probably because her voice was suddenly shaking with nerves. "It's okay, Kit Kat, whatever you've decided, it's okay."

"I'd like to." She looked up. "Stay with you."

His serious expression lightened. "Yeah?"

"Yeah. Well, not tonight, because I promised your mom—" She stopped. Flashed a grin. "I mean my grandma, that I'd spend the night with the cousins. But maybe we could start tomorrow night."

"I'd love that," he said, and somehow she knew he meant it.

"You don't think Harper will mind?" she asked worriedly. "I really like staying with her, but I also feel bad because she's done so much for me. Even after all she's been through. I hate that her dad ignores her and her ex took all their friends."

"I hate that too," he said. "But she has us now, and Shay and Abuela, and my brothers. The way she took care of you? We'll all take care of her. That's how this works."

Since that had her a little choked up, she just nodded, and he gave her a small smile. "I'm so glad you came tonight."

Shockingly enough, so was she. She couldn't remember ever being so relaxed and . . . happy. Usually, she managed to sabotage any happy that came her way, but this time she'd managed to keep it. It felt like Christmas in August. Well, not her usual Christmas, those were usually crap. More like the Christmases she saw on TV. And she wanted to never let it go.

CHAPTER 19

Someone knocked on Harper's upstairs apartment door, which, seeing as she knew exactly six people in town, almost never happened, especially late at night. She stilled in surprise, mouth full of the ice cream she was eating right out of the container. It'd been a long day, and she'd been very busy mentally processing the call she'd had earlier from Ivy, asking if it was okay if she moved in with Bodie.

She'd of course assured Ivy it was more than okay, it was *wonderful*. And it was. Really. She was going to miss her terribly, but that was the selfish part of her talking, and she was trying hard to ignore it.

She was also trying hard to ignore her feelings for Ivy's dad, but that was even harder. He made her laugh, he made her bones melt, but more than anything, he made her yearn for things she'd decided weren't for her.

When a second knock came, she looked at herself in oversize

pj's, covered in Ham fur, two messy space buns on the top of her head, no makeup, and Yoda slippers on her feet.

Setting aside the ice cream, she moved to the door, peering through the peephole.

Bodie, looking hot as ever in faded jeans and a dark blue long-sleeved lightweight—clingy!—workout shirt shoved up to his elbows.

"I thought you were at your mom's tonight," she said through the wood.

"I was. And now I'm here."

She closed her eyes and listened to her brain and body yell at each other.

Open the door . . .

Do not open the door . . .

"Where's Ivy? Is she okay?" she asked.

"She's good and spending the night with her little cousins at my mom's. We really going to hold this conversation with me standing out here and you in there?"

He sounded amused, but there was also something else in his voice. Affection, plus a good amount of sexiness. And if she hadn't looked like a walking advertisement for birth control, he might've made her feel sexy too. "So everything went okay?"

"It went great. Harper?"

"Yeah?"

"I want to see you."

Since the truth was that she wanted to see him too, she opened the door.

He took his time looking her over and smiled. "Cute."

"The space buns?"

"The face mask."

Oh dear God, she'd forgotten about the face mask, the one that had promised to take five years off her life. "Two minutes!" She ran like hell to her bedroom. Since it was all of fifteen steps, it was overkill, but *face mask*! She'd swiped it off and stripped out of her pj's and was in nothing but bikini undies searching for clean clothes when a throat cleared from the doorway.

With a squeak, she whipped around just as Bodie stepped into her bedroom, taking her hands in his and looking into her eyes. "This is my favorite look on you." Then he pulled off his shirt and dropped it over her head. This was a good deal for her because it held his body heat and smelled like him, which was to say delicious.

"I've spent the past six hours thinking about you naked," he said.

She had to laugh. "But thanks to you, I'm no longer naked," she said, voice husky.

"Maybe we'll work on that."

She drew a deep breath, because the truth was, she wanted that way too much, but it was getting harder to keep her heart safe with him.

He was looking at her, quietly assessing, probably trying to figure out where her head was at. Good luck to him, because even *she* didn't know where her head was at. "I'm not . . . easy, Bodie."

That got her a grin. "You are not."

She rolled her eyes.

He studied her face. "You're trying to tell me something."

"Yes." She drew a deep breath. "I'm impulsive and stubborn, and don't like to be told what to do. I've got zero patience. And I have trouble asking for help, even when I know I need it."

He took this in and nodded. "I like and respect your stubborn streak. I'm not impulsive, but I admire you being so. Maybe you can teach me. And I've got lots of patience. The rest is just details, but I can promise I'll never tell you what to do or make demands. I just want you, Harper. As is."

She was marveling over that when he spoke again. "It's not like I'm a cakewalk."

She laughed, and his brows went up. "So you've noticed," he said, and she couldn't help herself, she went up on tiptoes and kissed him until she heard herself moan. "Bodie?"

"Yeah?"

"Remember when I said I'd tell you when I was getting there?"

"I do."

"Well, I'm getting there." An understatement. Like it or not, he'd charmed his way right past her walls and into her heart. She reached for the button on his jeans. "You've got some catching up to do."

He kicked off his shoes and stripped down to nothing in seconds. Just like he did everything, he moved with economical grace, and she had to check for drool. Then he was on the bed with her, and . . . leaning back against her headboard, pulling her into his side.

"What are we doing?" she asked.

"You've yawned three times." He smiled. "You look done in. Go to sleep, babe."

"I'm fine."

"Okay," he murmured softly, running a big, warm hand up and down her back.

She yawned again. "I'm not going to sleep."

"Okay," he said again, and that was the last thing she remembered.

SHE WOKE UP wrapped in warmth and hard muscles. With a start, she opened her eyes and looked up into Bodie's.

"Morning," he said in a sexy, morning-gruff voice.

She'd slept the rest of the night without so much as stirring. She stared at him in marvel.

He smiled, but when he shifted, he winced like his shoulder was bothering him. She sat up and made him do the same, squeezing between him and her headboard.

"What are you—" His question was lost in his heartfelt groan when she began massaging his tight muscles. She worked them for long moments, wrenching another groan from him when those muscles finally gave into her pressure and relaxed a little.

"Please tell me I ordered the happy ending," he murmured, eyes closed, a small smile on his face.

She laughed. "If you're a very good boy."

He snorted, then pulled her around to his lap like she weighed nothing. His eyes were serious as he cupped her face. "Last night you told me what you think your faults are. It's my turn to do the same."

"What I *think* my faults are?" she repeated.

He smiled. "Yeah, because to me, the things you mentioned are all in the pro column."

"Okay, Mr. Smart-ass, what do you think my *real* faults are then?"

"You don't trust your instincts, even when they're spot-on. And you don't believe in yourself."

"Hey, I believe in myself plenty," she said. "I moved here, didn't I? Opened a bakery—" She broke off at that. Okay, yes, she'd begun baking and selling what she made, but she'd only had a soft opening, and really all she'd done was unlock her door. She still didn't have a sign up. She'd done zero advertising, hadn't connected with local caterers and restaurants, and she hadn't yet set up the front room for people to come in, browse, sit, and enjoy so they'd spread the word.

And she didn't even really know why.

Did she want to . . . not succeed?

He was watching her think and she sighed. "Fine. I could do better in those two regards." She shook her head at him. "All right, show-off, what are *your* faults—besides being a cocky know-it-all?" *And being exceptional in bed . . .*

His smile turned decidedly naughty, and she knew he'd read her mind. But then he let his smile fade away. "I'm closed off. Unwilling to engage with my emotions, or even acknowledge I have them."

"Those aren't faults," she protested. "They're a way of life."

He just looked at her.

"I'm serious."

"I know." His voice was low. Still sexy, but no longer amused. He was taking this seriously. He was taking her seriously. "I like to make jokes to avoid hard conversations. I also tend to not call or follow up, telling myself that my life doesn't lend itself to relationships. But that was before."

"Before what?" she asked.

"Before coming home and realizing that my job no longer puts me in constant danger, so my reasoning no longer exists." He paused. Held her gaze. "It was also before meeting you."

Her breath caught. Her heart caught. Hell, everything caught. "Bodie, I'm . . ." She paused. "I'm pretty sure I'm broken. At least in regards to relationships."

"Ours would be different."

She nearly swallowed her tongue, at both the words and his certainty. "You think we're in a relationship?"

"Yes." No hesitation.

She concentrated on breathing for a moment. "I'm not so good at them. And I'm even worse at losing them."

"I'm not going anywhere."

She shook her head, feeling a little panicky. "No one can promise that."

"Okay." He hugged her, running a hand up and down her back. "At your pace, Harper. Always."

His hair was more tousled than normal, and his jaw was dark with a couple of days beyond a five-o'clock shadow. He was desirable and fun, and far more trouble than she needed. Even knowing that, she wrapped him up tight in her arms. "Are you even real?"

"What else would I be?"

"A dream. A figment of my imagination."

He laughed as he rolled her beneath him. "Do I feel like a figment of your imagination?"

No. He felt like the best thing to ever happen to her . . .

"Any more questions?" he asked, his mouth busy at her throat, yanking a needy little whimper from her. "Good," he murmured. "Now shh, I'm about to have my breakfast . . ."

BODIE WOKE UP and reached out for Harper, but he was alone in her bed. He lifted his head and realized that he'd fallen back asleep. Then he realized what had woken him: the delicious scent of bacon and something cinnamony.

He looked at the clock. *Eight.* He'd slept for far longer than he intended to. He'd promised to pick up Ivy by ten to do something that until now no woman had ever gotten him to do: go shopping. Which, if he'd had a list of things he tried to never do, would be second on the list, right after being tortured. With a groan, he got out of bed and pulled on his jeans and checked his phone. He had a text from Ivy.

Bring Harper.

Since this was a full 180 from yesterday, he texted her back: you sure?

Her response came immediately: I was scared yesterday and took it out on her, and that wasn't cool.

He typed back: scared of what?

Her answer made him smile: Everything. I got over myself. Did you know your mom is pretty awesome?

He did know, and he'd never been more thankful. He located his shirt on the floor next to the scrap of black lace masquerading as Harper's panties. His phone buzzed again, a call this time. It was Harper.

"You alive, old man?"

He laughed. "Come back up here and let me prove that *nothing* about me is old."

"Got stuff in the oven. Can I bring you up anything?"

"Yeah, that sound you made when I—"

She laughed. "Okay, that's the last time I call on speaker. And anyway, I need assistance to produce that sound."

"Come back up here."

"You're dangerous." She laughed a little breathlessly. "I just turned off my oven and am heading up—"

He heard the knock on the back door through the phone and groaned. "Don't answer it."

"It's Shay," Harper whispered. "And Abuela. They're staring at me through the window."

"Shay's a bear in the mornings. Even Mace won't deal with her before ten a.m. Just toss her out a cinnamon roll."

"I'm hanging up now. You should probably stay upstairs so she doesn't see you and ask you questions you don't want to answer."

"What do you mean?"

"She told you I was a bad idea, remember?"

"Trust me, she was protecting you, not me. I'm the bad bet. Everyone knows that."

She paused. "*I* don't— Oh, shit, I gotta go." She disconnected.

He stared down at his phone as from downstairs he heard the back door open and Shay's voice. "I can smell the rolls from the bookstore. We want you to know we hate you because we've gained five pounds since you moved in. Is whatever you're cooking done yet? We need some."

"*Please*," Abuela said sternly. "You forgot the *please*."

"*Please* makes my jeans too tight."

"No, that's your lack of discipline and exercise," Abuela said. "Now Harper, she doesn't need exercise. At least not today. She got her exercise all night long."

Harper made a choking sound. "I don't know what you mean."

"It's your smile," Abuela said.

Shay sighed. "I wouldn't mind getting exercise all night long."

"Then you need to learn to argue better," her grandma said. "If you listened more and compromised even a little, you could put this whole mess with Mace behind you."

"Sugar," Shay demanded, presumably to Harper. "Quick. I need the shot of happy."

"You told me just the other day to *never* sell you anything ever again. You said you'd lifted up your shirt to check out your abs and donut crumbs fell out, and that you hated me."

"It's more of a hate-to-love-you sort of thing," Shay said. "Now hand over some goods." Shay paused. "*Please*."

"Consider me undone," Harper said dryly.

Bodie snorted and sat down on the bed to pull on his shoes. By the time he was done, all was quiet downstairs. As he got to the kitchen doorway, Harper's phone went off again.

She smiled at him, holding up a finger as she grabbed her phone. "Dad? Everything okay?" She listened for a minute, then turned her back on Bodie and said, "I've been gone a month, are you seriously just now noticing?" Another pause. "This is the first I've heard from you either. It goes both ways." The next pause was longer. "I'm sorry Michelle left you for her dentist, but didn't she leave her first husband for you? . . . No, I'm not trying to be sassy, Dad, I'm trying to—" She broke off and looked down at her phone. "Guess we were done." She shoved her phone back into her pocket and kept her back to Bodie. There was a tension in her shoulders that hadn't been there before, and he hated that for her. He and his dad had been incredibly close, and their relationship had meant everything to him. But then again, his dad hadn't treated him as Harper's dad had her. Well, okay, maybe a few times when Bodie had been a complete punkass dick . . . But never as a matter of course. "You okay?"

When she turned to face him, she had on a smile that didn't quite make it to her eyes. "Sure."

"Hey, you don't have to be." He pulled her into him. She pressed her face into his chest, and he nuzzled her hair, kissing her just above the ear.

"What do you do when you're not okay?" she asked quietly.

Nothing good. He looked away, not wanting to go there.

She lifted her face to his. Then gave a sweet but real smile. "Why don't you just tell me it's none of my business?" she said, nudging him with her shoulder.

"Because I want to be your business." Shaking his head, he relaxed. "I keep trying to take it slow, to ease back until you feel comfortable, but every time I get around you, I forget my good intentions." He paused. "What do I do when I'm not okay? Used to be, I'd pick a fight with one of my brothers and we'd go a few rounds. When I was ATF, the bad guys took my wrath. After I came back to Sunrise Cove . . ." He shrugged. "I guess I went back to picking fights with my brothers. It's kinda what we do." He smiled. "But this past month? I've been okay. Very okay."

She held his gaze. "Me too. I'm not used to it, but I'm working on it."

That made him smile.

"You probably already know this," she said, "but you in just those low-slung jeans and no shirt . . . I want to lick you like a lollipop."

He burst out laughing. He'd been half in love with her since that very first night in the surprise snowstorm, when popcorn had fallen out of her shirt. Her bravado hadn't quite masked her innate sweetness, a fascinating contrast. There hadn't been much sweet in his life then, and certainly no one who'd asked so little of him and rewarded him so well for what he'd given her.

Still, he'd originally had plans to maintain his emotional distance, but here he was orbiting Planet Harper, drawn in more each day by her gravitational pull. He was pretty sure he would burn up on entry, but it'd be worth it.

He gave himself a moment to imagine romancing her the way he wanted to: a fun adventure on Tahoe maybe, then a leisurely dinner, champagne by candlelight, holding her close on a dance floor, slow, lingering kisses. He wanted to give her everything that she had no idea she'd been missing. "Will you go shopping with me and Ivy today? She asked me to bring you, said she felt bad about yesterday."

She cocked her head. "Why do you sound so serious?"

"Shopping."

She laughed. "Not a fan then?"

"No."

"I could take her for you."

"I wish I could let you." And he really, *really* did. "But my daughter's asked something of me and I'm not going to turn her down."

She brushed a kiss over his lips. "You pretend you're tough, but you're really a big, old, sweet softie."

"I'm going to make you take that back later."

CHAPTER 20

Ivy followed Bodie and Harper into one of those staggeringly massive home goods stores. She'd never been inside one before. It reminded her of a flea market, but probably no one here was wondering whether someone's grannie had died in one of the chairs. The entire place was filled to the brim with things she'd never once given a thought to: useless decorative baskets, pig-shaped barbecue grills . . . sparkly lion statues. Like, what did one do with a sparkly lion statue that resembled a mirror-ball Mufasa?

There was wall art that said stuff like INHALE. *Who needs a reminder to inhale?*

Harper came up to her side. "I'd be more likely to buy one that said *Life is short, lick the spoon.*"

Ivy wanted to laugh but couldn't. "I'm so sorry about yesterday."

Harper hugged her. Right there in the store. "Honey, you

already said that in the car. And I said it's okay because I understand. I assumed you meant the apology, so please assume I meant it when I said I understand."

"So . . . we're okay?"

"Always," Harper said.

Ivy hugged her back, so grateful for this woman's easy forgiveness, which meant everything.

They found Bodie in the bedding section, eyeing the endless aisle filled with every possible different pattern of bedding under the sun. "Let's do this. Pick out whichever stuff you want for your bedroom."

"Oh," Ivy said. An involuntary exclamation. "But . . . it's your room, your house. You should pick out what you like."

"Nope, the room is now officially yours. Which means narrowing it down to something from all this is yours too."

"I couldn't."

He put a hand on her shoulder. "Kit Kat, if you like me, even a little, you'll spare me the migraine that choosing would cost me." He smiled at her to let her know he was kidding. Sort of. "It's important to me that you love it."

That meant a lot, but she wasn't stupid. At some point, likely sooner rather than later, she'd have to leave. Which was another reminder—if she didn't manage to ruin all this somehow, her mom certainly would. She was on borrowed time. She probably should've stuck to her original plan to take what she could from Bodie and be gone by the time her mom surfaced. It wasn't too late. She could still go. Should still go . . . But she couldn't stick to her plan to steal from him. She just couldn't do it. Just the thought made her feel sick, and she pressed a hand to her belly as a text from James came through.

We're going to a party tonight, you in?

She'd like to be, but she and Bodie had made plans to get pizza and set up her room, and she didn't want to blow him off on night one. Not when she had no idea how many nights she had left. So she reluctantly texted: Can't tonight, sorry.

She and Harper wandered up and down the aisle with Bodie waiting with a calm patience. But she'd quickly fallen in love with a thick, pillowy soft blue comforter set. What held her back was the price tag, which made her choke.

Bodie was looking at her. "So? Lay it on me."

She froze. Lay what on him? That she'd come here to steal from him? Or that she'd never planned on staying and getting to know him and her entire family, the one she already loved more than she'd ever loved anything? "What?"

"The bedding. What's it going to be?"

Relief nearly made her drop to the floor, but she pointed to one of the cheapest bed sets on the shelves—a perfectly functional multicolored set—so she wouldn't feel bad when this fantasy was over.

Bodie looked at Harper, then back to Ivy. "You sure?"

"Yep."

Bodie walked her back to the one she *really* wanted. "Not this one?"

"No, I'm sure," she said as casually as she could, startled that he could read her so well.

"Hey," he said softly, turning her to face him. "I want you to be happy in your room, with something special you've chosen. That one . . ." He pointed down the aisle to the cheaper one. "Says 'guest room.' But this one . . ." He picked up hers, which was twice the price. "This one seems like you. There'd be no mistaking which room is yours with this one."

Her heart was beating hard and heavy in her throat. "I just don't want you to spend so much money when we don't know how long I get to be here."

He held her gaze and gave a slow nod. "I hear you. But honestly, that changes nothing for me."

"I don't know what that means."

He pulled her into him by hooking an arm around her neck. "It means, Kit Kat, that whatever happens, I want you to know you have a room here, that you'll always have a room here."

She honestly had no idea what to make of this, other than it made her want to cry and she *hated* crying. Almost as much as she hated lying. Too bad she was good at lying and horrible at crying. She'd rarely, if ever, gotten her own room, and dammit, she wanted to remember every single moment of this before it ended. Because it would end. Good things did. "Always?"

"Always."

"Even if I'm back in Chicago?" Which, if she had her way, would be never . . .

"Even then," he said.

"Even when I go off to college?" A pipe dream, of course . . .

"Even then."

"Even when—"

"Let me save you some trouble," he said. "Always means always. Like forever. And ever." He picked up the coveted soft, cushy blue comforter set and dropped it into the cart.

"But—"

"Just say 'Thanks, Dad.'"

Whoa. She'd never called him Dad before, and that she wanted to surprised her. But she couldn't do this, not to him, and not to Harper. Not when she knew she had one foot out the door. "Thank you. Really, thank you. I'm just going to go . . ." *Freak out.* She just couldn't handle knowing she would eventually disappoint them both, the two people she'd come to love. ". . . check out some bathroom stuff," she managed, and her dad smiled at her.

Harper did too, and Ivy impulsively hugged her and held on tight. Harper made a soft sound of affection and squeezed her back. "Thanks, I needed that."

So had Ivy. Still way too close to a panic attack, she turned the corner to where they could no longer see her and drew in a few gulps of air. She knew they'd planned pizza and that she hadn't wanted to blow Bodie off, but she needed a moment. Maybe more than a moment. Hating herself, she pulled out her phone to text James.

I got free. Can you pick me up?

She went back to Bodie and Harper, who were now standing in front of the kitchen stuff. Harper was drooling over some sort of bakeware and telling Bodie a story about how she'd been coveting the set for years and how the minute she was in the black, it was hers.

"Hi," Ivy said. "So some friends want to pick me up to go hang out."

"Jessie and James?" Harper asked.

"Yes. If that's okay." She looked at Bodie. She could tell he wanted to ask her a bunch of questions, and she tensed for that.

"You'll be careful," he said. A statement, not a question, so she nodded, and then he nodded. "Call me for a ride home if you need one."

"Will do."

She made her way to the front of the store and outside. A few minutes later, James and Jessie drove up. James smiled, but it was short his usual wattage. Jessie didn't even try to smile, and Ivy was pretty sure she'd been crying.

"What's wrong?" Ivy asked as she put on her seat belt.

"We've got a problem." James drove them out of the lot and onto the main road that skirted the lake.

"Problem?"

James looked over at Jessie, who swallowed hard. "I wanted a laptop," she said quietly. "So I could do online college classes. I found a local woman who was selling her old one, and I bought it. With the money we'd been saving to get a place."

James didn't say anything, but he didn't have to. He looked . . . resigned. "I just wish you would've told me. I might've been able to get the laptop cheaper, leaving us less than, I don't know, *flat-ass broke*."

"Who cares about a stupid party anyway?" Jessie said flatly.

"I do," James said. "And you know why."

"Why?" Ivy asked.

"Because the guy holding the party's got a job for me if I show up tonight." James slid Jessie a dark look. "And it would've paid us enough to live off of for a long time."

"You don't know that," Jessie said. "Not for sure."

"Well, now we'll never know, will we?"

"James, it's dangerous to work for Rock," Jessie said plaintively. "Too dangerous. And you promised—"

"Doesn't matter now since you changed the game on me—twice. Or did you forget that you were the one who borrowed money from him in the first place? And we still have to pay him back. Or else."

Jessie's eyes glittered, with bad temper and also tears. "You know why I borrowed that money for tuition."

"Of course I do. But the second you picked school over survival, you left me powerless to protect you."

"I don't need protecting," Jessie said angrily. "I can handle Rock."

"You might think that, but you can't. And now I have to find a way to take care of you while you're living with your head in a cloud."

"Me wanting to go to college isn't me living with my head in a cloud. With a degree, I can get a good job."

James sighed. "How are you this naive after all we've been through. You know what Rock wants, right? He wants you."

"I can handle him," Jessie repeated softly, then turned away and stared out the window.

James looked like he'd just chomped on glass, and the air around them was tense and strained.

"How do you know Rock?" Ivy asked quietly.

"A few months ago, we were camping as usual." Jessie slid a quick glance at her brother, who was silent, driving. "And it got cold. Like super cold. So we sort of, um . . . found somewhere to stay."

"We were up in Palisades Tahoe," James said. "Ritzy, but there's also a lot of wooded land up there. Easy to park and camp without being seen."

"I was freezing." Jessie seemed to shiver with the memory. "So we walked through the woods until we came to some houses. We stopped at one that always seemed empty. We just assumed it was someone's second home, probably some Bay Area techie with too much money and too many fancy houses. The back deck had a bunch of comfy furniture on it and one of those outdoor heaters, so we thought we could sleep there and no one would know. But then . . ." She grimaced. "It's just that the house was so big, so beautiful. And one of the windows was cracked open. I just wanted to take a look around inside, that's all."

"If you give a mouse a cookie . . ." James muttered. Sighed. "She found the master shower, which was bigger than most houses."

"I wanted a hot shower." Jessie hugged herself. "I mean, how long had it been since we had a hot shower instead of sneaking into the campgrounds' bathrooms around the lake? I'll tell you. Forever, that's how long."

Ivy's heart squeezed, hard. She'd lived in a whole bunch of dumps with her mom, but they'd always had a roof over their heads. Who'd have thought she'd feel grateful to her mom for something, but in that moment, she did. Making her way here from Chicago had been terrifying, and she'd spent those three days trying to make due in bus station bathrooms and sneaking into restaurant bathrooms to wash up the best she could.

So she would never judge, not when she knew she wasn't all that different from the twins. After all, she'd come here to Tahoe to steal money from her dad. "Did you get caught?" she asked anxiously.

"The son of the owners came home and caught us raiding the pantry," James said.

"Rock," Ivy guessed.

"Yeah. He told us if we paid for using the house, he wouldn't call the cops. He even invited us back a few times. Then genius here borrowed money from him for tuition. Tonight's our deadline to pay him back, and if we don't do it, he'll be forced to take retribution, which he says is beyond his control, that he answers to his dad."

"And retribution would be what, exactly?" Ivy asked.

James flicked a glance at his sister. "Nothing good."

"I'm so sorry I got us into this," Jessie said softly.

James sighed. Shook his head. "Doesn't matter now. We know what we have to do. He said if we bring him five hundred dollars cash and the alcohol for this party, he'd let us off the hook. *And he'll hire me.*"

"What's the job?" Ivy asked.

James didn't answer.

Jessie was biting her lower lip. "Rock's an entrepreneur. The job is whatever he needs done."

Ivy didn't know much, but that sounded very ambiguous and, as Jessie had already pointed out, dangerous.

"We'll find a way to get him the cash and alcohol," Jessie said. "And then we can go south like we talked about. Find someplace cheaper to live, with more jobs."

James blew out a breath. "You know we can't get our hands on the money by tonight."

"I'll sell the laptop," Jessie said, tears in her eyes, sounding resigned. "I can put it up online and—"

James put his hand on hers. "No. You're not selling the laptop. You need it. You deserve it."

"But Rock—"

"I could lend you the money," Ivy heard herself say, unable to handle the look of carefully banked worry and fear on James's face for his sister. "I don't mind."

James pulled to the side of the road, and he and his twin sister both swiveled to stare at her.

"My dad put some money in his cash drawer for me to use as needed," Ivy said. "I can get it to you tomorrow."

"That's incredibly sweet," James said. "But I can't let you do that. This is our mess. Besides, tomorrow's too late."

Jessie's face was in profile now, but her fear was also clear, and Ivy knew that fear. "I'll call my dad and explain," she said softly. "I know he's got enough in the petty cash drawer. He could meet us there."

"Why would you do that for us?" Jessie asked.

It was a good question, but there was just something about these two, and the clear hopelessness they felt, that made her ache. "If it wasn't for Harper, and now Bodie, I could very well be in your position."

James studied her, then shook his head. "No. This isn't on you. It's on us. I like you too much to drag you into this. And even if I did, your dad isn't going to let you just hand over money to perfect strangers."

Jessie was crying quietly. The strongest girl Ivy knew, broken down by life. It hurt to see. "Then I won't tell him," Ivy said. "Take me to the bar," she said. "I'll get it myself. It's early, so the place is still closed, but I can get in."

"James," Jessie said softly. "We will find a way to pay her back."

James shook his head no.

Jessie burst into tears. James swore softly beneath his breath and then, without another word, pulled out and drove to Olde Tahoe Tap.

He cut the engine and turned to face her. "Ivy—"

"I'll be right back," she said, with more confidence than she felt. It was true, her dad had put money in the cash drawer for her. It was also true she had a way to get in. Mace had given her his code last week when she'd taken out the trash and needed to get back inside.

But that had been one thing. Helping herself inside and to the cash drawer was another entirely.

It's nothing you wouldn't have done weeks and weeks ago if you'd had the balls, she reminded herself. Drawing a deep breath, she hopped out of the car and walked around to the back of the building. She knew her dad and Harper were probably still at the mall, but she looked around anyway. Then she turned to the back door and entered Mace's code on the keypad.

CHAPTER 21

Don't mess this up," Abuela said. "It's muy importante."

"Gee, no pressure," Harper responded as she put the finishing touches on her great-grandma's red velvet cake.

Abuela snorted. "You young people know *nothing* of pressure." The older woman was carefully adding a chocolate Kiss to each of the cookies on her tray of chocolate Kiss cookies. "In my day, we worked our fingers to the bone twenty-four/seven."

"And I've been such a slacker?"

Abuela cackled. "Okay, no. You're a hard worker. It's why I'm willing to help you."

Harper had to laugh. "I pay you to help me."

"Yes, and there's that. You pay two dollars an hour more than I expected."

Harper gaped at her. "You said you wouldn't take a penny less!"

"And you believed me." Abuela came over to inspect her great-grandma's red velvet cake. "Looks good."

"It does, doesn't it?" she said with pride.

Shay walked in the back door, and Harper quickly shoved the cake into the fridge.

Shay divided a suspicious look between her and Abuela. "What?"

"No hablo inglés," Abuela said, and headed out to the front of the bakery.

Shay looked at Harper. "And you. Why do you look so sickeningly happy?"

"Because I'm baking to my heart's content in my own kitchen." Which she was never going to get tired of saying. "Only a few months ago, I was working my fingers to the bone for a horrible boss, hating my life. Coming here's been the best thing I've ever done for myself."

"Ugh, I so wanted to hate you," Shay said, heading to the fridge.

"No!" Harper yelled, and flattened herself to the front of it.

Shay blinked. "What's going on with you?"

Harper tried to look innocent. "What's up with *you*?"

Shay rolled her eyes. "Are you a toddler?"

"Stay out of my fridge."

"Since when?"

Since Harper had made the red velvet cake at Mace's request. He had plans, and for those plans, he needed Shay's favorite cake. "Since you've been eating me out of house and home."

Shay collapsed on one of the chairs at the small table. "I know! I can't stop! I think it's because I'm not getting any."

Harper's cell rang. "Don't tell her it's me," Mace said quickly in her ear. "I'm ready, so tell her you're hungry and you want company for a meal. Soon as you're headed over here, Zeke's gonna sneak into your place and get the cake. Abuela's going to cover your bakery."

"Okay." Harper hung up and turned to Shay. "You know what? I'm hungry too. Let's go get food."

Two minutes later, they were heading down the cobblestone walkway, Shay muttering something about how stupid she was for letting people into her stupid heart because it'd ruined her stupid life.

Harper understood the sentiment because not all that long ago, she'd felt that very same way. But with some distance and a new life, one she'd built for herself, she felt happier than she'd ever been. She was running her own bakery. Forging new relationships. More people had her back than ever before, and she couldn't imagine being anywhere else. Shay was one of them. Sure, they were unlikely friends, but it was very real. So was what she felt for Ivy.

And then there was Bodie. Putting a name to how she felt about him wasn't nearly as scary as she'd thought it'd be. There was something about how she felt when she was with him. She'd opened her heart to him, and he'd made himself at home there with an ease she'd honestly not believed possible. She knew she'd do anything for these people. Her people.

A minute later, she and Shay entered Olde Tahoe Tap. Bodie greeted them, first brushing a kiss to Shay's cheek, then pulling Harper in for a hug that warmed her from the inside out. "Mmm," he murmured in her ear. "Needed that."

"Me too. You hug almost as good as your daughter."

He gave a rueful laugh. "When I saw her hug you in the store this morning, it hurt my heart."

She pulled back to look into his face.

"In a good way," he assured her. "In the *very* best way."

She put her hand on his face, and he moved his lips over to kiss her palm.

"All right," Shay said. "Stop showing off."

Bodie took them to a table. Their server came over with menus.

It was Mace.

Shay froze in surprise. "What are you doing?"

"Hello, my name is Mace, and I'll be your server tonight."

"You've been avoiding serving me for over a month," Shay said.

"Our special cocktail tonight is the Gold Rush," he went on smoothly. "Is there anything I can help you with or answer for you?"

"Yes," Shay said, craning her neck, looking one way and then the other. "Where are the cameras? Are we on some reality show where exes get in a fight in a public place? Because that's what's about to happen."

Mace smiled. "As for food, we've got the gamut. Personally, I'd recommend the Mountain Burgers."

Shay opened her mouth, but Harper put her hand on Shay's arm. "We'll take two burgers," she said. "Sounds lovely."

Mace threw her a grateful glance.

"And at *least* two Gold Rushes," Shay said.

Mace bowed slightly, added a very charming, very sweet smile, and walked away.

Shay stared after him. "He's up to something."

Harper knew this to be true.

"The question is, is he going to use his powers for good or evil?"

"His powers?" Harper asked.

"He's charismatic, fascinating, and could enchant a nun."

Harper smiled. "Good thing you're no nun."

The burgers were indeed delicious, and so were the Gold Rushes. She and Shay were completely stuffed and slightly tipsy by the time they finished eating.

Bodie made his way over to them. "Everything going okay here?" He smiled at Shay, then turned to Harper and . . . *really* smiled, the warm, sweet, sexy, just-for-her smile that made her smile dopily back at him. He pulled her right out of her chair and gave her a hello kiss that stole her breath. "Busy tomorrow night?"

"No," she said. "Why?"

"Thought maybe we could go out and do something fun."

She was definitely not opposed to fun. "Okay. What should I wear?"

He smiled, his naughty smile. They'd been whispering to each other, and his voice was low and sexy. "Are you asking what I'd like you to be wearing when I pick you up?"

"Yeah," she answered a little breathlessly.

"Lipstick."

Oh boy . . .

"Seriously?" Shay said, waving a fork at them.

"What?" Bodie asked.

"You know what's worse than sitting in your ex's family's tavern and watching him smile and charm everyone in the place except you because you were stupid and let him walk away? I'll tell you what. Watching you two be stupid in love and making googly eyes at each other."

Harper started in surprise at the "stupid in love" part. Not Bodie. He looked unrepentant.

"*And*," Shay went on, still jabbing her fork in their general direction, "it's also annoying as hell to know that you're both getting laid and I am not."

Harper put her hands to her hot cheeks. "Please stop saying that."

"Hey, you're the one wearing that I've-recently-had-a-bunch-of-really-great-orgasms look on your face. You going to eat your fries?"

Harper pushed hers over, thinking if Shay's mouth was full, maybe she'd stop talking. "Maybe they weren't all that great. You ever think of that?"

"The fries?"

"The orgasms!" Harper realized she'd yelled that when several people looked over at her.

"They were exceptional," Bodie told Shay.

Harper rolled her eyes but also felt herself flush—not in embarrassment, but at the memory of just how exceptional.

"*Whatever*," Shay said, and lifted her hand. "Where's my waiter? You know, the one I *used* to sleep with, who *used* to give me some really great orgasms? I need more alcohol."

"How were the burgers?" Bodie asked. "Mace made them himself."

Shay shrugged. "They were all right."

They all looked down at Shay's plate, which she'd practically licked clean.

"So what?" Shay said. "The man can cook. He makes them for whoever orders them, not for me specifically."

"You don't know," Bodie said. "Maybe he's kissing up."

"Or he's trying to butter me up for some bad news."

Bodie tugged on a strand of her hair. "He's not. Try to enjoy yourself."

"I am."

Bodie studied her body language. "You're strung so tight you're going to snap."

"Yeah, well, your brother has that effect."

Bodie laughed, leaned over, and kissed Harper again, then moved off.

"I want that," Shay said.

"Well, you can't have it. It's mine."

"Not *that* that. Not *him*." She paused. "Okay, so I'd take him in a hot minute, but I really just want what you two have. And I want it with Mace."

"You remember that you let him walk away, right?"

"Dammit."

Mace came to clear their plates.

"Check, please," Shay said.

"It's on the house. Will you stay a few minutes?"

"Why?" she asked with her usual suspiciousness.

"I'd really like to talk to you," he said softly. "I just need to do something real quick in the back."

Shay looked up into his eyes, her own solemn. Serious. "Mace—"

"Please?"

She gave him a nod, and looking uncertain, she turned to Harper when he was gone. "Now that we're back to being friends and all, I think he wants to tell me he's going to start seeing other people. Which was implied when we broke up, but then neither of us did, so . . ." She bit her lower lip. "I'm strong as hell, but I don't think I'm strong enough for this."

"Maybe it's not what you think," Harper said, trying not to give anything away.

Shay looked doubtful as Mace came out with the cake.

"Wait—what's that?" she asked. "Is that what I think it is? Is that . . ." She turned to Harper. "Your red velvet cake made from your great-grandma's recipe that you won't share?"

"Yes."

Shay turned to Mace. "What's going on? It's not my birthday."

"No, but I'm hoping we're celebrating."

"Celebrating what?"

"Agreeing to see each other again."

She stared at him. "We 'see' each other all the time."

"You know what I mean." He looked at her, his eyes softening. "I'm sorry I pushed you away when you got scared. I should never have asked for something before you were ready."

"What if I'm never ready?" she whispered, looking heartbreakingly terrified.

Mace dropped to his knees at her side. "You love me. I love you. I don't need anyone else, ever. If you're never ready to sign a piece of paper pledging our love to each other, I'm okay with that. I know what we have."

Shay sucked in a breath. "Really?"

"Really, babe. I love you. I'm so sorry."

Her eyes filled. "No, I'm sorry for letting you go without trying to explain. I've regretted it every day since. But love has always sucked for me. *Always.*"

"I know," he said gently. "I've always known. I shouldn't have walked." He shook his head, looking disgusted with himself. "I've regretted my reaction every day since too."

Shay's voice was unbearably hopeful. "Yeah?"

"Yeah. So let's try this thing again." His voice was husky with emotion as he cupped her face and swiped away a few tears with his thumb. "Let's do this without any licenses or signatures, just let it have its way and take us wherever we want. What do you say?" He lit the sole candle on the cake.

Shay was quiet for a long time. For a really long time, until Harper started to worry about the cake melting. Or the bar catching fire. Everyone was holding their collective breath in the awkward silence until Shay finally spoke. "Are you doing this with an audience so I won't say no?"

Mace grimaced. "Yes?"

Shay held up a finger and closed her eyes for a long beat. Then she blew out the candle. "*Yes,*" she said, looking at Mace.

"Yes," Mace repeated carefully. "Yes to . . . a piece of probably melted cake? Yes to forgiving me? Yes to being with me again?"

"Yes. To all of it. Because love doesn't suck with you."

Mace hauled Shay right out of her chair and into his arms and kissed her as if his life depended on it.

Harper realized she had her hand to her chest, unbearably moved and happy for the two people in the world who were possibly more stubborn than she.

Bodie pulled Harper into his side, and she felt like she was a part of something wonderful, something she'd never known until she'd come here.

Shay finally broke free from Mace and swiped her finger through the frosting and then sucked it off her finger. "Oh my God. I've died and gone to heaven."

Bodie leaned into Harper and whispered in her ear, "Amazing."

"It's just a cake."

"It's so much more than that. And I meant you. *You're* amazing."

When she was with him, she felt amazing. "Bodie?"

"Yeah?"

"Remember that pace I set?" She looked up into his face. "Maybe we should kick it up to second gear."

Bodie laughed softly. "Babe, we've blown right past second gear." Then he lowered his head and kissed her.

"They keep doing that," Shay said.

Harper broke free and smiled up at Bodie.

His return smile lit up her heart. In fact, she was smiling so much her cheeks hurt when she felt her phone buzz in her pocket just as Bodie turned to say something to one of his servers.

Harper pulled out her phone. Ivy. "Hey, babe."

"Are you with my dad?"

The worry and stress in the teenager's voice had the smile gone from Harper. "Yes, are you okay?"

"I have to tell you something, but you have to promise you won't tell him."

Oh boy. "Ivy, you know I can't do that—"

"Promise me, or I'm hanging up right now."

Harper looked up in time to see Bodie moving into the kitchen. She sucked in a breath, caught between a rock and a hard place. If she didn't promise and Ivy hung up, they'd have no idea what was happening. If she did promise, it would mean not telling Bodie something about his kid. "Ivy—"

"I knew it. Bye, Harper—"

"No!" She lowered her voice. "I won't say a word. Where are you?"

"Promise me!"

"I promise," she said, moved by the genuine fear and panic in Ivy's voice. "Are you hurt?"

"I blew it. I totally blew it."

"Ivy, just tell me where you are."

"Not until you're alone."

Harper stood up. "Okay, I'm walking outside now. Send me a

pin of your location. Stay on the line with me." The music had been cranked up and everyone had moved onto the dance floor, living it up. She eyed the swinging doors to the kitchen where she'd seen Bodie go.

"Hurry," Ivy whispered.

She started moving, and Zeke looked over at her, a question in his gaze. "You okay?"

"Yep," she said, knowing Ivy was listening. She headed outside, starting to type a text to Bodie: Gotta go, call me.

"Harper?" Ivy asked, voice thin. Scared. "You still there?"

"Right here." She got into her car while accessing the pin of Ivy's location. "My ETA's seventeen minutes."

"Hurry."

GPS led her up to Hidden Falls and a dirt road off the highway that was narrow and rutted. She hadn't gone very far when Ivy said in her ear through the phone, "Stop!"

There was no room to pull over, so she just hit the brakes. Dust rose around the car, and before it'd cleared, Ivy had jumped into her passenger seat.

Harper looked her over as much as she could in the dark confines of the car. The teen looked the same as she had earlier, in simple jeans, a tee, and beat-up sneakers. No sign of injury. "You okay?"

"Can we just get out of here, please?"

Harper managed to turn the car around, executing a zillion-point turn on the narrow road. They didn't speak until they were back on the highway.

"Where are you taking me?" Ivy asked.

"To your dad. He's at Olde Tahoe Tap."

"No!" Ivy looked over at her. "Please, can you just take me home? I'll wait for him and tell him everything when it's just him and me, I promise. He's not expecting me before midnight anyway."

Harper tried to find the fault in that but couldn't. "Okay, but start talking."

Ivy drew a deep breath. "James and Jessie got themselves in trouble with a guy they owed money to. So I lent them the money Bodie had set aside for me to spend."

Harper looked over at her. "The money he left in the cash drawer for you?"

Ivy winced. "I'm going to pay it back, I promise."

"You stole from your dad's bar?"

"Borrowed. And I had no choice."

Harper shook her head. "Ivy, there's always a choice."

"No, you don't understand!" Ivy cried. "They're like me, only not as lucky. They don't have a you or a Bodie. They have no one. I *had* to help them. They had to bring five hundred dollars to a party, and . . . somealcoholwhichIalsotookfromthebar."

Harper's head swiveled to Ivy. "What?"

"And then the cops came and everyone ran, and I got separated from James and Jessie. They're safe, they've been texting me, feeling so bad about losing me. They would've come back for me, but I called you." *Because I needed the comfort . . .*

"What were you thinking?" Harper demanded. "You could've been arrested."

Ivy slumped into the passenger seat. "If I'd wanted a lecture, I'd have called Bodie."

"Was that *attitude*?" Harper glanced over at her. "Because that sounded like attitude, to the person who just risked a lot to come out here for you, no questions asked."

"You asked plenty."

"And you told me nothing, and yet I still came. And now I'm an accomplice in your lies."

Ivy sniffled. "I'm sorry!" She covered her face. "I knew that everything was too perfect. Bodie and his entire family. You . . ."

Harper gave her a look of shocked disbelief. "So you *chose* to mess it all up?"

"Yes!" Ivy cried. "I'm stupid, okay? And it doesn't matter. I took money from the bar's cash drawer. And alcohol. Soon as he finds out, I'm good as gone anyway. I should've stuck with my original plan: show up, get the child support owed to me from my sperm donor, then go and start a new life on a beach in Santa Barbara or San Diego. But then I liked it here, so I stayed. I thought I'd stay forever. So stupid."

"Wait—*that's* why you came?" Harper sucked in a breath. Bodie would be heartbroken when he found out. "First off, he's not just your sperm donor. He's your dad. And if you can't tell that after everything he's done to show you he loves you unconditionally and on first sight, then you've not been paying attention. And take it from someone who spent her teenage years alone, I'd have given *anything* to have a dad who loves me the way yours loves you." She pulled up to Bodie's house.

It was dark.

Ivy sank down in the seat. "Are you going to tell on me?"

"No, *you're* going to tell on you, first thing tomorrow morning since he'll be home late."

"Fine." Ivy got out of Harper's car.

"I know it doesn't feel like it right now," Harper said. "But I care about you, Ivy. A lot."

The teen's eyes filled as she nodded, shut the door, and walked into the house.

Harper waited until her bedroom light came on upstairs before she pulled out of the driveway.

When she got home, she waited for Bodie to call her.

She fell asleep waiting on that call.

CHAPTER 22

vy didn't sleep much, in spite of her new awesome bedding. It was hard to relax when she knew come morning, she'd be in the hot seat. She texted briefly with the twins, who'd promised to get her money back to her as soon as they could, but she knew they were going to have to leave the area rather than risk Rock's wrath.

When she heard Bodie in the kitchen, it was still dark outside. She sucked it up and pulled on some clothes. Everything inside her told her to get her backpack and run, just like she'd planned in the beginning. But she didn't want to. She wanted to believe it would all be okay. She wanted to believe Bodie Campbell, her *dad*, was everything he'd presented himself to be, that he'd understand and forgive.

But she knew she didn't deserve it. She'd broken their pact to be honest with each other. She'd lied about where she was going, then she'd not only stolen from him, she'd pulled his girlfriend in on it. And she'd done all that willingly.

God, she was so stupid.

At the bottom of the stairs, she stopped in the hall because she could hear him on his phone in the kitchen. He was on speaker and making coffee at the same time, and when she heard her mom's voice, shrill and angry, she froze.

"You haven't been there for her in sixteen years," she was saying. "You don't get to just step in now and be the hero parent."

"Whose fault is it that I haven't been there, Jenny?" This was her dad's voice, low and controlled. "Look, let's just deal with the now."

"Well the *now* is that she starts school next week. She needs to be home."

Ivy didn't move, didn't blink, waiting for him to say, *This is her home now.* Or *She's not coming back, I want to keep her.* Instead, he said, "Understood. I'll cover the flight."

Feeling stupid that she'd believed anything he'd ever said, Ivy whirled around and ran back up the stairs, furious at herself for having to swipe away tears. Grabbing her backpack, she went to the window, reaching for the huge tree branch from the lodge pine a few feet from the house. She had just begun to shimmy down when she heard her dad—nope, her sperm donor—call out to her from the other side of her closed bedroom door.

"Ivy? You up? I'm making blueberry pancakes."

For a beat, she hung there, suspended in her lost hopes and dreams. He'd led her to believe they'd have a ton of mornings just like this, but she hadn't been the only one to lie and break their pact.

She didn't want to feel bad or guilty about leaving. But she did. She felt awful. He clearly couldn't wait to get rid of her, and she'd never even guessed. She should've known it was just a matter of time before he did what her mom had always done: gotten involved with someone and then no longer wanted her around. She knew the drill, and yet she'd *still* delayed her plan, and for what? *Nothing*, as it turned out.

"And if you're wondering, yes, the pancakes are a blatant bribe," he said through her bedroom door. "Because I think we both know we need to talk."

Oh hell no. Sliding down the tree, she hit the ground at a run, putting Bodie in her rearview mirror.

JUST A FEW minutes past dawn, Harper was in the kitchen kneading dough while trying to ignore the fact she'd never heard from Bodie last night. She was feeling the strain on her shoulders, which was more from stress than from the physical activity, when the back door opened.

Bodie.

Ham hopped up from where he'd been sleeping in the sole sunspot, scrambling like a cat on linoleum to get his paws under him so he could run to one of his favorite humans.

Bodie squatted and hugged the dog, but for a much briefer time than he usually did, which had Ham letting out a whine of protest. Bodie left a hand on the dog's head when he lifted his gaze to Harper. "Is Ivy here?"

"For work? Not yet." Relieved and happy to see him, she also moved toward him, keeping her hands out at her sides so as to not get him dirty when she went up on her tiptoes to kiss him, but he took a step back.

"She's gone," he said flatly.

Harper's heart stopped and then sank all the way to her stomach. "What?"

"When I went upstairs to wake her, the window was open, and she and her old backpack were gone."

Harper let out a breath. "So she didn't come downstairs to apologize to you this morning?"

His eyes bore into hers. "For what? Taking money from the bar?"

She stared at him, a very, very bad feeling coming over her. "You know?"

"We have cameras, Harper. Jason discovered the missing cash late last night at closing and we checked the recordings. She used Mace's code to get in before we opened. I'd hoped she'd come to me to explain this morning. She didn't." His eyes were laser focused. "Now you."

"She called me when I was at the bar last night."

"Zeke said you left looking like a runner. I didn't believe him at first."

"I left you a text," she said.

"I don't have a text from you."

"No, I . . ." She pulled out her phone and accessed her texts, scrolling to his name. The "call me" was there—*not* sent. "Oh my God, I forgot to send it." She looked up into those intense eyes and bit her lower lip. "I haven't seen her since last night."

"What do you mean, last night?"

She sucked in a breath. "Ivy was with Jessie and James at a party when she got into some trouble. She called me to come get her. She was scared. She wouldn't tell me where she was until I promised not to tell anyone. So I went and got her and dropped her at your place. She promised me she'd tell you everything first thing this morning."

"Okay." His face was devoid of emotion, and so was his voice. "Now explain why *you* didn't tell me."

"She was upset and ready to hang up. In the moment, it seemed more important that she have someone to help her than ratting her out to you."

"I'm her dad. There's no ratting her out. You should've told me. Where was she going?"

"*Nowhere.* She promised not to leave."

"Funny how promises get broken so easily."

Direct hit, but now wasn't about them. Not with Ivy missing.

Bodie hadn't moved. Not a single muscle. "Is there anything else you've neglected to tell me about my daughter that will help me find her? Did she give you any hint on where she might go? I know she wouldn't go back to Chicago. At least I don't think she would."

She met his gaze and held it, which wasn't easy. But she felt like they had been building something, something good. He'd helped her believe that. "Ivy came looking for back child support so she could run away and start a new life somewhere south and somewhere warm like Santa Barbara or San Diego, but . . ."

"Hold on." He ran a hand over his eyes, clearly shaken at the idea of a sixteen-year-old doing that on her own. "Jesus," he said, barely audible.

"But, Bodie, she'd changed her mind. She loved it here. She was no longer planning on leaving."

He took this in, and when he spoke, his voice was deadly calm and deadly quiet. "Apparently things changed. It's thirty degrees outside and my kid's out there, and you not only knew this was a possibility, you kept it from me."

His expression sliced right through her. "I was just trying to help—"

"If this is your idea of help, please don't ever try to help us again." He started toward the door, but then paused. "You promised to give us a shot."

"I *am* giving us a shot. We blew past second gear, remember?"

"You just took us right off the map."

"A teenager calls you scared and maybe in danger and says she'll only let you help her if you promise not to tell . . . What would you have done?"

"This isn't a hypothetical. You chose to uphold a promise to a *minor*, over the much bigger promise you'd made to her dad."

That it was 100 percent true hurt her almost as much as his anger did. "At least let me help you find her."

"I think you've done enough." He met her gaze, his own giving nothing away. "You didn't trust me to do the right thing by Ivy, and I can't get past that. But worse, I trusted you when you said—*promised*—you wouldn't hide anything about Ivy from me ever again." He gave a slow headshake. "We're done here."

Her heart hit her toes. "Just like that, you decide it's over?"

"No, you decided the moment you didn't pull me in last night."

And then he was gone.

She had no idea how long she stood there, frozen in place, mouth literally hanging open. Maybe she'd screwed up, but he'd been wrong about her not trusting him. She *did* trust him. And she'd believed he would trust her. But if he had, he'd have understood why she'd done what she had. Last night she'd acted rashly, yes, but also from her heart, believing she was putting *both* Bodie and Ivy first.

And once again, she hadn't been enough. That was always the bottom line, wasn't it, her coming up short, never quite being enough? And apparently, she was also quite easy to walk away from. Locking the door, she slowly slid down to the floor, still covered in flour.

Ham tried to crawl into her lap, and she buried her face in his fur and held on to the only man who'd never let her down.

BODIE'S BRAIN CLOSED off from everything except the mission: find Ivy. He went into hunt mode. From the bakery, he went directly to the one and only bus station in town and showed the guy at the ticket counter a picture of Ivy. "Have you seen her?"

"Dude, it's fucking freezing this morning, no one's coming or going."

"Can you just look at the picture?"

The guy took in the pic, his eyes hooded now. "No one's here, and no buses have left since yesterday midday."

Bodie thought about yanking the guy out of his little window, but he didn't have time to be arrested right now. "You've seen her," he said with a calm he didn't feel.

"Fine. She was here."

"When?"

"Half hour ago. She looked at the schedule, saw no buses were leaving until two p.m., then left without buying a ticket. And no, I don't know where she went."

Bodie's phone buzzed, and he yanked out his cell to see a text.

MOM: Ivy just showed up. Don't tell her I told you.

BODIE: She okay?

MOM: Honey, she's a teenager, they're never okay.

BODIE: Don't let her leave, I'm on my way.

MOM: When you get here, LEAD WITH LOVE.

What the hell does that mean? Lead with love . . . He drove to his mom's, thoughts racing faster than his truck. By the time he turned on his childhood street, he'd figured out what his mom meant. He'd been emotionally unavailable since losing Tyler and his dad. He couldn't remember the last time he'd told his mom or brothers or *anyone* that he loved them. He'd never told Ivy either, which was even worse, because at least his family *knew* he loved them.

But Ivy would have no way of knowing how he truly felt, even though she completely owned his heart.

Nor Harper—not that he could go there at the moment.

Still, the fist gripping his heart in his chest loosened very slightly. Ivy hadn't gotten on the bus. She was safe at his mom's. He had no idea how he was going to fix this, but he would. He sure as shit wasn't going to have *another* mission failure.

Again, his mind wandered to Harper, but he wasn't ready to open that door. One at a time . . .

He pulled into his parents' driveway and got out to find his mom standing in the doorway. He jogged up the steps and hugged her tight, kissing her on the cheek. "I love you, Mom."

"I'm not the one who needs to hear that right now."

"She turned off her phone. I've been sick with worry."

His mom let out a short laugh. "You'll never get the joy my generation had as a kid, knowing our parents had literally no way to get ahold of us until we decided to go home."

"Times were different then."

"Not so different." She cupped his face. "She's going through a lot, and what she needs to know is that she can trust you. She needs to learn from you how to be loved. Can you understand that? She's been through so much, baby, and right now what she needs more than anything is to know how much she matters to you."

"How can she doubt it?"

His mom gently patted his cheeks. Then not so gently. "Think hard. *Real* hard."

Bodie shook his head. "I don't know what happened. One minute we were okay, and the next minute she was gone."

"You're missing a piece of the puzzle."

"Mom." He ran his hands through his hair. "You obviously know more than I do. Just tell me."

"I believe you said more to Jenny this morning than you're remembering."

Bodie stared at her. "Ivy heard the call."

"How many times have I told you heathens that it's rude to answer a call on speakerphone? And it wasn't her mom who upset her either. She knows her mom and how she is."

"Oh shit." Bodie blew out a breath. "It was me."

"It was you."

"But what did I say? I barely said a word."

"Silence in her mind is agreement to whatever was being said."

Bodie reran the call through his head. "I was trying not to argue because I didn't want Ivy to have to leave."

"I'm taking it that you didn't say that part, or we wouldn't be having this conversation." His mom squeezed his arm. "She's asleep in your old room. Maybe you should go tell her what you want her to know."

Bodie thunked his head on the doorjamb a few times, stopping when his mom snorted. "This is funny to you?" he asked, heavy on the disbelief. "We never put you through *half* of what she's putting me through."

His mom laughed, *hard*. "Are you kidding me? Do you know how many nights I stayed awake waiting for you to come home after you'd sneaked out your window? And yes, I know. Zeke always let me in on your stupidity."

He'd deal with his asshole brother later.

"No, you won't," she said, making him realize he'd said that out loud. "And hey, you boys gave me a full head of gray before I was forty. Welcome to parenthood."

Bodie closed his eyes. "I don't know what I'm doing, Mom. Not with Ivy. Not with Harper. Not with anyone."

"Oh, honey, don't you get it yet? *No one* knows what they're doing. Even people who love each other are going to act irrational or get mad, and sometimes you're just going to have to realize that you"—she gently poked him in the chest with her finger—"yes, *you*, are the asshole."

He choked out a laugh.

She smiled. "All I can tell you is that if you show up every single moment of every single day, and you love her for exactly who she is, that little girl will come out of her shell. I promise you. You weren't lucky enough to be in her life for her first sixteen years, but the universe has given you a chance to be there now, for better or worse. Don't do what so many people do and lose sight of what's important."

Too late. He'd managed to do that on two notable occasions now. When Tyler had died, and when he hadn't been there for his dad after his heart attack. So hell yeah, he was going to do whatever was needed to be a good dad for Ivy. God knew, she deserved that much. "I've got this," he said, not sure if he was trying to convince her or himself.

His mom, who apparently believed in him far more than he did, smiled and hugged him hard. "I know."

He headed up the stairs toward his childhood bedroom, knowing he was going to have to open a vein and bleed. Ivy deserved no less.

Harper too. Because instead of letting her in, letting her see his fears, telling her that everything felt so out of control and was terrifying him in a way that facing down a gang of bad guys never had, he'd used the opportunity as a way to lock her out, like she didn't even matter, when she mattered a hell of a lot. In fact, outside of his family, she'd become the most important person in his world.

And how had he repaid that? He'd walked away, knowing full well that was *her* biggest fear.

He didn't deserve either Ivy or Harper, but he no longer was going to let that stop him from trying to keep both.

If they'd have him.

CHAPTER 23

vy opened her eyes. She'd pretended to be asleep when her grandma checked in on her. *Her grandma.* She'd wanted one of those her entire life, had dreamed about what it might be like to have someone at her back no matter what. Someone warm, and maybe sweet and even silly, someone who'd always be there for her.

Even if she'd tried, she could never have dreamed up a grandma as great as Suzie Campbell.

Or uncles like Mace and Zeke.

Or friends like Harper and Shay, who'd welcomed her, pulled her into their circle, and wanted nothing but the best for her.

And then there'd been Bodie, who'd treated her like a member of the family far before she'd let him in on the truth.

Sitting up in the childhood bedroom he'd once shared with Zeke, she hugged the pillow to her chest and looked around. There was a scarred old desk with stickers all over it. Some posters on the wall. An old snowboard leaning in a corner. A pic on the desk of him and his brothers, including Austin.

And this world had been kept from her.

Next to the bed, beneath the nightstand, was a thick photo album. She pulled it up and, sitting cross-legged, set it in her lap. It was filled to overbrimming with family pictures, from when her dad had been a kid growing up on the lake: jet skiing, snowboarding, rock climbing, mountain biking. All the things she'd missed out on because her mom had lied.

All the things she was going to miss out on because, like her mom, *she'd* messed everything up. She was so stupid. She'd found something here, something more valuable than money. *This* was where she wanted to start over, not some nameless place she'd never been, where she wouldn't know a soul and would be so scared. She buried her face in her pillow, devastation sitting like a weight on her chest. She was really effing tired of ruining everything that was good in her life.

She startled at a knock on the door, and then it opened. Bodie looked as he always did, perfectly calm and at ease . . . except today there was a new tightness to his features, and though his eyes were warm and he was clearly happy to see her, he wasn't smiling.

Because you stole from him . . .

"Can I come in?" he asked.

Heart pounding because she had no idea how he would deal with her stupidity, she did her best to give a careless shrug. "It's your room."

"It's okay to say no if you're not ready to talk."

"I don't know what I am," she whispered, and heard the tears in her own voice.

He came in and sat next to her. Like her, he leaned back against the wall and then . . . didn't say a word.

Since this was the opposite of anything her mom had ever done, she wasn't sure what to do with that. She braced herself for him to call her out on what she'd done and ask her to leave.

Instead, he nudged his chin in the direction to the opened photo album. "That picture on the left was taken before we went snowboarding one day. I ate shit—" He caught himself. "Er, I wiped out. Spectacularly, I should add. Like a real garage sale, which means I lost my board, my gloves, my helmet, *everything*—" He broke off when a helpless giggle escaped at the image he'd painted. "Yeah," he said on a smile. "It was probably something to see. I was going way faster than I should've been. Broke my leg."

Her amusement faded. "Oh no!"

"It was a fracture really, nothing too bad." He shook his head. "But Mace has never let me forget it."

"You mean you weren't always perfect at everything?"

He snorted. "Trust me, I'm not perfect. Not even in the ballpark. If there's one thing you can take away from this time we've had, it's that."

This time we've had. Past tense. "Is that the way this family works? They never let you forget your mistakes?"

He turned to fully face her and put his hand on hers. "Do we like to give each other a hard time? Yes. One hundred percent. But Zeke carried me down that hill. Stayed with me in the ambulance, even faking his own injury to do so. He felt really bad that I got hurt because I was on his watch. Austin and Mace attempted to do my schoolwork that first week when I was in a lot of pain. They turned my A in algebra to a C, but they tried. So no, family isn't about rubbing our faces in our mistakes. It's also not sneaking out the window and running away in thirty-degree weather without a jacket and without telling anyone where you're going either. It's about being at each other's back no matter what, even if you've forgotten that you're not alone. *That's* how this family works."

She nodded, but then remembered her new no-lies pact to herself and shook her head. "I don't know that kind of family."

"I know. And I'm sorry I didn't understand the depth of that." He paused and put a hand to his chest. "You left without talking to me, but what nearly killed me was that you took only what you'd shown up with, which was almost nothing. I was scared for you."

Her chest was so tight she could scarcely breathe. The emotion in his voice . . . it told her just how much she'd hurt him. And still she did what was habit—went on the defensive. "You lied to me too."

He shook his head. "I've never lied to you."

She was too mad to even touch that one. No, wait. She wasn't mad. She was hurt, which was even worse. "Look, I'm sorry about last night, okay? But I don't want to be here if you don't want me." Her words literally burst out of her, and she wouldn't take them back. "I know you're too busy for me, I get it."

"Ivy."

She was staring at her hands clasped in her lap. She was white-knuckling it in a way she hadn't in a long time, not even last night.

"Kit Kat, look at me. Please?"

Dammit, the "please" got her every time. She looked up, telling herself if she let even one tear fall, she was never going to forgive herself.

"My life will *never* be too busy for you," he said with quiet intensity.

And *there* went a few tears. "Please don't say that unless you mean it," she managed.

He opened his mouth, but she rushed to say the rest before she couldn't. "Do you know how many times in my life I've heard it? Well, probably not as many as you might think, but no one's meant it. Ever. *Everyone* always goes back on their word." She tossed up her hands. "Why do you think I risked crossing the country to a place I've never been to hunt down a dad I never met?"

"Is that really why you came?" he asked. "To forge a relationship with me?"

She felt the heat of her truth scald her face.

"How about this?" he said quietly. "We try again with that deal of ours about no lying. I'll start. I know you think that when I was talking to your mom this morning I alluded to not wanting you here, but that couldn't be further from the truth. I was following Serena's advice to be agreeable so the conversation didn't turn hostile."

Ivy let that soak in. "But Mom's always hostile. And even

though I know she doesn't always want me around, she doesn't want to look like a bad mom either. She's never going to let me live here."

"Ivy, where do *you* want to live?"

She drew a deep breath. "Here. With you."

He nodded. "I'd like that too. But we've got to go through the process. You have a say in this. If she digs in, wanting something you don't want, I believe a judge will take your age and your opinion into consideration, both of which will matter to them."

"I stole money from you last night," she said quickly, needing him to know everything before he said anything else. "A lot of it."

"I know."

Her gaze flew to his, which were warm and calm. Hers filled. "I'm so sorry," she whispered. "I was stupid. I should've gone to you or Harper, I know that."

"It's okay. I forgive you. And you can trust *me*. Always, Kit Kat. And the rest of the Campbells. Harper too. Can you believe that?"

"I used Mace's code number," she said in a very small voice. "Without asking. I used Harper. What if neither of them forgives me?"

"You plan to be big enough to apologize?"

She nodded.

"Then they'll forgive you. I hope you can believe that too."

She nodded, because it was actually starting to sink in. "So . . . what now?"

"You come home with me."

She wanted that. Badly. "You still want me to live with you? Really?"

"Really."

She had no idea how she'd gotten so lucky when she didn't deserve it. "Can Harper live with us too? I know she loves her bakery so much, but she's always working. I think it'd be nice for her to live somewhere other than work, but I don't think she can afford it yet. And since you two are sorta together . . ." She tapered off at the quick flash of . . . *something* on his face. Regret? No, it was grief. "What?"

"I don't know about Harper," he said quietly. "You weren't the only one who ran away."

"She ran away from you?" Ivy asked in disbelief. "Why? I mean she's always giving you the moon eyes, so . . ."

"It wasn't her who ran. It was me."

Stunned he'd admit such a thing, she blinked. "You could apologize. Isn't that what you just told me family does when they love each other? Forgive?"

He stared at her and then let out a rough laugh. "Yeah. Although I didn't actually realize it until right this very moment."

She felt a small smile on her face, which felt good because a few minutes ago she hadn't known if she'd ever have something to smile about again. "You mean I know something you don't?"

His lips quirked. "I'm sure there's a lot you know that I don't."

"You knew better than to trust my friends." Her smile faded. "People suck."

"Not everyone sucks."

Hope was a painful knot in her chest. "I was so stupid."

He let out another rough laugh. "Do you have any idea how many incredibly stupid things I did as a teenager alone? I hope you never find out about half of them, though I'm sure your uncles will be happy to embarrass me any time."

"Do you miss Austin?" The question popped out before she could bite it back, though she wanted to kick herself when his face went serious again.

"Every single day." He looked at her. "I want to say one last thing about last night, okay? You could've called me. You can *always* call me. Even if you're afraid you can't, you can. I'll come for you, no matter what. Please, if you believe nothing else, believe that."

She couldn't have stopped the tears now if her life had depended on it. But he'd laid it all out for her and she needed to do the same. "Even if I came to get money from you?" she whispered.

"Even then." He held her gaze. "Fresh start, yeah?"

She nodded, and the hope expanded, making her heart feel too big for her chest. "Yeah," she breathed. "Fresh start." And when they hugged on it, she held on super tight.

And so did he.

CHAPTER 24

Harper knew how to do this. Knew how to pick herself up and keep breathing, even after a direct hit to the heart. It hurt. It hurt like hell. But she was, if nothing else, resilient. Even if it didn't feel like it right now.

The trick was digging deep and finding a way to forgive herself for her part in what had happened, and then accept that there were certain things she couldn't control.

Such as what someone else thought of her.

Her phone buzzed, and she made herself calmly pull it out of her pocket, ignoring the leap in her pulse.

BODIE: I've got her.

Harper nearly collapsed with relief before she texted back: thanks for letting me know.

Ivy's text came next: I'm so sorry about last night.

HARPER: are you okay?

IVY: Yes. I'm with my dad. I'm really sorry. I
shouldn't have involved you.

Harper thumbed an immediate response: I have zero regrets
about getting you out of a bad situation. I'll always help when you
need it.

Taking a deep breath, she slid her phone away and looked
around. So she'd been walked away from. Again. So what? She'd
survived before, and she'd survive now. She still wanted to be
here. That hadn't changed. She'd come here to Sunrise Cove to
find joy, and she had. But she'd also come to get her act together.

Time to concentrate on doing that. Past time.

Yes, she'd been baking up a storm and selling okay, but she
hadn't done any of the things she kept reminding herself to do in
order to be truly successful. Which meant that what Bodie had
said to her might actually be true. She hadn't believed in herself,
not 100 percent. And if she didn't, who would?

Okay, so where to start? One thing she knew: in order to get
return customers, she had to catch them—hook, line, and sinker.

Takeout only wasn't going to do that.

So she splashed water on her face, put on her big-girl panties—
well, mentally, because it was laundry day and she was in her
last pair of clean undies, which read: *I'm good at getting things
to rise.*

Two hours later, she stood in the middle of the bakery. She'd
just done more to make strides for the bakery—and herself—

than in the month-plus she'd been here. She'd placed ads, posted on social media, and contacted local wedding planners and caterers, offering her services. She'd created a real menu. Well, it was on a self-standing chalkboard, but still. She'd set up her four cute little round tables with equally cute mismatched chairs. She hung pictures on one wall from the building's past, the ones she'd found in the kitchen closet. Another wall held her own culinary past and fun bakery sayings.

DON'T BE AFRAID TO TAKE WHISKS.

BAKING, BECAUSE MURDER IS WRONG.

BAKE IT HAPPEN.

And her personal favorite: I'M THE SECRET INGREDIENT.

She needed to remember that one. It didn't matter what a man thought of her. She was a strong, independent woman who didn't need a man. Drawing a deep breath, she turned in a slow circle, smiling with pride at her cute place.

She still had a sick, hollow feeling in the pit of her stomach, but doing something for herself had helped some. She no longer felt like she wanted to throw up. That was a bonus, right? Right now was about getting ready to open, because ready or not, she'd decided today would be her grand opening. It was time.

She ran upstairs to change really quick out of her jeans and into a cute sundress and a pair of wedge sandals she'd splurged on because they made her look taller. Hopefully that would distract anyone from the fact that her hair was fluffed in all its bird's-nest glory. Even pulled back in a ponytail, it was reaching critical mass. Her eyes were blurry and scratchy, but crying did that to a person. And oh, how she hated to cry. Especially over a man. She'd thought those days were long behind her, but apparently she hadn't learned her lesson yet.

She had it down now. And maybe a small part of her wanted to go back to bed, because if she let her pessimism take hold, she knew today had the potential to be shitty.

No. No, she wasn't going to do that, assume the worst. She was going to assume the best.

If it killed her.

She looked at the clock: 7:50 a.m. She was going to open in ten minutes. She'd be offering free cookies to every customer, and it would be a good day. A *great* day.

"What are you mumbling about?" Shay asked, coming in the bakery kitchen door.

"Nothing."

"Uh-huh." Shay grabbed a cupcake for each hand. "Spill."

Harper sighed. It didn't help that Shay looked great as always, and adding insult to injury, she had a certain look. "You're wearing a honeymoon glow."

Shay grinned, stuffing her face. "Enough about me. Talk."

"You're eating my goods."

"Put it on my account."

"Your balance is approaching the national debt." Harper narrowed her eyes. "Wait a minute. Why are you being so nice?"

"Because when *I* was an idiot, as you so helpfully pointed out, I was lonely. And now you're the idiot. Or so I'm guessing, by your splotchy face, red eyes, and woe-is-me posture. I figure you need me to help you through whatever fight you and Bodie had."

Harper immediately straightened her spine to resemble a steel rod. "How do you know *I* was the idiot?"

Shay shrugged. "It takes two idiots."

"A lot you know," Harper said, picking up a knife to slice into her banana nut bread. "*He* walked away from *me*. We're done. His words, bee-tee-dub, not mine." And, as it turned out, even saying so felt like someone was physically stomping on her heart.

Shay frowned. "Are you sure?"

"Yes, I'm sure!"

"Are you aware you're waving a knife and yelling at your best friend?"

Harper set the knife down with a whole bunch of effort. "Best friend? You don't even like me."

"I like you more now that you put the knife down. And since when is that a requisite to be BFFs anyway?"

Whelp, she had her there . . .

"Spill," Shay said, waving the cupcake at Harper as she inhaled it.

Harper started to open her mouth, but her eyes filled so she shut it again.

Shay pointed at her. "No. No tears for boys."

"Says the person who cried over Mace every time we drank together."

"As my BFF, it's pretty effing rude to point that out." Shay took another bite and moaned. "Damn, you can bake." She wiped her mouth with a napkin. "Okay, so fine, Bodie walked. Did you let him? I mean, who didn't keep who?"

Harper stared at her. "Are you listening? *He* walked away

from *me*. And yes, I let him. I've had enough of being walked away from in my life. Why would I try to stop him?"

"Well . . . there's walking. And then there's needing some space to think. Which isn't the same thing at all as not wanting to be with you anymore. Trust me, I confused the two myself, so I get it."

"Well, I don't," Harper said. "I'm not you, and at the risk of sounding like a broken record, *you don't even know the story*."

"You're right." Shay hopped up on the counter and sat back like she was about to watch a reality show unfold.

Harper crossed her arms.

"What? It's not like I'm glad you're hurting. I'm just relieved to be the watching side of the drama for once." She gave Harper a "go on" gesture with her hand.

Harper sighed. "Last night at the bar, Ivy called me upset, beyond upset. She needed help and a pickup, so I rushed out to go get her and took her home."

"Okay. That was incredibly sweet of you. What's the problem?"

"It's twofold." Harper grimaced. "She asked me not to tell her dad, and . . . I didn't. And two, I didn't go inside Bodie's cabin with her when I dropped her off and wait for him to get home to make sure Ivy stayed put."

"Hey, Ivy's sixteen. Old enough to be left alone at home. That's a nonstarter as far as I'm concerned. But the not-telling him . . . wasn't he with you at the time?"

"He'd gone into the kitchen. Ivy was crying, and definitely not okay. She asked me not to tell him, and given how she sounded, I just rushed out. I was worried and scared for her. When I dropped her at Bodie's, she promised me she'd tell him everything."

"Only . . . she didn't, I'm guessing. And he got pissed at you."

"Yeah." There was more to the story, of course, like Ivy taking money from the bar and then running off on Bodie this morning, but that was their story to tell.

"Look," Shay said. "He was probably just worried and scared too. I love the guy, but it sounds like he took it out on you, which isn't cool. Sometimes the Campbells . . . well, they don't handle not being in control very well. And they often have to be confronted before they'll talk about what the real problem is, especially if emotions are involved. Which they're not a fan of."

Harper knew Bodie had been stunned and terrified for his daughter, someone he'd go to the mat for every time. His life for hers, no price, not ever. That was the unspoken promise between parent and child, something she hadn't really understood until she'd watched them find their way in each other's lives. Feeling suddenly a little nauseated, she put down the knife and started to plate the slices of banana bread.

"Can I have one?" Shay asked. "No, two."

Harper handed over two slices. "I think you're right."

"Of course I am. About what?"

"About why Bodie reacted the way he did, and about needing to be confronted to talk about it. He confronted me this morning." Blindsided, more like. "While avoiding any of the real stuff." Like how he'd become an insta-dad without the benefit of experience or warning, and it was hard. Really hard. "But I was

wrong too. I should've found a way to tell him, not exclude him."
She didn't know why she'd done it. Nope, scratch that. She did
know. She loved Ivy. Her first instinct had been to react to the
fear in the teen's voice and let it dictate her moves.

But the fact was, she loved Bodie too. When that had happened exactly, she wasn't sure. But it was every bit as real and
true as her love for Ivy.

"Well, the good news," Shay said around a mouthful, "is that
this is *not* all on you. He should've trusted that you had her best
interests at heart. Just talk to him, be your annoyingly sweet self,
and—"

"I'm not all that sweet."

Shay laughed. "You're *literally* the sweets girl. Actually, make
that the *sweetheart* girl, because everyone likes you."

"Stop."

"Like you don't know you're at the top of everyone's list of
favorite sweethearts. Harper: the Sweetheart List girl."

Abuela walked into the kitchen. "Flapping your jaws when
there's only two minutes before opening? There's a line outside."

"Oh my God, really?" Harper asked.

"No," Abuela said. "Not really. You'd need ads and incentives
and an area for customers to actually sit and enjoy to earn a line."

"Ha," Harper said. "Done and done and done. Can you unlock the front door? I'll be out there in a minute."

"Put some blush and lipstick on first," Abuela said. "Or you'll
scare people."

Harper drew a deep breath and tried to find some calm and
patience. Both were in short supply. She looked at Shay.

"She's right. You look like death warmed over."

"You always kick someone when they're down?"

"Sorry," Shay said. "Bad habit. You look . . . great."

Harper realized Shay was trying to be nice. It made her heart hurt even more, and she hugged her tight. "Thanks."

Shay sighed dramatically. "This is why I don't have girlfriends. Guys don't ever want a hug. They want to sleep with you or eat. That's it."

"Listen, I'll be right back, okay? Take over for Abuela? Don't let her serve any customers. The pricing's on my new cute menu, you'll see it. And give everyone a free cookie."

"You do realize you don't have to bribe people to like you with cookies, right? I told you, everyone loves you. Don't give your shit away. And don't leave me alone in here."

Shay was wrong. Not *everyone* loved her. "No one ever shows up before nine. I'll be back way before then." She was searching her pockets for her keys. She realized she needed to do something before she could move on. She needed to apologize to Bodie for her part in last night. As for if Bodie was open to hear her or not, that was on him.

Shay got between her and the door, frowning at the look on Harper's face. "Where are you going? You're finally having a grand opening and you're going to leave?"

"I need to talk to Bodie so I can go into this grand opening with a clear mind and know I did the best I could. That I will always do the best I can." She met Shay's gaze. "He's important to me."

"Well, duh. But what am I, chopped liver?"

"Not even close. You're a part of my new family, and trust me, I don't say that lightly."

Shay stared at her, her eyes going a little bit shiny. "Oh," she said softly. "Well, then carry on. But if someone pays cash and needs change, don't expect me to do math. I never do math for free."

"Noted. I'll be right back." Harper yanked open the back door, thinking even if a bear was in her driver's seat, it wouldn't stop her.

But she *did* stop, and not because of a bear.

Bodie stood there, hand raised to knock.

"I was just coming to find you," she said.

He looked surprised. "But it's your grand opening."

"How did you know?"

"I saw it on TikTok."

In the back of her mind, a few brain cells stood up and cheered that her marketing was working. But wait a second. "I didn't put it on TikTok, just Instagram and Twitter."

"You're welcome!" Shay yelled from inside.

"Is that why you're here?" she asked Bodie. "The grand opening? Because the free cookies are all out in the front with Shay and Abuela—although they're probably all gone by now. Shay was pretty hungry."

"Hey, I'm not that much of a freeloader!" Shay called out. "And what did I tell you about those cookies! We don't need them to love you!"

Bodie gave a hint of a smile. "Truth."

Harper got a sense of exhaustion pouring from him, emotional as well as physical, and had to work hard not to give a shit. Finally, he gave a slow, solemn shake of his head. "I'm not here for the free cookies."

She tried to look into his eyes, but they were covered by his dark sunglasses. He was still as stone, and she couldn't get a bead on his mood with those glasses. Not that it mattered, because she was going to tell him what was on her mind regardless. "I shouldn't have kept Ivy's call from you, and I'm sorry for that, more than I can ever say, but I can't . . . I won't apologize for keeping a promise to her. Yes, I should've included you, but in the moment all I knew was that I couldn't betray Ivy that way. Not after all she's been through, not even for you." There it was, her heart laid bare before him, all her emotional baggage condensed into that one sentence, leaving her feeling incredibly vulnerable. Everything in her wanted to take a step back inside and shut the door to protect herself. Well, except for her feet, which had turned into two blocks of concrete.

For a beat, nothing moved, not him, not her, not the air, nothing. Then he shoved the sunglasses to the top of his head. "I understand," he said quietly. "And I'm grateful." Gone was his protective wall, and his eyes were full of regret. "I let my fear for Ivy . . ." He shook his head and drew in a deep breath.

"She's okay?" Harper asked quickly.

He nodded and ran his hand over his eyes. "Yeah. Thanks to you. And I'd have done the exact same thing in your position. I'm just thankful you were there for her when she needed you. I'm so sorry, Harper. I should never have left like that."

"I mean, I get it. You were worried sick," she said through

a thick throat, nodding. Then slowly, she changed to shaking her head. "It was the way you . . ." She drew a deep breath. "You walked away from me, Bodie. You said we were done. But you'd promised you weren't going anywhere. And then when the going got tough, you said goodbye and left."

He closed his eyes for a beat, and when he opened them, they were filled with a grim remorse. "I know. I let myself go into a free fall and took it out on you. I hate that I did that to you. I'm so sorry, Harper. If I could take it back, I would. But I can promise you that I'm figuring my shit out, and I learn from my mistakes. If you let me, I can prove I'll never do that again."

The words were shiny and pretty. But there was something she needed to know. "Your mom told me something about you when she came to meet me at the bakery."

He grimaced. "Oh boy."

"She said you learned to protect yourself by hiding your emotion and by disengaging. That you could protect people with your own body without hesitation, but you also believed you could further protect people's hearts by shutting them out."

"My mom talks too much."

"She loves you. Is what she said true?"

"Shit." He ran a hand over the scruff on his jaw. "Yeah. Probably. Definitely." He drew a deep breath. "But I mean it when I tell you I won't shut you out again. You deserve better. You deserve . . . everything."

It was her turn to take a deep breath. "If we're being honest, I was scared last night. Before Ivy called. I was watching Mace and

Shay, and you with your brothers, and . . ." She shook her head. "I suddenly was afraid that I was in it alone, that you had so much love in your life that you could never feel the same things for me that I felt for you. When I had Ivy on the phone, I knew I needed to tell you in spite of what she wanted." She swallowed. "But I didn't. I purposely kept you out of the loop. I think it's because I knew it would mess things up between us." She looked away from the intensity in his gaze. "My only excuse is that falling in love with you is the most terrifying thing I've ever done."

He was suddenly very still. "You love me?"

Shay stuck her head out. "Bodie, are you kidding me? That's all you heard?"

Ivy pushed past Shay. "Oh no, I'm missing it!"

"Yes," Harper said to Bodie, barely audible to her own ears over her heartbeat pounding through her. "I love you." She let out a breath. "I wasn't sure I would ever tell you until right now, but that doesn't make it any less true."

"He loves you back," Ivy said breathlessly as Bodie opened his mouth. "He didn't figure it out until this morning."

"Guys are always slow like that," Shay said helpfully. "Well, not my guy, because he's got his shit together. But all the others are."

Ivy put her hand on Harper's arm. Her mouth was smiling, but her eyes were serious. Worried. "For grown adults, you two can be pretty dense."

"I've got another word for it," Shay offered. "But sure, let's go with dense."

"They're wrong," Bodie said to Harper. "I knew I loved you. I just let it mess with my head. So much that I never told you how you're the glue. You made me and Ivy possible."

Ivy's eyes filled at this. "He's right. And I'm so, so sorry about last night—"

"Honey, I told you, it's okay."

"No." She shook her head. "I put you in a terrible situation."

"Actually, I put myself in that position," Harper said. "I should have never agreed to keep something regarding you from your dad. That wasn't okay."

Ivy threw herself at Harper in a hard hug that felt so sweet, Harper nearly lost it. "Don't hate me," she whispered.

"Are you kidding?" She wrapped her arms around Ivy and squeezed. "If I had a daughter, I couldn't love her more than I love you. I'm so happy you found family." When they pulled apart, Bodie took Harper's hand, his other gently lifting her face to his. "You're a part of this family too, Harper."

"Even though you know I don't always make the best decisions?"

He shook his head. "You don't have the market cornered there."

She snorted. "Oh, so you're able to make a bullet-point list of the things you've screwed up?"

Without preamble, he ticked off his bullet points. "Blew up an op that cost a friend his life, got a stranger pregnant and never knew my daughter, kept you at arm's length and hurt you as a result." He shook his head. "*Everyone's* got a long list of things they'd redo, Harper. Would you like to know what I'd redo?"

She nodded.

He stepped into her, running his hands up her arms to cup her face. "I'd start with not overreacting with fear when Ivy was gone, which led me to do one of my top two stupidest moments ever—walking away from you."

With each word, her heart got lighter. "And the other stupid thing?"

"Believing I couldn't fall in love." He smiled that just-for-her smile. "You sparked joy in my life from the moment you told me to take a hike when I tried to help you with your chains." He brushed his lips to her forehead, and she felt him smile against her. "When I'm with you, I'm reminded that I'm more than the things I've seen and done. I can feel. I can love. And I love you, Harper. So much."

Knees a little wobbly, Harper backed to a chair and sank into it.

Ivy shifted, looking like a teenager who'd just caught her parents necking. "Is this going to get much mushier? Cuz I'm going out front for this part. Do I still have a job? I know I don't deserve it, but—"

"You still have a job," Harper said, both laughing and maybe crying. "You have a place here, and in my life and heart always."

Ivy's eyes filled as she bit her lower lip, then nodded shyly and headed out to the front room.

"I missed you last night," Bodie said. He crouched on the balls of his feet to look her in the eyes. "I want you in my life. Now you. What do *you* want, Harper?"

She'd come to a decision about her life. Starting now, maybe not all the time, maybe not with everyone, but definitely with this man, she wasn't going to drop hints, hope for a sign, or ask for less than she wanted. "I want you to need me."

His eyes met hers with a whisper of surprise in them. "Babe, I need you more than my next breath. You're the most incredible woman I've ever met, and I can't imagine my life without you in it. I know you've been through a lot when it comes to relationships, and you deserve better. I hope you believe that. I want to love you, Harper, just as you are, for as long as you'll let me."

Ivy popped her head back in. "Oh my God, did you just propose? *And* you did it wrong!"

Bodie's mom's head appeared next to Ivy's. "*Did* he just propose to her? Where's the ring?"

Shay's head was there as well, the three of their faces lined up in the doorway, squished together like animated characters. "It sure sounded like a proposal."

Serena became the fourth head, nodding in agreement. "It was lovely."

Zeke was eyeing the place. "Look, I'm just here because I heard there were going to be free cookies."

"I still don't see a ring," Bodie's mom fretted. "What son of mine would propose without a ring?"

"The son who *didn't* just propose," Bodie said, "because he understands Harper wants and deserves more time to make sure I'm not always such a dumbass." He never took his eyes off Harper. "The son who wants her to have all the time she needs, but also wants her to know I'm an option when and if she decides she wants to take that step with me."

Harper smiled at him. "Bodie?"

He smiled back. "Yeah?"

"I love who you are too."

He pulled her into him, one hand palming the back of her head, the other sliding across her shoulders for a warm hug that had her wanting to climb him like a tree. Well, except for their audience. She was starting to understand that with the Campbells, there wasn't going to be much privacy, but she'd had enough privacy in her life. This was better. This was everything.

"We're going to need more sourdough bread!" Abuela yelled from the front. "In case anyone here happens to care about business!"

Harper pulled back from Bodie but kept a hand in his as she wrapped an arm around Ivy's neck and hugged her tight too. Then they all went out front.

The place was packed. Bodie turned a slow circle and smiled at Harper. "You made some changes. I love it." He caught sight of her chalkboard menu, and item #3—Austin's Moose Tracks Pie, and looked incredibly moved. "Harper."

"More bread!" Abuela repeated. "And cupcakes. And some croissants too. Oh, and a raise for me, stat!"

Harper stood there, marveling. She'd found her place. Her people. Her life. "I'm going to need a list."

Bodie's eyes were warm and serious and full of so much emotion she didn't know how to process it all. Then he gave a slow, beautiful smile, took her hand, and brought it to his mouth, brushing a kiss over her fingers. "A list, Harper? From you?"

"Yeah." She'd never been so happy in her life. "Go figure,

right? But I'm developing a real fondness for liking where I am and where I'm going. And to keep it all together, the occasional list might be helpful. For instance, apparently I need more sourdough bread, cupcakes, and croissants. And, last but most definitely not least, *you*."

His grin was instant, though when he spoke, his voice was rough, telling her how important this was. How important she was. "I like being in your plans. It's convenient, since you're in mine."

"You'll have to excuse them," Shay said to the people in line. "They always forget they're not alone."

Bodie squeezed Harper's hand. "You ready for all this?"

"As long as I've got you and Ivy." She smiled. "Always."

EPILOGUE

Two and a half years later
Christmas Eve

At eighteen and a half, Ivy was technically an adult. And as such, she could live wherever she chose. She spent most of her time at the South Tahoe Culinary Academy, living in a really tiny apartment in South Lake Tahoe with two roommates and loving every second of her life. She flew back to Chicago for some holidays and her mom's birthday, and with some distance, they had a much better relationship. It was even better now that Ivy felt grown up, because while maybe she didn't understand why her mom had made some of the choices she had, she no longer had the need to judge her for them. In return, her mom actually seemed interested in Ivy and her life, which felt . . . good.

But Ivy was her happiest in Sunrise Cove at her dad's cabin, with him and Ivy and Ham.

She had two weeks off for Christmas, and she planned to ski

with the fam and eat to her heart's content. Shouldering her duffel bag, she let herself into the cabin.

Ham was waiting at the front door as always, and as always, she had to thrust her hand through the cracked door to budge him because he still didn't understand he had to move so his precious human could get inside.

Once in, she was accosted with slobber and love. Laughing, she jokingly yelled out, "Honey, I'm home!" Tossing her bag to the couch, she smiled at the huge but undecorated Christmas tree.

They'd waited for her.

Harper got to her first, rushing out of the kitchen, a streak of flour across one cheek and in her hair as she enveloped Ivy in a warm hug.

"You smell like chocolate." Ivy laughed and squeezed her back.

Two more arms came around her as well; longer and stronger. Her dad in a tool belt, holding a hammer. "Just in time," he said.

Ivy pulled back. "Yeah? What's up?"

"Come look," he said, and vanished down the hallway.

Ivy looked at Harper, who smiled and reached out a hand.

Ivy ducked with a dramatic gasp worthy of a soap opera star, pretending to be blinded by the diamond her dad had put on Harper's finger last year.

They were both laughing as they followed him down the hall. Ivy had been swamped with school for the past month, so Harper and Bodie had come to her weekly. In fact, the last time Ivy had been home was October, since she'd flown to Chicago for Thanksgiving. So she was shocked to see that the hallway was longer than before.

With a gesture of great flourish, Bodie pointed to the door that used to be their linen closet. "Can you get that for me?"

Raising a brow, she eyed his two perfectly good hands, but she dutifully stepped forward and opened the door.

No longer a closet, but a bedroom. The ceiling and window trim matched the shiny hardwood floor. There was a bed and dresser and a small love seat, but the real heart-stopper was the sliding glass door opening to the backyard and a view of the woods and majestic snow-covered mountains.

"Do you like it?" Bodie asked quietly.

"You mean it's for me?"

"Yes."

Ivy couldn't believe it. "It's so beautiful. And big. My entire apartment could fit in here." She looked at him. "You didn't have to, I was fine with the room I had."

"It was small. It'll make a better baby room."

Ivy whipped around to stare at Harper, watching her eyes mist. "You're . . ."

Harper nodded and put her hands to her still-flat belly. "Are you okay with that?"

"Are you kidding me?" Ivy hugged her again. "You're giving me a baby sister for Christmas. There's nothing else I could want."

"It could be a baby brother," Bodie said, slinging an arm around each of them, grinning down into their faces. "Campbells make a lot of boys."

Harper and Ivy ignored this. "In any case, she won't be here for a while yet," Harper said. "I'm only seven weeks. We haven't told a soul other than you. We wanted you to know first, and make sure you were okay with it."

Ivy waited for the old anxiety to hit her, along with the age-old fear of being cut out of the family unit. Neither came. "She's going to love it here with us."

"Or, you know, *he*," Bodie said as Harper and Ivy walked toward the kitchen, arm in arm.

The rest of the gang showed up. Zeke and Serena and the heathens. Mace and Shay. Ivy's grandma. They ate pizza and decorated the tree, and then after, when everyone had gone home, the three of them opened presents to one another.

Months ago, Ivy had sneaked a stack of Harper's childhood photos out of the house, which she'd created a scrapbook with.

When Harper opened it, she stilled, then her eyes filled. "Oh my God, it's so beautiful." She sniffed. "And incredibly thoughtful." A few tears escaped as she began to flip through the pages.

"I didn't mean to make you cry," Ivy said, her stomach going all ugly squishy with worry.

Bodie slid an arm around Harper while smiling at Ivy. "It's pregnancy hormones. This morning she cried because her toast tasted so good."

"Well, it did taste good!" Harper mopped her face on her husband's T-shirt, then went back to looking through the photo album, telling Ivy and Bodie about each pic.

Bodie was leaning in, expressing interest in the way he always did when it came to them.

Ivy loved him ridiculously for that alone.

"These next few pages are the Tahoe trips I took with my mom," Harper said.

Eight-year-old Harper looked adorable sitting on a paddleboard on the lake, her mom standing on the board behind her, steering them through the water. "We had so much fun."

The next picture was a close-up of the two of them sitting on the shore, wrapped in towels.

"I realized when I was making the scrapbook, that's the park that I always take Ham to," Ivy said. And where she'd first met James and Jessie. After that long-ago disastrous party, the twins had moved south where it was warmer. They still sent Ivy twenty-five bucks faithfully every month, working toward paying off what they owed her dad, even though he'd told them he'd forgiven the debt.

Which meant that Ivy sent the money back to them every month. Her version of paying it forward. Jessie was in school, which she loved, and James was working happily as a mechanic. They had a small apartment and were doing well. Ivy had plans to go visit them on her next break and couldn't wait.

Bodie leaned in to study the park. "I don't think I ever told either of you, but I used to hang out in there as a kid as well." He ran a finger over the huge jungle gym. "I still like to run there."

"'Like' and 'run' don't belong in the same sentence," Harper said on a laugh. She pointed to the jungle gym. "Right after this pic was taken, I climbed that thing all the way to the top, then got too scared to move."

"How did you get down?" Ivy asked.

"A boy a few years older than me tried to help, but I wouldn't let him. I was too scared."

Bodie's attention shifted from the album to Harper's face, an odd expression on his own.

"What happened?" Ivy asked.

"He—"

"—Talked you down," Bodie said. "Stood at the bottom, pointing out the handholds to you."

"Wait—how do you know that?" Ivy asked.

"Because it was him," Harper said softly, staring at him. "*It was you.*"

"You came back the next year," he said. "You were part of a summer camp. Everyone climbed the jungle gym."

"Except me." Harper shook her head. "I refused to do it. Until one of the older kids, the same boy the year before, offered to talk me through it. Again."

"And you did it," Bodie said.

"The next year too." Harper looked both full of marvel and almost unbearably moved. "I'm sorry, I still can't believe it. The boy who showed me such kindness was you."

"The last year you came, you'd shaved your head."

She nodded. "My mom had gotten cancer that last year. She'd lost her hair. I shaved mine in solidarity, and then was horribly bullied in school about being bald. We couldn't afford it, but she brought me here anyway that summer because she wanted me to feel happy, even for a little while. She died a month after we got home."

Ivy was dividing her gaze between her two favorite people, surprised but also somehow not surprised. They'd fallen in love as adults, never realizing they'd already known each other. Cared about each other.

Bodie took Harper's hand. "I looked for you the next year, but you didn't show. I never saw you again."

She brought their joined hands up to her chest, over her heart, blinking back more tears. "You probably had no idea how much your kindness meant to me during a heartbreaking time in my life."

Bodie shook his head. "Anyone would have helped you down that day on the jungle gym."

"But not just anyone did. *You* did. And I never forgot it." She smiled. "I think in some ways, I've been waiting to see you again my whole life."

He looked emotional when he hugged her. "Know what I love?" he asked when he pulled back. "That it was you who gave my daughter a safe place to stay." He took Ivy's hand in his much bigger one. "You brought us together."

"Anyone would have helped her," Harper said softly, repeating his words back to him.

Ivy shook her head. "Not just anyone, and I'll never forget it."

Harper took Ivy's other hand and placed it on her still-flat belly. "You're going to make the best big sister to your little sister."

"Or brother," Bodie said.

Harper and Ivy smiled at each other, and Ivy had never felt more at home in her life. "I could never have guessed how much

I'd gain by coming here," she said. "You've both changed my life."

"Just as you've changed mine," Bodie said. "I guess it's all too easy to go through life without knowing what you mean to someone. But I want you to know, Kit Kat, you mean everything to me, to us."

And for the first time in her life, Ivy Campbell believed it.

ABOUT THE AUTHOR

New York Times bestselling author Jill Shalvis lives in a small town in the Sierras full of quirky characters. Any resemblance to the quirky characters in her books is, um, mostly coincidental. Look for Jill's bestselling, award-winning novels wherever books are sold and visit her website, jillshalvis.com, for a complete book list and daily blog detailing her city-girl-living-in-the-mountains adventures.